MURDER
ON THE
LUSITANIA

MURDER
ON THE
LUSITANIA

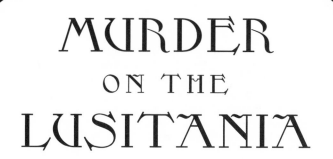

Conrad Allen

ST. MARTIN'S MINOTAUR 🐎 NEW YORK

A))

Design by Nancy Resnick

Library of Congress Cataloging-in-Publication Data

Allen, Conrad, 1940-
    Murder on the Lusitania / Conrad Allen. — 1st U.S. ed.
      p.   cm.
    ISBN 0-312-24114-3
    1. Lusitania (Steamship) Fiction.   I. Title
    PR6063.I3175M88 1999   99-34003
    823'.914—dc21   CIP

First Edition: December 1999

10 9 8 7 6 5 4 3 2 1

"Extremely amusing."

"In the *Westminster Gazette*?" continued the other with un-feigned contempt. "That is a Liberal newspaper."

"I care nothing for its politics," explained the podgy man, anxious not to give offense. "I chose the *Gazette* because of its competitions."

"Competitions, sir?"

"Intellectual diversions."

"Indeed?"

"Some, quite serious. Others, mere trifles."

"They would not be enough to entice me to buy such a periodical. It is bad enough to have to endure a Liberal government without paying to read its insidious propaganda."

"There is no propaganda in this quotation from Shakespeare," said the other defensively. "A prize of two guineas was offered for the best rendering into Greek iambics of this passage from the Bard. The winning entry shows remarkable scholarship."

"Is that what provoked your mirth?"

"Good heavens, no. I am a Balliol man. I revere a Classical education. What tickled me was this sublime piece of nonsense under the heading of 'Advice in One Dozen Emergencies.' Twelve problems were set and each competitor had to provide twelve pithy answers. The winner has a true sense of the ridiculous."

"Oh?"

"Take number six, for instance," said the portly man, eager to share his pleasure. " 'Question: G., engaged to Ethelinda, cannot afford to marry her, and would be relieved if she would break the engagement. How would he induce this?' "

Dillman saw the scowl on the face of the man opposite him and elected to supply the encouragement that the other frankly denied. He turned to his neighbor.

"What is the answer given, sir?" asked Dillman.

"It is so droll."

"How *does* a man induce his fiancée to break the engagement?"

" 'Answer: Wear ready-made clothes, and grow a beard.' "

The podgy man chortled again and Dillman gave a quiet

chuckle but the trio opposite were not amused. The mother pursed her lips in disapproval, the father retreated pointedly behind his own newspaper, and the daughter seemed on the verge of tears, but the conversational ice had now been broken and Dillman felt able to speak openly.

"You mentioned a competition involving Shakespeare, sir."

"There are three, my friend," said his companion. "Apart from the winning entry in Greek iambics, there are two new competitions relating to the Bard. In the first, they are offering two guineas for the best rendering of a Shakespearean sonnet into Latin elegiacs in the manner of Catullus or Propertius."

"Which sonnet might that be?"

" 'When in disgrace with fortune or men's eyes . . . ' "

Dillman closed his eyes and whispered the next few lines. " 'I all alone bewail my outcast state, /And trouble deaf heaven with my bootless cries, /And look upon myself and curse my fate . . . ' "

"Well done, sir! You know it by heart."

"Shakespeare is my first love," admitted Dillman, opening his eyes again. "I was reared on his plays and sonnets."

"Then an American education may not be as flawed as we have been led to believe," teased the other gently. "Ignore my levity," he added quickly, removing his pince-nez. "I do not mean to be facetious. My name is Cyril Weekes. I am delighted to meet you."

"George Dillman," said the other, shaking the proffered hand.

Dillman was then introduced to Ada Weekes and one side of the compartment was soon engaged in polite but lively discourse. It was only a matter of time before Dillman's accent parted the red-faced man from his newspaper. He gave a patronizing smile.

"I had a feeling that you were not English," he observed.

"Not for want of trying, sir," replied Dillman. "I bought my suit and hat on Bond Street and do my best to ape your behavior but I will never taken for a true-born Englishman. I fear that I am stamped for life as an irredeemable Bostonian."

"With a surprising knowledge of Shakespeare's sonnets," noted Weekes, giving him a complimentary nod.

6

MURDER
ON THE
LUSITANIA

ONE

G eorge Porter Dillman caught his first glimpse of her at Euston Station. Even in a crowd as large and volatile as that, she stood out, albeit for the briefest and most tantalizing of moments. As he picked his way through the mass of bodies, Dillman was suddenly confronted by a slender young woman in a green straw hat trimmed with white flowers and a blue velvet ribbon that matched the color of her dress. What struck him was not the sudden beauty of her face or even the delicate sheen of her blond hair. It was her unassailable confidence. Amid the swirling crowd with its buffeting shoulders and its jostling elbows, she was completely at ease, moving with the grace of a dancer and blithely ignoring the admiring or lustful glances that she collected.

Dillman had never met anyone with such an air of self-possession. He stepped back to allow her to pass, touching the brim of his hat and offering a polite smile, but she did not even notice him. A porter trailed in her wake, pushing her luggage on his trolley and warning people to "Mind yer backs, please!" in a voice that rose above the cacophony. Dillman watched her until she was swallowed up in the throng. Even his unusual height did not permit him to keep track of her for long. The white flowers

1

on her hat soon merged with the vast expanse of floral decoration on the assembled headgear in the station concourse.

It was as if a huge garden was on the move, rippling and surging like a multicolored wave, bearing, along with it, on the heads of male passengers and well-wishers, a motley collection of top hats, bowlers, homburgs, straw boaters, and flat caps of every description. But flowers predominated on that September afternoon and, in Dillman's mind, her white posies on that green straw hat took pride of place among them.

Two minutes later, he was climbing aboard the train and making his way along the corridor in a first-class carriage. It was one of the three specials that had been laid on to take passengers to Liverpool to board the *Lusitania* on its maiden voyage, an event that had caught the public imagination in the most extraordinary way. The excitement aboard the train was palpable. Even the most phlegmatic travelers were imbued with a sense that they were setting off on a great adventure. They were not merely sailing to New York on the biggest ocean liner in the world. They would be taking part in a voyage of historic significance. Dillman shared the anticipatory delight, though for somewhat different reasons.

The compartment he chose already had five occupants, and Dillman had difficulty finding a space on the luggage rack for his valise and his hat. When he sat down with a book in his hand, he distributed a nod among his companions but got no more than one noncommittal glance in return, convincing him that he was part of a wholly English gathering and could expect conversation from none of them until they were well on their way. The magic of the *Lusitania* had no doubt touched their souls but it had as yet failed to break through their natural reserve. He marveled again at the strange capacity of the English upper middle classes to suppress any hint of the wild enjoyment they must be feeling. In the third-class carriages, he was sure, passengers were already surrendering to the thrill of the occasion, talking volubly, sharing expectations, and forging new friendships. Among those with first-class tickets, pleasure was kept on a much shorter leash.

His back to the engine, Dillman was seated at the corridor end of the compartment. When he looked out at the tumult on the platform, he was able simultaneously to take stock of his traveling companions. Beside him on his left was a short, podgy, well-groomed man in his fifties with thinning hair that had already taken on a silver hue and a snub nose on which his pince-nez was rather perilously set. His head was buried in a copy of the *Westminster Gazette* and a quiet smile played about his lips. Beyond him was a lady whom Dillman took to be his wife, a small, slim woman in a fashionable dress of navy serge edged with black braid. Since she was gazing through the window, her hat obscured most of her face from Dillman.

Seated opposite the American were three people who quite clearly composed a family. Even if the occasional muttered remark was not passed between them to indicate togetherness, Dillman would have linked them instantly. The young woman who sat between the two older passengers so patently embodied the features of both that she simply had to be their daughter. Her mother, a handsome woman in a gown of French lace, was alternately scanning the platform and turning to look at the young woman with a distant maternal concern. The father, by contrast, a big, red-faced man with side whiskers and a permanent chevron etched into his brow, was lost in thought, his hands folded across his stomach, his eyes fixed on some invisible object on the rack opposite him.

It was the daughter who really interested Dillman. She had inherited her mother's good looks and her father's prominent chin but she lacked the animation of either parent. Flicking her head to and fro, the one seemed to be buzzing with controlled energy and, even in a reflective mood, the other exuded a kind of dormant vitality. Their daughter, however, dressed in a smart blue frock of striped zephyr, was so lackluster as to appear almost ill. Her face wore an expression of grim resignation and it occurred to Dillman that she looked less like a girl about to undergo a thrilling maritime experience with her parents than a female prisoner being escorted by two warders.

The pandemonium outside increased audibly as late arrivals

hurried to join the train and porters trundled past with the last of the trunks and suitcases. Tearful farewells took place the entire length of the platform before a warning was shouted and a whistle was blown. The engine then came to life, displaying its power with a series of thunderous emissions of steam, inching away, then slowly gathering speed. A great concerted cheer went up from those on the platform as they sent friends and relations off on the first stage of their journey of a lifetime.

It was only then that the young woman came fleetingly awake. She sat bolt upright and flung a wistful glance through the window. Dillman noted the color that rose to her cheeks. When the train pulled clear of the station, however, her interest vanished at once and she sagged back into morose introspection. After subjecting her to careful scrutiny, her mother gave a gentle sigh of relief, then traded a knowing glance with her husband, who had been jerked out of his reverie by the movement of the train. He gave a satisfied nod, then reached for a copy of the *Times*, which was tucked in beside him. Letting out an occasional grunt of approval, he read his way through the correspondence columns.

The train steamed on through the afternoon sunshine and settled into a jolting rhythm that was punctuated by the clicking of the wheels over the track. The small woman eventually dozed off to sleep, the two men remained immersed in their respective newspapers and the mother had a muted conversation with her daughter. Unable to hear anything of what they were saying, Dillman opened his novel and began to reacquaint himself with the joys of *Nicholas Nickleby*. No journey was ever complete without Charles Dickens beside him to stave off boredom.

A contented silence soon descended on the compartment, broken only by the rustling of the newspapers and the subdued clamor of the train itself. It was the short, podgy man who finally spoke aloud.

"By Jove!" he said, and let out a chortle.

The *Times* was immediately lowered and dark eyes inspected him.

"You find something amusing, sir?" said the red-faced man.

"Actually, I am much stronger on his plays."

"We may civilize you yet, then," said the red-faced man, baring his teeth in a condescending grin. He gestured at the book in Dillman's hand. "And I see that you have discovered Dickens as well. Far too unsavory an author for my taste, but one has to concede the fellow's talent. Shakespeare and Dickens, eh? English literature clearly has charms to soothe the savage American breast."

Dillman had to endure a whole series of such inane comments from the *Times* reader, but he did so willingly because they broke down the last social barriers and brought the whole compartment into the general conversation. The novelty of his American nationality initiated a flurry of questions from both men and from their wives. Instead of being the outsider in the group, Dillman now became its focal point. In due course, he learned the names of Matthew and Sylvia Rymer. Their daughter, Violet, was less forthcoming but even she took a gradual interest in the tall stranger with the exquisite manners. It was Violet Rymer who asked the most obvious question.

"Which ship did you sail on to get here, Mr. Dillman?"

"The *Lucania*."

"She is leaving for New York today before the *Lusitania*."

"Yes," agreed her father, "and part of me wishes that I were aboard her. The *Lusitania* is the finer vessel but I believe that the *Lucania* has the most precious item in its cargo."

"What do you mean, Matthew?" asked his wife.

"It is not a question of what but of whom, my dear. The details are here in my newspaper. Sailing on the *Lucania* is the MCC cricket team. They are having a five weeks' tour of America." Rymer looked across at Dillman. "I daresay that you have no idea what MCC stands for, do you?"

"I fear not, sir," said Dillman deferentially, knowing quite well that the initials stood for the illustrious Marylebone Cricket Club but playing the ignorant foreigner so that Rymer could resume his lofty tone and sermonize. "Perhaps you would enlighten me."

Matthew Rymer needed no more invitation. One thumb in his

waistcoat pocket, he described the game of cricket in detail and spoke of the MCC's seminal place in its history. The recital drew a few respectful complaints from his wife and put a glazed look into his daughter's eye, but he plowed on relentlessly and Dillman learned even more about the structure of the family who sat opposite him. Matthew Rymer was a preeminent example of a man who was master in his own house.

Cyril Weekes could not be kept silent for long, but his wife was happy to contribute nothing but the odd smile and stray remark. Weekes volunteered the information that he and Ada were sailing to New York to celebrate his retirement from business, though he did not specify the nature of that business. Rymer announced that the trip was a present for Violet on the occasion of her forthcoming twenty-first birthday but Dillman saw no sign of enthusiasm for the voyage in her eyes. The expensive gift instead seemed to depress her. The most she could rise to was a wan smile.

"What is it like to sail the Atlantic, Mr. Dillman?" asked Weekes.

"Invigorating, sir."

"Are we in any danger of seasickness?"

"Not in a vessel as large as the *Lusitania*," said Dillman confidently. "You will feel as comfortable as if you were in the Ritz Hotel. It is first-class travel in every sense."

"So it should be, at those prices," mumbled Rymer.

"Tell us about New York, Mr. Dillman," said his wife. "How does it compare with London, for instance? What should we aim to see?"

As the conversation gathered pace and intimacy, Dillman stroked his mustache and basked in the warmth of acceptance. Long before they reached Liverpool, he received separate invitations from the Rymers and the Weekeses to join them for dinner during the voyage. Friendship was secured. Dillman had the camouflage he needed. He was in.

It was a good start.

TWO

Few cities in Europe had as impressive a maritime history as Liverpool and none could match the pride and fervor with which the port sent off each successive ship on its maiden voyage. But even Liverpool had never known such an occasion as the departure of the *Lusitania* on its first Atlantic crossing. The latest addition to the Cunard Line excited such curiosity and inspired such patriotic feeling that people came from all over the country to witness the event. Huge crowds milled along both banks of the Mersey, swelling in numbers until they passed the two hundred thousand mark. The object of their veneration, the elegant giant known as the *Lusitania*, had been anchored in midstream throughout most of the day while the *Lucania* took on passengers. Once the pride of the line, the latter now looked small, old, and dowdy when seen beside the looming beauty of the new vessel.

When the *Lucania* set sail at 4:30 P.M., the *Lusitania* moved slowly into its vacant berth, drawing a gasp of awe from the spectators as they watched a ship that was longer than the Houses of Parliament glide effortlessly over the water. It was a marvel of marine engineering. Many in the crowd wondered how a vessel with a gross weight of 31,500 tons could remain so buoyant in the water. Here was a ship that was not only the biggest and most luxurious in the world; its quadruple screw propellers were powered by four direct-acting steam turbines and were capable of generating speeds in excess of anything ever seen in an oceanic liner.

None of those now staring at the huge vessel with its four red funnels gleaming in the sunshine doubted for a moment that it would regain the Blue Riband—the unofficial prize for the fastest Atlantic crossing—from the unworthy hands of the Norddeutscher Lloyd Line. British pride had been severely dented when its maritime ascendancy was usurped by Germany with technically advanced liners such as the *Kaiser Wilhelm der Grosse* and the *Deutschland*. Centuries of dominance came to a juddering halt, a situation compounded by the fact that the German navy was now growing at an alarming rate. Political motives came into play. Government subsidies were hastily offered to Cunard. The *Lusitania* and its sister ship, the *Mauretania*, due to have its own maiden voyage in November, were built expressly as a means of reasserting British supremacy on the high seas and of sending a clear message to the German government.

Activity around the ship reached a peak as passengers converged eagerly on the pier. The customs sheds worked at full stretch, port officials were out in full numbers, a sizable police presence had been drafted to control the crowds, and a small army of hawkers moved among the spectators to sell food, drink, flags, postcards, and assorted souvenirs. The majority of passengers arrived by train but several were delivered by horse-drawn cabs or spluttering automobiles, each competing for space in the congested traffic. Electric trams brought those who could afford no better transport, and open carts emblazoned with the name *Lusitania* were pulled by pairs of horses from the hostels where emigrants had stayed overnight with their meager belongings.

Rich and poor alike streamed aboard the vessel, caught up in the heady excitement and determined to savor what was self-evidently one of the most important events in their lives. Coal barges had already filled the bunkers, and the decks had been swept clean of any lingering dust. The crew looked smart and alert. There was a reassuring sense of readiness about them. Wearing trim uniforms and welcoming smiles, stewards waited to conduct passengers to their cabins and to provide basic information about the regimen aboard. In the ship's kitchens, the chefs and their staff were already preparing the first meal. Saloon bars were well stocked and barmen were at their stations.

George Porter Dillman gazed around the pier to take it all in. As he strolled toward the ship, he looked at the shining faces of well-wishers and listened to constant barrage of noise. He had never known such an atmosphere of excitement. It was intoxicating. When the shadow of the *Lusitania* fell across him, Dillman paused to stare up at its massive hull and shook his head in wonder. Unlike most of the other passengers, he had already had a privileged tour of the vessel, but its sheer proportions still took his breath away. With an overall length of 785 feet and a breadth of 88 feet, she dwarfed every craft in sight. The river was dotted with steamboats, fishing smacks, motor boats, yachts, and dozens of rowing boats that had come to wave the *Lusitania* off. Against the great Cunard liner, they were minnows beside a whale.

"Awesome, isn't she?" said a voice at Dillman's elbow.

He turned to see Cyril Weekes standing there with his wife on his arm. The two of them looked up at the ship with controlled glee.

"Incredible!" said Ada Weekes. "Quite incredible!"

"Yes," agreed Dillman. "Truly magnificent."

"We are so fortunate to be here."

"It is a great day for all of us, Mrs. Weekes."

"Let us see if she has an interior to match," suggested Weekes, moving forward. Dillman fell in beside them and joined the queue for the first-class gangway. "I must say, I did not expect to see crowds as large as this. Liverpool is such a friendly city. Rather drab and undistinguished in many ways but undeniably friendly."

"You have been here before, sir?" said Dillman.

"Oh, yes, Mr. Dillman. We come to Aintree every year."

"Aintree?"

"For the Grand National."

"A famous steeplechase," explained his wife.

"I know that, Mrs. Weekes," said Dillman. "Its fame has spread across the Atlantic. I am just grateful that it was not mentioned in the presence of Mr. Rymer," he added wryly, "or he would no doubt have felt obliged to lecture me on the whole history of the turf in England and the mysteries of bloodstock. With the very best of intentions, of course."

They shared a laugh. Weekes gave an apologetic shrug.

"Do not be too harsh on us, Mr. Dillman," he said. "Not all Englishmen are quite so arrogant as Rymer. I fear that he suffers from the national disease of insularity. This voyage may broaden his mind, though I beg leave to doubt it. You may have to endure more tutorials from him."

"I don't mind," said Dillman. "I just wish he didn't raise his voice every time he speaks to me. Mr. Rymer seems to think that being an American is akin to being both deaf and stupid."

"Whereas you are patently neither," observed Weekes shrewdly.

"Indeed not," reinforced his wife.

Dillman acknowledged the compliment with a smile then followed them up the gangway. He liked Cyril and Ada Weekes. They struck him as a pleasant couple with a marriage that was happy without being too cosy. Weekes was an educated man, a Classical scholar from Oxford, yet he carried his erudition lightly. His wife was a quiet, watchful woman with a twinkle in her eye. Though he liked the Rymers less, Dillman nevertheless found them more intriguing. They seemed to be carrying a lot of emotional problems with them and Dillman looked forward to finding out exactly what they were. Behind the easy pomposity of Matthew Rymer, he sensed, was a bristling anger, and he wondered what had caused it. One thing was certain. Both his wife and daughter were afraid of him. And something even more than fear lurked in the eyes of Violet Rymer.

There were eighty-seven special cabins in the first class, most of which were situated on the promenade deck. The remainder of the first-class cabins were on the main, upper, and boat decks, all of them accessible by the grand staircase, which more than justified its name. The entrance to the staircase was on the main deck and thus convenient for gangways from docksides, landing stages, and tenders. When they left the amiable turmoil of the quayside, first-class passengers entered a palatial world of woven carpets, embroidered curtains, paneled walls, dazzling mirrors, ornate light fittings, windows glazed with specially etched glass, and upholstered furniture of the highest quality.

It was truly a luxury hotel on the water.

Genevieve Masefield stepped aboard with an elation tempered with mild regret. Traveling alone, she was looking forward to the voyage and to setting foot on American soil, but a few uncomfortable memories still clung to her. Genevieve accepted that it might take time to shake them all off. Meanwhile, she could enjoy the pleasures of being a first-class passenger on the most remarkable ocean liner ever constructed. The steward who led her to her cabin on the upper deck was a tall man in his thirties with brilliantined hair and a flashy handsomeness that was kept in check by a submissive manner. One glance at Genevieve was enough to ignite his interest and he did his best to ingratiate himself with her, carrying her valise and assuring her that the rest of her luggage had already been brought aboard and stowed in her cabin.

A veteran of Atlantic crossings, he knew the importance of first impressions. Single women appreciated an attentive steward. Who knew where that appreciation might lead? Experience had taught him that social etiquette, so inflexible ashore, was sometimes abandoned at sea. The romance of an Atlantic crossing could turn single ladies into viable targets for the right man. When he unlocked her cabin door, he stepped smartly back out of her way so that she could go in first to appraise her accommodation.

Sweeping into the middle of the room, Genevieve pirouetted and looked around the whole cabin. It was sumptuous. The colors were tasteful, the decor superb. The bed had a comforting solidity, with its headboard quilted, its valance embroidered. Genevieve could not resist trying the springs with her hand. She gave a nod of approval, then moved to study herself in the gilt-framed mirror as she removed the green straw hat to reveal lustrous fair hair parted in the middle and gathered into a small bun at the rear. The steward watched with growing fascination and ran his tongue across his upper lip.

"Is there anything I can get you?" he asked softly.

"Not at the moment."

"Are you sure, miss?"

"Quite sure."

"Would you like to be shown around the ship?"

"In time, perhaps."

"Call me when you're ready," he said, gaining in confidence.

"But I understood that I was to have a stewardess."

"Yes, miss. A stewardess will look after your cabin." He flashed a knowing grin and took a step toward her. "But she may not be able to provide you with all that you want."

Genevieve turned to confront him with an inquiring smile.

"All that I want?"

"Extras, miss."

"Extras?"

"Personal attention."

"Ah, I see," she said, torn between amusement and annoyance.

"Just ring the bell and I'll come running."

"I'll bear that in mind."

"My name is Eric," he said, taking a bolder step toward her.

"Eric?"

"Yes."

"I'll bear that in mind as well," said Genevieve sweetly. "And if you ever come near my cabin again, Eric, I will mention your name to the chief steward. I require no 'personal attention' from you, young man."

"Oh."

"Considerate as your offer is."

The steward backed away, crestfallen. He groped for an apology.

"No offense was intended, miss."

"Are you in the habit of bothering female passengers?"

"Of course not."

"I'm glad to hear that," she said softly, "because some of them might not be as forgiving as I am. Let us pretend that we never even met each other, shall we? Goodbye, Eric. Close the door behind you, please."

He removed the key from the lock, set it down on the table and scurried out before shutting the door gently behind him. Genevieve turned back to the mirror to scrutinize herself for a moment. A hand fluttered up to touch her hair. She then adjusted the brooch at her neck. She was pleased with the way in which she had dealt with the steward. Eric would no doubt describe the encounter to his colleagues and the word would go out. Her territory was inviolable. She would have no further trouble from amorous young stewards with inflated ideas about the power of their masculinity. Eric's advances had been so direct and presumptuous that they were almost comical. Genevieve laughed aloud.

Expectation built steadily to a climax. At 9:00 P.M. precisely, the deep boom of the Lusitania's whistle echoed right across the river. With her cargo, her mail bags, and over two thousand passengers aboard, she was ready to begin her momentous journey. Standing on the bridge with his officers, Capt. James Watt checked his watch then gave the order to set his ship in motion. The maiden voyage began. Assisted by tugs and wafted along on the cheers of the watching audience, the Lusitania moved slowly away from the landing stage, ablaze with lights to fend off the approaching dusk. Hats, handkerchiefs, flags, and walking sticks were waved madly along both banks. Horns were tooted on every vehicle within sight. Hundreds of cameras recorded the scene. Shrill hoots of acclaim went up from the Mersey ferries and from the other steam craft on the river. Oars were brandished in rowing boats. Fireworks were set off aboard a small yacht. The harbor gulls added their own distinctive cries of joy as they dipped and wheeled in the air. Liverpool was sending yet another ship off on a rolling tide of goodwill.

The passengers shared the sense of exhilaration, crowding the decks to view the scene below and acknowledging the ovation with raised palms. The intensity of the experience surpassed anything they had envisaged. Whatever individual reasons they might have for making the trip were submerged in the general euphoria. They were all one now. First, second, or third class, they were making history on the churning water of the river. It was an unforgettable moment.

Dillman reveled in it. When he looked along the rail on the promenade deck, he saw that even Violet Rymer seemed to be deriving some pleasure at last. Her eyes were alight, her hands clasped tightly together and her hair blown gently by the breeze. For the first time, he noticed how attractive she could be. It was only when he moved closer to her that Dillman realized that she was not, in fact, relishing the occasion at all. Violet was raking the quayside with a mixture of hope and despair. Deaf to the remarks of her parents beside her, she was looking for someone among the masses on the shore. The ship moved on, the faces below became white dots in the gloom, and Violet Rymer bit her lip in disappointment. Whomever she had expected to see was not there. Turning away from the rail, she dabbed at a tear with a lace handkerchief.

Dillman moved solicitously across to her.

"Are you all right, Miss Rymer?" he inquired.

"Yes, yes," she said, recovering quickly. "I'm afraid that I find it all rather overwhelming. So many people, so much noise."

"They came to wish us bon voyage."

"Don't let me spoil it for you, Mr. Dillman. Go back to the rail."

"I'd prefer to talk to you."

"Would you?" she said with surprise. "Why?"

"Because we didn't have time for a proper conversation on the train. Not that we can have one here," he said, putting his hands to his ears as another blast of sound came from the other craft on the river. "But I would like to think that we might speak at some stage."

She rallied slightly. "Thank you, Mr. Dillman."

"There is one condition, mark you."

"Condition?"

"I want no more lectures about the MCC."

She laughed for the first time since he had met her, a strained, involuntary, high-pitched laugh, but a clear indication that she had a sense of humor. Violet looked guiltily across at her father to make sure that he had not heard her, then she rolled her eyes with relief. Dillman gave a sympathetic smile. She appraised him with real interest until her shyness got the better of her curiosity.

"I think I'll go back to the rail now," she said.

"Savor the moment while you may, Miss Rymer. I doubt if either of us will ever see anything quite like this again."

"No, Mr. Dillman. We shan't."

"Violet!" called her mother. "Where are you?"

"Coming!" she said, and rejoined her parents at the rail.

Dillman saw her shrink back into anonymity, like a flower whose petals suddenly closed. He felt sorry for Violet Rymer and suspected that her twenty-first birthday would bring her little joy. All he could hope was that her coming of age might, in the fullness of time, give her confidence to stand on her own feet and to escape the vigilance of her parents. When he looked at the back of Matthew Rymer's head, he thought about his own battles with a dictatorial father and he was reminded that nobody ever won such encounters. Victories were illusory. Each combatant limped away with permanent battle scars.

The *Lusitania* surged on. Though not engaged in a formal race with the *Lucania,* she was expected to overhaul the older vessel sometime during the night and to reach Queenstown Harbor well before her. But nobody was looking that far ahead. Crew and passengers alike were still luxuriating in the first magical hour of the maiden voyage.

Dillman strode the length of the deck, simply enjoying the enjoyment of others. Over five hundred first-class passengers were

17

aboard and every one of them seemed to be on the promenade deck. They included Mr. E. H. Cunard, grandson of the company's founder and a director of the Cunard Line. Since he had been allowed to peruse the full list, Dillman knew that he traveled in distinguished company. English aristocrats like Lord Carradine graced the ship along with diplomats, Members of Parliament, international financiers, senior churchmen, and foreign dignitaries. A name Dillman noted was that of Itzak Weiss, the renowned violinist. The great, the good, and the very wealthy were there in abundance. So were representatives of the press.

One of them accosted Dillman with a smile.

"Good evening, sir!"

"Good evening," returned Dillman.

"Ah!" said the newcomer, brightening at the sound of Dillman's voice. "An American passenger. How fortuitous! My name is Henry Barcroft, sir. I'm a journalist, reporting on the *Lucy*'s maiden voyage and trying to talk to as many people as possible. What are your impressions so far?"

"Extremely favorable, Mr. Barcroft."

"In what way?"

"Every way. She is an astonishing vessel."

"A floating palace."

"I was not thinking of her passenger facilities, Mr. Barcroft. They are beyond reproach. The real glory of the *Lusitania* lies out of sight, in the engine room. That is where true innovation is taking place."

"Indeed?" said the other, his interest quickening. "May I ask if you have any knowledge of marine engineering?"

"As it happens, I do," confessed Dillman modestly. "I was born and brought up less than a mile from the sea and worked in the family business for a while. We design and build oceangoing yachts."

"Then I've obviously stumbled on the right man. I have a happy knack of doing that. By the way, I did not catch your name."

"That is perhaps because I did not give it."

Dillman spoke with polite firmness. There was something about Barcroft that he did not like, a beaming familiarity that set off warning bells. The journalist was a stocky man of medium height in a dark brown suit. His features were pleasant enough but his careful grooming suggested vanity. Dillman put his age at around thirty. Barcroft was quite undaunted by the mild rebuff.

"You prefer to remain a man of mystery, do you?" he mocked. "So be it, sir. I will not intrude on your privacy. But since you have a special interest in the subject, you might care to know that this astonishing vessel, as you call it, has not been without its problems."

"Problems?"

"Yes," said the other airily. "It is something which Cunard would prefer to hide, but the *Lucy*'s final sea trials were not—if you will forgive an outrageous pun—plain sailing.

"Is that so?"

"The engineers discovered that she had an unfortunate vice. At high speeds, her stern vibrated. And I do not refer to mild trembling. She positively shuddered. From what I hear," said Barcroft in a confidential whisper, "the stern more or less went into convulsions. Steel plates rattled, strakes and stanchions shook violently. The noise was deafening. They could never put passengers through an ordeal like that."

"I am sure that the problem has been completely overcome."

"Indeed, it has, sir. You can probably guess how."

"With an assortment of arches, pillars, gussets, brackets, and any other form of bracing, I should imagine. Much of it cunningly disguised behind built-in furniture, I daresay. Cunard would not bring a ship into service until every deficiency was rectified."

"Quite so. But the cost was phenomenal. Over a hundred forty second-class cabins had to be gutted to cure the vibration in the stern."

"You seem well informed, Mr. Barcroft."

"I am a journalist. It is my job to be well informed."

"Does that mean it is safe for me to believe everything I read in your newspaper?" said Dillman, raising a cynical eyebrow. "The American press is nowhere near as reliable. Fact and fiction intermingle there."

Barcroft's face hardened, then an appeasing smile surfaced.

"You are an intriguing man, sir," he flattered, watching Dillman closely. "There cannot be many passengers aboard with your professional expertise. I would value a tour of the ship in your company."

"That will not be possible, I fear."

"But you could point out all of its salient features."

"I think that you know them already, Mr. Barcroft," said Dillman levelly. "There is nothing I could add which could possibly interest someone as well informed as you."

"Your comments would be invaluable."

"I only helped to build yachts, Mr. Barcroft. That is a far cry from marine architecture on this scale. It is the difference between journalism and literature. Between the sort of article you write and the major novels produced by a Dickens or a Thomas Hardy." He saw that he had caught the other man on the raw. "For which newspaper do you work, sir?"

"Any and every one. I am a freelance."

"Then I will not keep you from your duties. I am sure you will want to employ your happy knack of meeting the right man elsewhere."

Barcroft's eyelids narrowed for a second and he bit back a rejoinder. Then he gave a mirthless laugh and reached forward to pat Dillman on the arm before turning on his heel and moving away. Dillman watched him go. Barcroft insinuated himself into the crowd at the rail and engaged a young couple in conversation. The journalist had soon drawn them into an impromptu interview. There was something relentless and predatory about Henry Barcroft, but that was not the only quality of his that Dillman resented. He sensed a vengeful streak in the man and had a strong feeling that he had not seen the last of him. During the train journey earlier in the day, Dillman had taken the trouble to make friends with fellow passengers. In Henry Barcroft, he had just made his first enemy.

THREE

A carnival atmosphere prevailed aboard until well after midnight. First-class passengers lingered among the potted palms in the dining saloon, which was decorated in the style of Louis XVI with the predominating color of *vieux rose*. One of its outstanding features was a vast mahogany sideboard, ornamented with gilt metal and glistening like a huge beacon. Above the saloon was a circular balcony supported on Corinthian columns and taking the eye up to the magnificent grand dome with painted panels after Boucher. Those who chose to recline in the lounge found themselves in an equally resplendent room, decorated in the late Georgian period, and featuring fine inlaid mahogany panels, a richly modeled dome ceiling, and superb marble fireplaces.

Second-class passengers enjoyed comfort without opulence. The public rooms were large, well appointed, and tastefully decorated, the facilities comparing favorably with first-class quarters on smaller ships. Public rooms in third class were unashamedly functional with bare wooden chairs and benches in abundance and a distinct absence of the luxurious fixtures and fittings that proliferated elsewhere. Almost twelve hundred people—more than half the number of passengers—would cross the Atlantic in third class and its shortcomings might in time prove irksome. In those early hours of the voyage, however, they were so buoyed up by the general feeling of elation that they had no complaints and were as happy as anyone aboard.

Genevieve Masefield chose to have supper with the Hubermanns, two sisters whom she had befriended on the train from Euston and who seemed to think that someone as young and beautiful as she needed a chaperon. Accordingly, they took her under their wing. Carlotta and Abigail Hubermann had been on a grand tour of Europe and were returning to their native Virginia with an endless supply of anecdotes, souvenirs, and objets d'art. Genevieve warmed to them immediately. Both in their early sixties, they were lively companions, pleasantly garrulous but never to the point of boredom, kind, considerate, and always eager to listen to others. Ladies of independent means, they were extremely generous with their time and money.

"How long do you plan to stay, Miss Masefield?" asked Abigail.

"A month or so, probably."

"Bless you!" said Carlotta. "You must stay longer than that. What can you see of America in a month? We will expect you to spend at least that long with us, won't we, Abigail?"

"We insist. You simply must come to Virginia."

"That's a very tempting offer," said Genevieve. "I don't wish to spend the whole of my time in New York and it would be unfair to impose on my friends indefinitely. By the same token, I would hate to outstay my welcome in Virginia."

"There is no danger of that," said Carlotta. "Is there, Abigail?"

"None whatsoever. It is settled."

"Abigail Hubermann has spoken. No argument will be allowed."

"Well," said Genevieve, smiling. "If you put it like that . . ."

"We do," they said in unison.

They were seated in the lounge, ensconced in plush armchairs beside one of the marble fireplaces. The Hubermanns presented a strange contrast. Though they could be identified as sisters at once by certain facial similarities, the resemblance ended there. Abigail, the elder of the two, was a thin, angular woman with bony wrists and a delta on blue veins on the backs of her hands. Yet there was no suggestion of fragility. Her energy seemed inexhaustible. Carlotta Hubermann was big, plump, and jovial, her fat cheeks tinged with red, her eyebrows arching expressively whenever she spoke. Both were maiden ladies but Genevieve had the impression that Carlotta's private life had not been without its share of romance. Even in her portly state, she was still a very handsome woman.

Abigail sipped her coffee, then regarded Genevieve for a moment.

"I still think you should have reported him, dear," she said.

"Who?" asked Genevieve.

"That steward about whom you told us. That kind of behavior is intolerable. In your place, I would have had him severely reprimanded."

"I didn't wish to make too much of it, Miss Hubermann. Besides, it was not so much what the fellow did as what he was contemplating. I found it all rather amusing, to be honest. To be so open about it, he must have had success in the past."

"Have the man dismissed," urged Abigail.

"Don't be so ruthless, Abigail," said her sister. "It sounds to me as if Genevieve took the right course of action. She put him firmly in his place!"

"Yes, Miss Hubermann. I have a stewardess now. There will be no further problems of that kind."

"None of this would have happened if you traveled with your own maid," argued Abigail, setting her cup and saucer down on the table. "Carlotta and I would never go anywhere without Ruby. She is a positive jewel. I daresay she is turning down the beds in our cabin right now."

"I prefer to travel alone, Miss Hubermann," said Genevieve.

"Except that you are no longer alone," added Carlotta a with a grin. "You have acquired two strong bodyguards. And the first thing you must do is to stop calling us Miss Hubermann all the time or it will get very repetitive. We answer to Abigail and Carlotta."

"I will remember that."

"Carlotta," prompted the other.

Genevieve gave an obedient nod. "Carlotta it is."

"Which part of England do you hail from?" wondered Abigail.

"I was born in Canterbury but my family moved around a great deal. We lived in Italy for a few years."

"Which part of Italy?"

"Florence."

"One of our favorite cities!" said Abigail, clapping her hands together. "Wasn't it, Carlotta? We bought that painting of the Doge in Florence."

"I thought that it was in Ravenna," said her sister.

"Florence, dear."

"I think you will find it was Ravenna."

"We bought the painting of the three musicians there."

"That was definitely in Venice."

"I hate to contradict you, Abigail."

"Then don't. Because you are wrong."

"Not this time, dear."

"Carlotta!"

It was not really an argument but it allowed both of them to display their characteristic gestures. Abigail used her hands to reinforce her points but Carlotta relied more on facial expressions, raising her eyebrows, pursing her lips and occasionally wrinkling her nose. Watching the two of them, Genevieve marveled at the way they could dispute a simple point without any rancor. In the end, they agreed to refer the matter to their maid, Ruby, for arbitration but Genevieve was sure that it would be the older of the two sisters who would turn out to be right. There was something quietly decisive about Abigail Hubermann. Slighter in build, she carried much more weight in argument.

The three women were enjoying each other's company so much

that they did not notice they were under observation. Sitting within earshot of them, Henry Barcroft caught snatches of their conversation while trying to hold one himself with a senior member of a Christian Science delegation traveling to America in order to attend a conference where they would meet the founder of the movement. As soon as he caught sight of Genevieve Masefield, the journalist lost all interest in Mary Baker Eddy but he pretended to listen while his companion extolled the virtues of *Science and Health*.

"A seminal book," said the man reverentially.

"So I understand," murmured Barcroft.

"Mrs. Eddy writes so cogently. It is inspiring. Would you care to borrow my copy of it?"

"Not just now, sir."

"I could fetch it from my cabin."

"Tomorrow, perhaps," said Barcroft, rising to his feet. "If you will excuse me, I must try to interview some more passengers. Thank you so much for talking to me."

Before the Christian Scientist could detain him, the journalist strode across to the trio at the table beside the fireplace. Barcroft put a tentative note into his voice.

"Forgive this interruption, ladies," he said with oily politeness. "I don't mean to intrude but I couldn't help overhearing those delightful American accents. My name is Henry Barcroft. I'm a journalist and I've been commissioned to write an article about this voyage. I wondered if I might trespass on your time to get your impressions of it?"

"Now?" said Abigail, sizing him up. "It's very late, young man."

"We were just about to retire," said Carlotta.

"Might I make an appointment to speak to you sometime in the morning, then?" asked Barcroft. "I am told that the Veranda Café is an ideal place for an informal chat."

"I am not sure that I wish to be quoted in a newspaper," continued Abigail guardedly. "Journalists have a habit of twisting one's words."

"I would send nothing off without your approval."

"That is different," said Carlotta reasonably. "But what do you mean about sending your article off?"

"The ship has a wireless room. They will transmit whatever I give them. Even in the middle of the Irish Sea, as we are now, I could get through to my editor." Barcroft turned to Genevieve. "What about you, miss? May I ask for the privilege of an interview with you as well?"

"I'm not sure about that, Mr. Barcroft."

"What is your objection?"

"I have no wish to see my name in a newspaper."

"That objection is easily overcome," he promised. "You'll remain completely anonymous. If I quote you in the article, I'll simply refer to you as a charming young lady on her first trip to America." He fished gently. "I take it that it *is* your first trip?"

"Yes, sir."

"May I ask the purpose of the visit?"

"To stay with us," said Abigail bluntly. "And if you must ask us questions, confine them to the *Lusitania*. You are not entitled to probe into our private lives. Remember that, young man. As far as you are concerned, we are just three more faceless passengers."

"You could never be that," he said with gallantry, looking around all three of them. "I have never seen three more distinctive faces."

Abigail sniffed but Carlotta's cheeks dimpled at the compliment. Genevieve, too, mellowed slightly toward the stranger as the idea occurred to her that he might be useful.

"Whom else have you interviewed?" she said.

"Dozens of people," he replied, keen to impress. "I spoke with Mr. Cunard himself, of course, and with the Countess of Dunmore. Then there was Mr. Jacob Rothschild, the MP Mr. Robert Balfour and his wife, Sir William Wiseman, and so on."

"All this for one article?" said Abigail tartly.

"I am very thorough."

"Do you really need our opinion, Mr. Barcroft?"

"Indeed, yes," he insisted. "The more reactions I can glean, the better. As American passengers, you have a special interest for me because you must already have made one transatlantic voyage in order to get to Europe. You have a point of comparison. You can measure the *Lucy* alongside the *Lucania* or whichever ship brought you over."

"The *Ivernia*," corrected Carlotta.

"How did she compare with the *Lucy*?"

"Oh, she is not in the same class."

"I thought this interview was going to take place tomorrow?" said Abigail, who still had reservations about the journalist. "My sister and I need to sleep on it before we decide if we will speak to the press."

"What harm can it do?" asked Carlotta.

"None," said Genevieve, "if our names are not to be used. Actually, I would rather get it over with now. If you would prefer to go to bed, I'll remain here with Mr. Barcroft and answer his questions."

The journalist beamed and took pencil and pad from his pocket. An interview alone with Genevieve was exactly what he sought. Abigail Hubermann forced him to moderate his pleasure.

"If you stay, Genevieve," she affirmed, "then so will we."

"Yes," said Carlotta loyally. "For as long as it takes."

"Good!" said Barcroft with false affability. "May I sit down?"

A light meal with the Rymers was less of a trial than Dillman had anticipated. Though still in homiletic vein, Matthew Rymer was much more relaxed, and even ventured, albeit with plodding slowness, into the realms of humor when he described the recent purchase of a property. Dillman learned that his host had amassed a small fortune by means of property speculation, enabling him not merely to travel first class with his wife and daughter on the *Lusitania* but to take one of the coveted regal suites, comprising two bedrooms, a dining room a drawing room, bathroom and toilets, with an adjoining cabin for their maid, a bosomy middle-aged woman called Mildred. Dillman did not know of her existence until he joined the Rymers in their private dining room and he assumed that Mildred must have traveled to Liverpool with them in a second- or third-class compartment of the same train.

Sylvia Rymer was also more personable, delighted with their accommodation and liberated from the nervous tension that Dillman had remarked earlier. Like her husband, she was able to open up now that the ship had actually left port, as if some major obstruction had finally been negotiated, allowing her to enjoy the voyage. Dillman was certain that the obstruction was related in some way to Violet, who still sulked whenever her parents spoke to her but who showed a genuine curiosity in their American guest.

"Did you actually design yachts?" she said, eyes widening.

"Not really," he admitted. "My father kept me very much in a subservient role. It was one of the reasons I felt that I had to get away."

"What was his response?" asked Rymer.

"Let us just say that he opposed the notion."

"So what will you do now, Mr. Dillman?"

"That is what I am going home to discuss with my family, sir. There are several options to consider, but I don't wish to worry about them now. I had the most pleasurable vacation in the old country and mean to wring every ounce of enjoyment out of this maiden voyage before I have to contemplate the prospect of a new career."

"What will you most remember about England?" asked Sylvia Rymer.

"The dreadful weather!" answered her husband.

"Not at all," said Dillman. "It has been unusually kind during my stay. I was warned about the likelihood of rain but it kept off for the most part. No, my most treasured memories are my visits to the theater."

"What did you see?"

"Whatever I could, Mrs. Rymer."

"We went to the theater ourselves last night," she explained.

"To the Hicks Theatre on Shaftesbury Avenue. A play by Henry Arthur Jones."

"Yes. *The Hypocrites.*"

"You saw it as well, Mr. Dillman?"

"I enjoyed it immensely."

"So did we," said Rymer, and then he flung a glance at his daughter. "Some of us, anyway. It was a waste of a ticket to take Violet."

"I was not in the mood, Father," she muttered.

"You might have preferred the play at the Duke of York's Theatre," said Dillman helpfully. "*Brewster's Millions.* It's a hilarious farce about the business of making money."

"There is nothing farcical about making money," said Rymer seriously. "Who wrote the play?"

"A fellow countryman of mine called Byron Ongley."

"Ah! An *American* play!"

"And not the only one in town, sir. Had you gone to the Comedy Theatre, as I did, you could have seen Miss Marie Tempest in *The Truth,* an astonishing performance in a fine play by Clyde Fitch. He is perhaps best remembered for a play called *Captain Jinks of the Horse Marines,* another comedy about American social life. Believe it or not, we do have our own dramatists, you know."

"But they pale to insignificance beside our playwrights."

"That is a matter of opinion, Mr. Rymer."

"No American can hold a candle to Pinero or Henry Arthur Jones."

"I would dispute that, sir, though I would happily yield the palm to another British dramatist. He is a comic genius. We certainly have nobody who can get within touching distance of him."

"Do you refer to this new fellow—whatsisname? The one who wrote a play called *The Golden Box?*"

"*The Silver Box,* Matthew," reminded his wife. "We saw it last year. The author's name was John Galsworthy."

"Well, I wouldn't call him a comic genius."

"No more would I," said Dillman patiently. "The man who has

really taken the stage by storm is George Bernard Shaw. I've had the pleasure of seeing his work both here and in New York. Mark my words, he is the playwright of the future."

Rymer was appalled. "But the fellow is an *Irishman*."

Dillman could see that it would be unwise to take a discussion of drama any further and he swiftly backpedaled. After thanking them for their hospitality, he took his leave. As they waved him off, Sylvia Rymer was gracious and her husband uncommonly civil, but their daughter was hurt by his departure and shot him a wounded look. Violet obviously did not wish to be delivered up once more to the less-than-tender mercies of her parents.

Pleased that she had identified him as a friend, Dillman felt a twinge of guilt at having to abandon her. He consoled himself with the thought that there would be time to make amends in the days ahead. Meanwhile, he felt the need of a stroll on deck to clear his lungs. At the end of their meal, Matthew Rymer had smoked a cigar and its acrid smell still haunted Dillman's nostrils and clung to his clothes. It was a mild night with a welcome breeze. As he walked along the promenade deck, he inhaled deeply. Most passengers had started to disperse to their cabins by now but a few were still on deck. Dillman strode past them until he spotted a uniformed figure at the rail. He recognized the profile.

"Rather late for you to be up, isn't it?" he said jokingly.

Lionel Osborne turned round. "Oh, hello there, Mr. Dillman."

"Early to bed. Doctor's orders."

"What is the point of being the ship's surgeon if you can't ignore your own advice?" said Osborne with a grin. "Besides, who could resist being on deck on an historic night like this? Sea air is so bracing."

Osborne was a dapper man in his forties with a clean-shaven face that tapered to a point at the chin. Dillman had only met him once but had taken to him immediately. Osborne had a blend of expertise and resilience that was vital in his profession. Unlike some of the ship's complement, he treated Dillman as an equal and not as a rather minor employee whose presence was a necessary insurance.

"Do you expect to be busy?" said the American.

"Doctors are always busy on transatlantic crossings."

"Seasickness?"

"That is the least of my worries, Mr. Dillman. No, what we are up against is the law of averages."

"I don't follow."

"Work it out for yourself, old chap. Five days on board with over two thousand passengers. There's bound to be at least one heart attack, brain hemorrhage, or other serious problem. And some people will overindulge in the dining saloon, so there'll be everything from cases of acute indigestion to more serious gastric disorders." He waved a hand at the rolling waves. "I'm enjoying the view while I have the chance."

"There is not much to see in the darkness."

"Maybe not," said Osborne, "but it is an improvement on the swollen ankles, inflamed throats, and distended stomachs which I'll have to look at in due course. Not to mention the odd broken bone. Whenever I'm on duty, someone always manages to fall down some steps. It's uncanny."

"What is the worst emergency you had to face?"

"Difficult to say, Mr. Dillman. If you pressed me, I think it would be a toss-up between performing a tracheotomy on the floor of a cabin and delivering a baby in a force nine gale. Oh," he recalled, "then there was the lady with the sick poodle."

"Are you expected to be a vet as well?"

"A ship's surgeon is supposed to be able to cure anything from malaria to foot-and-mouth disease." Osborne grimaced at the memory. "But that poodle was vicious. It almost bit off my finger. When I told its owner that there was nothing wrong with the animal, she turned on me as well. I had the pair of them yapping away at me."

"Occupational hazards."

"I daresay that you have your share of those, old chap."

Dillman smiled. "I enjoy a spot of action."

"Has there been any to report so far?"

"Not really. I conducted one brief search of the ship earlier on but found nothing untoward. To be honest, I still haven't mastered the layout of the vessel."

"Nor I. It's like the Hampton Court maze."

They chatted amiably for a while, then Dillman excused himself and resumed his walk. Seven decks were designed for use by the passengers, from the lower deck up to boat deck. Though his responsibility was largely confined to the first-class areas, Dillman had an interest in the whole vessel and he spent some time exploring it while it was relatively uncluttered by passengers. Eventually, he made his way up to the boat deck, the largest open area on the ship and the one that would be most populated during good weather. It was almost deserted now and the cooling breeze he felt on the covered promenade deck had stiffened markedly now that he was more exposed. Dillman liked the way that it ruffled his hair and tugged at his clothing. It brought back happy memories of his yachting days.

The only people he could see were a young couple, arms entwined, gazing into the void over the stern of the ship. They were far too much in love to notice the cold. Dillman glanced at the lifeboats, secure on the davits and covered with tarpaulins. In the days to come, he knew, they would assuredly be brought into use for clandestine assignations. Those who had designed the boats showed little consideration for the needs of lovers but true passion made light of discomfort. During his crossing to England on the *Lucania,* Dillman had found a stowaway in one of the boats but he knew that the *Lusitania*'s set had been carefully searched before leaving port.

He raised a palm to cover an involuntary yawn. After a valedictory glance around the boat deck, he made his way back to his cabin, feeling the need for sleep. On his way, he had to walk past the first-class lounge and he popped his head in to see if anybody was still there. Several people were still up, talking in groups or, in one case, dozing fitfully in an armchair, but the people who immediately caught his attention were beside the fireplace. There were four of them. Two were elderly ladies and a spasm of excitement went through him when he looked at the fair-haired young woman seated between them. He had seen her once before, at Euston Station, a blur of loveliness. Shorn of her straw hat, she was even more beautiful and had a natural poise that defied the late hour.

Unfortunately, she was deep in conversation with a man whom Dillman also recognized. Henry Barcroft was in his element, quizzing her and simultaneously showing off by displaying his knowledge of the first-class passenger list. To Dillman's jaundiced eye, they seemed almost like a couple. It was galling. The young woman he most wanted to meet was ensnared by the journalist he most wished to avoid.

It was time to go to bed.

The superior speed of the *Lusitania* allowed her to overhaul her sister ship, the *Lucania,* at 4:30 A.M. the following morning before a blanket of fog obliged both vessels to slow down considerably. Not long after 9:00 A.M., the *Lusitania* anchored at the entrance to Queenstown Harbor. Fifteen minutes later, the *Lucania* floated past it to take up its berth. Large crowds had been gathering since dawn on both east and west headlands around the harbor and craft of every shape and size had assembled to give the ships a true nautical salutation. On that southernmost tip of Ireland, sailors and citizens alike appreciated the real significance of the maiden voyage of the *Lusitania* and they were determined not to miss a sighting.

After taking on board passengers and mail, the *Lucania* set sail first and passed Daunts Rock Lighthouse at 11:35 A.M. The *Lusitania* took on more than a hundred passengers and almost eight hundred bags of mail before setting off, shortly after noon, in pursuit of the other ship. The watching crowd cheered themselves hoarse as the narrow beam of the new vessel cut cleanly and purposefully through the dark water. An attempt to win back the Blue Riband, and the enormous kudos that went with it, was now properly under way.

The new passengers were eager to stow their luggage in their cabins so that they could get swiftly back up on deck in order to enjoy the true, heartwarming Irish send-off they were being given. One of them, however, showed no interest in the proceedings. He was a tall, slim young man with a swarthy complexion and large brown eyes. While others had tripped excitedly up the gangplank, he had more or less slunk aboard the ship, head down and face largely covered by the peak of his cap. When he was shown to his cabin in the second-class quarter, he locked the door behind him before swinging his suitcase up onto the bed. Opening it at once, he took out a small photograph of a young woman and kissed it softly before placing it on his table.

From inside a silver frame, Violet Rymer smiled back at him.

FOUR

By midafternoon, the *Lusitania* was steaming across the Atlantic Ocean with thick black smoke belching furiously from three of her funnels. Passengers on the boat deck who wondered why no smoke came from the fourth funnel were unaware of the fact that its function was purely decorative and that it had been added by the ship's designer for reasons of symmetry. A vessel on that scale needed massive funnels, each one so large that it was possible for two cars to drive through them side by side when their individual sections had been riveted together at the shipyard. Photographic proof of this capability had been released to the press and many newspapers had startled their readers with the pictures. Other details of the ship's construction, however, were jealously guarded. The giant was ready to display its muscles to the world, but its vital organs were kept largely secret so they could not be copied by rivals.

It did not seem like a Sunday. Though services had been held aboard and hymns sung with Christian gusto, there were few outward signs of the Sabbath. People promenaded on the decks or made use of the various leisure facilities. Cameras were much in evidence and a few amateur artists worked on their first sketches.

The busiest men aboard were the trimmers and stokers down in the engine room, the former making sure that the latter had an endless supply of highly combustible bituminous coal from the bunkers. There were almost two hundred furnaces and their appetite was voracious. In order to maintain the top cruising speed of twenty-five knots, the best part of a thousand tons of coal a day had to be shoveled into the flames. For those down below, the Sabbath was no day of rest.

George Porter Dillman spent most of the morning familiarizing himself with the vessel and mingling with the other passengers. Some new acquaintances were made and he was on nodding terms with several other people. Though technically a member of the crew, it was important for him to be accepted as just one more first-class passenger so that he could move unseen around his territory and monitor it more effectively. Late afternoon found him taking tea in the Veranda Café with Cyril and Ada Weekes. The couple had acquired a new friend in Jeremiah Erskine, a big, ponderous man of middle years with a luxuriant black beard and a scattering of ugly warts on a high forehead. Extensive business interests in the United States made Erskine a regular transatlantic traveler but he seemed to derive no pleasure from his voyages.

"I sense trouble ahead," he said darkly. "Everything has gone far too smoothly so far. That is a bad omen."

"What do you mean, Mr. Erskine?" asked Weekes.

"The Cunard Line is fraught with danger, sir."

"That is not true at all," said Dillman defensively. "Its safety record is beyond reproach and no more stable vessel has ever been launched than the *Lusitania*."

Erskine remained lugubrious. "They said the same of the *Umbria* when it came into service over twenty years ago. Yet it went badly adrift in 1892 and was later involved in a major collision in New York Harbor. As for the much-vaunted *Etruria*," he continued, hitting his stride, "that, too, was involved in a collision. When I sailed on her four years ago, she was the target for gangsters who tried to blow her up."

"Heavens!" exclaimed Ada Weekes.

"You are causing unnecessary alarm, sir," warned Dillman.

Erskine was unrepentant. "I believe in facing facts, Mr. Dillman."

"What was that about gangsters?" asked Weekes. "Who were they?"

"Italians," said Erskine. "Members of the Mafia Society. An evil organization which swore to destroy all British ships leaving New York."

"But they failed miserably," said Dillman, wanting to reassure the others. "Security aboard all Cunard vessels was far too tight. On the occasion to which Mr. Erskine refers, the *Etruria* crossed the Atlantic without incident."

"That was not the case earlier this year," said Erskine solemnly, scratching at his beard. "Did you know that two members of its crew were killed during bad weather in January? Then there is the *Campania,* another Cunard ship with a reputation for safety. It was involved in a bad collision in 1900 and, a mere two years ago, it was struck by a freak wave which killed some of its passengers."

"That's dreadful!" cried Ada Weekes.

"But highly atypical," insisted Dillman.

"I had no idea that an Atlantic crossing was so perilous."

"It's not, Mrs. Weekes. Believe me."

"Inclement weather is only one hazard," said Erskine, settling into his role as a prophet of doom. "Bad seamanship is another problem. Only two years ago, the *Caronia,* biggest and newest ship of the line, ran aground off Sandy Hook. Size is no guarantee of safety."

"So it seems," said a meditative Weekes, patting his wife's arm to calm her. "But I am sure we are in no danger here. The Cunard Line will have learned from its earlier mistakes."

"Indeed it has," emphasized Dillman, wondering how two such affable people as Cyril and Ada Weekes had been drawn to such a melancholy individual as Jeremiah Erskine. "What you have heard are isolated examples. Hundreds of thousands of people have sailed across the Atlantic without any whiff of danger. As for the tragedy aboard the *Campania,* it was caused, as Mr. Erskine told us, by a freak wave. What he did not say was that it was the first time in sixty years that any passengers were killed on the Cunard Line."

"You seem to know a great deal about this subject, sir," said Erskine, annoyed at being robbed of his ability to spread unease. "May I ask what allows you to speak with such apparent authority?"

"I come from a maritime family, Mr. Erskine."

"You have been an officer aboard a liner?"

"No, sir. But I have helped to build oceangoing yachts and that has given me great insight into the safety features of any vessel as well as the vagaries of weather."

"Yet you have not crossed the Atlantic as often as I have."

"I concede that," said Dillman. "What suprises me is that a veteran like yourself would not wish to offer a degree of reassurance to passengers, like our friends here, who are crossing for the first time."

"When I sense disaster, Mr. Dillman, I must speak out."

"Even if it causes willful distress?"

"I have a premonition, sir."

"Then why sail on the vessel in the first place?"

"It is a business necessity."

Weekes stepped in to change the subject to the dinner menu for that evening and Erskine was diverted from his gloomy prognostications. Ada Weekes visibly relaxed. Dillman took the opportunity to excuse himself. The teatime session with Jeremiah Erskine had left him feeling the need for more cheerful company. Since the weather was still relatively mild, one side of the café had been opened up so Dillman simply had to step a few yards before he was out on deck. Many passengers were sauntering along in the sunshine, some with dogs on leashes. Dillman strolled in the direction of the stern but he did not get very far before he recognized the two people who were coming toward him. They were the elderly ladies whom he had seen in the lounge on the previous evening with the mysterious young woman and the egregious journalist. It gave him the chance to do some detective work on his own account.

Wearing coats, hats, and scarves to ward off the breeze, the Hubermanns walked along arm in arm. They had slept well the night before, eaten a hearty breakfast and an even more delicious luncheon, then spent the afternoon in a leisurely tour of the ship. When the tall young man confronted them with a polite smile, they came to a halt. Dillman touched the brim of his hat.

"Good afternoon, ladies," he said.

"Good afternoon," they chorused.

"Ah, fellow Americans!"

"There seem to be a lot of us aboard, sir," said Carlotta, eyeing him with approval and noting his immaculate suit. "My sister and I are thinking of forming an American Society aboard the *Lusitania*."

"It was only a fanciful notion," said Abigail dismissively.

"An interesting one nevertheless," observed Dillman. "I'm sorry to interrupt your stroll but I have the feeling that I saw you both in the lounge last night, talking with a British journalist."

"Yes!" said Carlotta ruefully. "He kept us up until all hours."

"Both you and the young lady with you."

"He was far more interested in her than in us."

"What did you make of Mr. Henry Barcroft?"

"Why do you ask?" said Abigail suspiciously.

"Because he set on me earlier in the voyage. I must say, I found him uncomfortably persistent. His manner was far too intrusive for my liking. I shook him off as soon as I could."

"I wish that we had done the same," said Carlotta.

"Yet your companion seemed to find his conversation interesting."

"It was for her sake that we tolerated him."

"Is the young lady traveling with you?"

"Oh no. We met her on the train to Liverpool."

"She looks oddly familiar."

"Does she?" said Abigail, eyelids narrowing.

"Her name would not happen to be Violet Weekes, would it?"

"No," said Carlotta. "It is—"

"It is not," said Abigail, interrupting firmly. "But, then, you already know that, sir. Had she really been the person whom you mention, you would have come across and spoken to her in the lounge last night. Let us be honest here," she said, fixing Dillman with a withering gaze. "You caught sight of a beautiful young lady and wondered what her name was. That is why you accosted us just now, in the hope that you could trick the information out of us." She took a tighter grip on her sister's arm. "You have not succeeded."

"Allow me to explain," he said.

"No, sir. Allow *me* to explain. You are the fourth man today who has tried to wrest her name from us under false pretenses and you will not be the last. It is very ignoble of you. Stand aside, please." Dillman moved out of their way. "Come along, Carlotta."

They swept past him and he touched his hat once more. His plan had gone awry but he was not abashed. His brief encounter with the Hubermann sisters had been stimulating. They were a formidable pair and seemed to be the self-appointed guardians of the young woman in question. If they kept him at arm's length, they would also protect their friend from the attentions of Henry Barcroft. It was some consolation.

Barcroft was ubiquitous. Having talked to a wide variety of first-class passengers, he spoke to several officers and crew members, even taking the trouble to chat to deckhands, window cleaners, stewards, linen keepers, hairdressers, and musicians. But the man he was most anxious to interview was the chief engineer. Fergus Rourke seemed to have been designed in proportion with the vessel. He was a huge man with a barrel chest and shoulders so wide they they looked as if they were about to break free from his uniform. A red beard fringed his chin. Proud of his appointment as chief engineer, he was keen to fulfill his duties and found the visit by the journalist increasingly irritating.

The clamor of the engine room obliged them to raise their voices.

"It's very warm down here, Mr. Rourke!" shouted Barcroft.

"You get used to it, sir."

"Those pistons are earsplitting."

"They go with the job, Mr. Barcroft."

"It's not one that I would care to have. But I take my hat off to you and your men. It takes the most enormous effort to keep the ship sailing at this speed. What sort of power is generated exactly?"

"We have four direct-drive steam turbines, sir. In all, the machinery develops some sixty-eight thousand IHP and revolves at a hundred eighty RPM." Rourke towered over him. "Do you need me to explain exactly what that means?"

"No, sir. I did my homework before I came aboard. I think I've mastered most of the technical terms. Including PSI."

"Steam is provided at one hundred ninety-five PSI by twenty-three double-ended and two single-ended cylindrical boilers, situated in four separate boiler rooms. That's how the *Lusitania* can travel at such a lick."

"Could I take a closer look at the boilers?"

"I'm afraid not, sir."

"But my editor is a stickler for detail."

"No passenger is allowed beyond this point."

"I'm a journalist, Mr. Rourke. A man with an inquiring mind."

"Then I suggest you take it back up on deck, sir. I was happy to answer your questions but you are now interfering with my work."

Barcroft would not be shaken off. "Keeping the British press well informed is *part* of your work, surely?" he said. "Don't you want us to celebrate this engineering marvel? We can hardly do it if we are not given the complete freedom of the ship."

"Take the matter up with Captain Watt, sir."

"This is the domain of Chief Engineer Rourke. I was told that you rule the roost down here. Only you can give me permission."

"No chance of that, sir."

"Why not?"

"I must ask you to go back up on deck."

"May I come again, Mr. Rourke?"

"I've told you all that I may."

"One final question. What happens during the night?"

"The night?"

"Do these stokers still work at the same manic pace?"

"Of course, sir," said Rourke. "These furnaces are tended twenty-four hours a day. My men work in shifts throughout the night. While you and the other passengers are tucked up in your cabins, the engine room will be as busy as ever."

Henry Barcroft looked at the dust-covered trimmers and the gleaming sweat on the arms and faces of the stokers. Each time a furnace door was opened, he felt the heat surge up at him like a punch.

"It's hell down here," he concluded. "Thank you, Mr. Rourke. You've been extremely helpful. But I'm ready to go back up to the other place now. Yes," he said brightening, "that could be the opening line of my article. 'The difference between the boiler room and the first-class areas is the difference between hell and heaven.' Now, what does that make you, Mr. Rourke?"

The chief engineer gritted his teeth, held back a stream of ripe expletives, and hid his exasperation behind a gruff civility.

"You tell me, Mr. Barcroft," he said. "You're the journalist."

As soon as he received the message from him, Dillman went straight to the purser's cabin. Charles Halliday was a thin, almost ascetic-looking man with hollowed cheeks and piercing eyes but he was an efficient and resourceful purser. There was a touch of self-importance about him, but Dillman ignored that. Purser Halliday was a crucial figure aboard the ship and the American had to work in harness with him and with the other purser. When his guest arrived, Halliday poured him a drink of whiskey, then sipped from his own glass.

"Thank you for coming so promptly, Mr. Dillman."

"Problems, Mr. Halliday?"

"One or two. I had a chat with the chief steward earlier. He's spotted one of our regulars."

"Regulars?"

"Chap by the name of Collins. Edward Collins. At least, that is the name he always travels under. Passes himself off as an art dealer but the only art he practices is at a card table."

"A professional gambler?"

"Yes, and a highly successful one at that."

"What do you want me to do, Mr. Halliday?"

"Keep an eye on the rogue," said the other. "There's no law against playing cards but we have to make sure he doesn't fleece the other passengers and we don't want them signing IOUs which they can't honor. Not everyone in first class is a millionaire."

Dillman grinned. "I can vouch for that."

"Collins will repay watching. If he goes too far, you may need to step in with a quiet warning. Can't have him upsetting people. It will give the *Lusitania* a bad name."

"Leave it to me, Mr. Halliday." He tasted his own drink. "This is an excellent malt whiskey, by the way. Thank you."

"I needed something to revive me," said Halliday. "A purser is always in the line of fire and the bullets have been coming thick and fast today." He drained his glass. "The other problem concerns a British journalist who's been making a bit of a nuisance of himself."

"I think I can guess whom you mean."

"We had to have the press aboard on a maiden voyage. Necessary evil, I'm afraid. Most of them hunt in packs and are easy to control but this fellow is something of a loner. Wanders off where he's not wanted. Pries into parts of the ship which are out of bounds."

"Would his name happen to be Henry Barcroft?"

"You know him?"

"I had a rather abrasive meeting with him yesterday. Mr. Barcroft is indeed a nuisance. He pops up in the most unwelcome places."

"Put him on your list for surveillance."

"I will, Mr. Halliday. Anyone else?"

"Not as yet. But there will be, I fear."

"Yes." Dillman sighed. "The pickings are too easy. People tend to be off guard on a transatlantic voyage. Far too trusting. An ideal situation for gamblers and confidence tricksters."

"That's why the passengers need our protection, Mr. Dillman."

"I know." He finished his drink. "That was very welcome, sir."

"No time for another, alas. Have to see to the needs of the ladies."

"Ladies?"

"Yes," said Halliday wearily. "Dress was very informal on our first night at sea but it will be different this evening. The men will be in their best bib and tucker and the ladies will want to wear their jewelry. That means I'll have to take it out of the safe and get them to sign for it. I tell you, Mr. Dillman, we have a veritable treasure chest under lock and key. Diamonds, rubies, emeralds, sapphires, and goodness knows what else. Much of it will be on display in the dining saloon this evening." He wagged a finger. "Let's make sure that none of it goes astray."

"I'll keep my eyes peeled."

"*Nothing* must go wrong on this voyage."

"No, Mr. Halliday."

"Nothing at all."

Genevieve Masefield took extra pains that evening. Always careful with her appearance, she knew that she had to make a real impact over dinner and she had chosen her most striking dress for that purpose. It was made of rippling silk and its turquoise hue matched her eyes perfectly. Much as she liked the Hubermanns, she was beginning to regret that she had let them get so close to her. They might keep away unwelcome suitors but they would also deter gentlemen in whom she might actually take an interest. Carlotta Hubermann was not the stumbling block. If a romantic entanglement did present itself to Genevieve, she felt sure that Carlotta would both encourage her into it and support her throughout it, but Abigail Hubermann was a totally different matter. She was more likely to scupper it before it even got started. Genevieve needed to be tactful.

When she finished her makeup and brushed her hair, she stood up to examine the results in the full-length mirror. Highly satisfied, she twirled around to inspect the rear view and made the silk dress swish. Genevieve reached for her purse, checked its contents, then snapped it shut. With the purse under her arm, she let herself out of the cabin and walked down the corridor. At that precise moment, a man came around a corner ahead of her and tossed her a casual glance. Henry Barcroft stopped when he recognized her and gave her a broad grin.

"Good evening, Miss Masefield!"

"Good evening."

"I didn't realize that your cabin was along here."

"Didn't you?" she said, wondering if his appearance was the result of accident or clever timing. "I hope you will not try to interrogate me any further, Mr. Barcroft. I have no more to add to what I said last night."

"Rest assured there will be no more questions," he said warmly. "And I do apologize for keeping you up the way that I did. You and your friends must have been dropping with fatigue."

"We survived."

"Yes, they were tough old birds, those two."

"The Hubermanns are delightful ladies."

"Oh, I meant no criticism," he said, appraising her dress and the diamond necklace above it. "It was a privilege to meet them— and to meet you, of course. May I say how ravishing you look this evening?"

"Thank you, Mr. Barcroft."

He waited for an answering compliment from her but it did not come. Wearing white tie and tails, the journalist preened himself for a moment. He gave her an admiring smile.

"Will you be dining with the Hubermanns this evening?" he asked.

"Yes, Mr. Barcroft."

"Well, I hope they will release you at some stage, Miss Masefield."

"Why?" she said coldly.

"I remembered your saying that you would be interested to meet Lord Carradine, the tobacco baron. As it happens, I interviewed him this afternoon. A most approachable man. I'd be very happy to introduce you to him if the notion appeals to you."

Her manner softened at once. "Thank you, Mr. Barcroft."

"We might even catch him before dinner."

"Lead the way."

Barcroft offered his arm but Genevieve ignored it, preferring to walk beside him. Other couples were also converging on the dining saloon and there was a small queue when they reached the entrance. Barcroft saw the tall, elegant man in evening dress who was talking nearby to one of the stewards. He waved a hand.

"The mystery man returns!"

"Good evening," said Dillman, peeved to see whom the journalist was accompanying. He extended a hand to Genevieve. "I don't believe that we've met."

"No," she said, looking past him. "We haven't, sir. Excuse us."

"Enjoy your meal," added Barcroft.

Then the two of them brushed past him and went to join a group of people who were standing in the middle of the room. Dillman was taken aback. He watched the journalist introduce his companion to a balding man in his thirties with a monocle in his right eye. Dillman could see that she made an immediate impression on him. He sidled across to the head waiter and spoke in an undertone.

"Who is that man?" he asked.

"Which man, sir?"

"The one with the monocle. In the center of the room."

"That is Lord Carradine, sir."

Dillman ransacked his memory. "Carradine? That name rings a bell. Isn't he something to do with tobacco?"

"I believe that he is *everything* to do with it, sir."

The headwaiter moved off to welcome some newcomers and Dillman was left to study the group from the sidelines. Lord Carradine was evidently charmed by his new acquaintance and was introducing her to his friends. Henry Barcroft floated discreetly away. Dillman was still watching the scene when the Hubermanns came up behind him.

Abigail summed up the situation at a glance.

"Are you still lurking, young man?" she said accusingly.

"Oh, good evening!" said Dillman, turning to see them. "No, I was just looking around for some friends."

"We know whom you had in your sights, don't we, Carlotta?"

"Yes, Abigail," agreed her sister.

"How many times do you need to be told, sir?"

There was an asperity in her tone that made Dillman step back. They moved past, shooting him separate looks of disdain, then went to collect their young friend from the attentions of Lord Carradine. It had been an unpromising start to the evening for Dillman and there was worse to come. Cyril and Ada Weekes suddenly appeared at his elbow. When greetings had been exchanged, Weekes gave his arm a squeeze.

"Ada and I are so glad that you're joining us for dinner. We took the liberty of inviting someone you already know to sit beside you."

"Who is that, Mr. Weekes?"

"Mr. Erskine. The two of you seemed to get on so well."

Dillman's heart sank, but he contrived a grateful smile.

"Yes," he lied bravely. "I look forward to meeting him again."

Philip Garrow spent most of the day finding his way around the ship and learning something about its rules and regulations. Anxious to make contact with Violet Rymer, he knew that he would have to bide his time. She would still be under the close supervision of her parents. Since the three of them were traveling first class, he opted for a second-class ticket so there would be no accidental meeting. Matthew and Sylvia Rymer had to be avoided at all costs or there would be severe repercussions. The problem lay in eluding them and reaching their daughter. It would not be easy. Clear demarcation lines existed between the different classes of passengers. Warning notices kept interlopers out of forbidden areas.

Garrow obviously needed an accomplice. He chose one of the older stewards, a man seasoned in the ways of the world and accustomed to hearing odd requests from the passengers.

"What's your name?" asked Garrow.

"Albert, sir."

"Do you like being a steward, Albert?"

"'ave to like it, sir. It's my calling."

"Does it bring in a decent wage?"

"Not so as you'd notice, sir."

"But there must be extras. Tips and so on."

"Now and again," admitted the other, curiosity aroused. "Why do you ask, sir? You don't look as if you want to be a steward aboard a liner. Where's all this leading?"

"That's up to you, Albert."

They were standing outside Garrow's cabin and he fell silent while a quartet of people went past on their way to the second-class dining saloon. Sensing a chance to make money, the steward waited patiently. He was a short, stout man with graying hair. A florid complexion hinted at a fondness for alcohol. His eyes were bloodshot.

"Well, sir?" he nudged.

"Are you allowed into the first-class quarters?"

"Not unless I want to lose my job, sir. I'm confined to the second-class and, to tell you the truth, I prefers it that way. Too many airs and graces in first-class. The passengers there can be very demanding. Some of them treats you like dirt. No, sir," he decided. "I'm 'appier here."

"But you must know some of the stewards in first class."

"Dozens of them. My own brother for one."

"You have a brother on the ship?"

"Two, sir. Tom and me's second-class. Jack's first."

"Can you get in touch with Jack?"

"Easily." A considered pause. "If there was a good reason."

"I'd like him to do a favor for me."

"What sort of favor, sir?"

"A very simple one, Albert. I have a special friend aboard this ship. In first-class. I just want to know which cabin she's in."

The steward sniggered. "Like that, is it?"

"Do you think that Jack could help me?"

"'e's not supposed to," said the other, shaking his head. "What you asks for is confidential information. Jack'd be taking a risk."

"I'll make it worth his while."

"Would you, sir?"

"And you'll get the same, of course. After all, you're the go-between. What do you say, Albert? Can you and your brother help me?"

"I'll 'ave to think it over, sir."

"Don't be too long about it. This is important."

"I gathered that, sir. Sweetheart, is she?"

"I need the number of her cabin."

"Then what?"

"I might need a second favor."

Another snigger. "Thought you might, sir. You'll be wanting our Jack to deliver a message, I daresay. Better warn you now, this'll cost you. A sovereign apiece won't cover this. Risks, see? Dangers."

"Name your price."

The steward squinted up at him. Philip Garrow was patently a driven man with an edge of desperation about him. He was ripe for exploitation. At the same time, Albert felt inclined to help him. The thought of playing Cupid appealed to a romantic streak in his nature.

"Let me speak to Jack," he said at length. "Me and 'im needs to chew this one over. Who knows? Maybe we can do a bit more for you than is being asked of us. That suit you, sir?"

FIVE

The mood of celebration continued and intensified throughout the evening until the *Lusitania* seemed to be hosting one enormous party. People who would normally have been attending Evensong at that hour or reading to their children from the family Bible were happily ignoring all precepts about the nature of the Sabbath. Passengers in first class might be attending a banquet but those in third class were not excluded from the sense of occasion. Jollity and camaraderie ran along the serried ranks of wooden benches, and a cheer went up when someone began to play a concertina. The vessel was traveling in international waters. It was outside time and outside the normal restraints of social life.

Decorum was, however, still maintained to a degree in the first-class dining saloon. Notwithstanding the festive atmosphere, there was a visible display of hierarchy with the most distinguished guests seated at the captain's table and others of note also taking up favored positions. George Porter Dillman was at once a participant in, and observer of, the glittering occasion, enjoying a splendid meal for its own sake while keeping the entire room under observation. Seated near one wall of the saloon, he was well placed to let his gaze roam, and his first general impression was one of dazzling opulence. Purser Halliday's prediction had been accurate. The ladies had reclaimed their jewelry from the safe with a vengeance. There were so many diamond tiaras, costly earrings, sparkling necklaces, and gold brooches on show that Dillman felt he was attending a royal function.

Lord Carradine was at the captain's table, dispensing small talk with consummate ease and evincing all the attributes of a bon vivant. Dillman was interested to see that the Rymers had forsaken their private eyrie to dine in public. Matthew Rymer seemed to be delivering one of his lectures to the rest of the table with occasional comments from his wife but Violet Rymer was as reserved and distrait as usual. Alone of the dinner guests, she was clearly suffering.

Whenever he looked around, Dillman's eye always ended up on the same person. Seated between the Hubermanns, she was poised and yet vivacious, taking a full part in the general discussion and entrancing every man at the table. Dillman thought she was the perfect example of English beauty. What surprised him was that there was no sign of the journalist who had escorted her into the saloon. Unless he was hidden by one of the pillars or potted palms, Henry Barcroft had vanished. Dillman half expected him to have wangled himself a place at her table, but Fortress Hubermann had obviously proved impregnable.

Two other surprises lay in store for Dillman. Steeling himself to endure an evening's proximity to the morose Jeremiah Erskine, he instead found the man in an almost lighthearted vein. Champagne was the main reason for this transformation but the other was the presence of his wife, Dorothea. She was the biggest surprise of all. Years younger than her husband, she was a slender woman in a most striking pink evening gown and wearing a diamond necklace the equal of any piece of jewelry in the room. Dillman was amazed that Erskine was even married. The man's funereal manner suggested a lonely and disappointed bachelor. That his wife should be so young and handsome was astonishing, but it certainly made for a more pleasant meal as far as the American was concerned.

Dorothea Erskine was an alert, intelligent woman with firm opinions on every subject that came up. She was even ready to contradict her husband from time to time. Instead of resenting her opposition, Erskine reveled in it, chortling into his beard at each new polite rebuke. Cyril Weekes also came into his own at the table, revealing a gift for humorous anecdote that brought titters of amusement from all of them, including his wife—even though the stories must all have been wearisomely familiar to her. There were five other people at the table and Dillman was glad of the opportunity to widen his circle of friends. As the only American present, he came in for some gentle ribbing and fielded the inevitable questions about New York.

"Is it really as different as they say?" asked Ada Weekes.

"In some ways," replied Dillman.

"New York is surprisingly civilized," added Erskine with a muted guffaw. "One might almost be in London!"

"I hope not," said Weekes. "I want it to be delightfully *foreign*."

"I'm sure that none of you will be disappointed," said Dillman, looking around the table. "Visitors from England are always given a warm welcome. You just have to allow for the idiosyncrasies of the American way of life."

Dorothea Erskine agreed with him and started a debate about national characteristics. It carried them right through the main course. Dillman was just about to eat his dessert when he became conscious that someone was watching him. It was a strange feeling, and he could not make out if it was pleasant or unsettling. His initial hope was that he was arousing interest in a certain person between the Hubermanns, but he saw that she was, in fact, giving instructions to one of the waiters. His gaze searched the saloon until it finally rested at the Rymers' table. It was the pale blue eyes of Violet Rymer that were fixed on him with a mixture of curiosity and appeal. Dillman felt that she was issuing a silent cry for help. When he met her gaze, she gave a brief smile, then seemed to lose her nerve and look away. It was puzzling.

When the meal was over, some guests remained at their tables to prolong their conversations but most began to disperse. Dillman saw the alacrity with which Lord Carradine crossed to the Hubermanns' table to extend an invitation to his new young acquaintance. Since he wisely included the two sisters in his invitation, it was readily accepted and all three ladies rose from their seats. Dillman accepted that she was beyond reach for the rest of the evening. Lord Carradine would have a private lounge to which he could adjourn with his select friends. Dillman had already noted that the aristocrat was unencumbered by a wife or a partner. It allowed him to be singularly attentive to the young lady who had sparked his interest.

"I feel the need of a cigar," declared Erskine.

"Then go to the smoking room," urged his wife. "You know how much I hate the smell of those foul cigars."

"Of course, my dear." He glanced up. "Anyone care to join me?"

"I will," said Weekes.

"Anyone else? Dillman?"

"No, thank you, Mr. Erskine. I don't smoke."

"How bizarre!"

Everyone at the table rose to their feet and made for the door. Cyril Weekes fell in beside Dillman and gave him a companionable nudge.

"Keep an eye on the ladies, old chap, will you?"

"With pleasure."

"Don't want them being abducted, do we?"

"How long do you expect to be?"

"One cigar leads to another. You know how it is. Besides," he said, lowering his voice. "Much as I adore the fairer sex, I do like to retreat into a male preserve on occasion. No ladies in the smoking room."

"Quite so, Mr. Weekes."

"Old Erskine was in fine form this evening, wasn't he?"

"Yes," said Dillman.

"I meant to ask you about something he said this afternoon."

"Mr. Erskine?"

"Over tea. What exactly is this Mafia Society?"

"Why?" teased the other. "Do you wish to become a member?"

Weekes burst out laughing, then shared the joke with Erskine as he led him off to the smoking room. Watching them go, Dillman began to see the affinity between the two men. He suspected that they had a bond that went far deeper than a mutual passion for cigars. Most of the ladies in the group repaired to the powder room and the American was left to settle into an armchair and chat with two abandoned husbands and a lone banker. He was rescued by the appearance of Violet Rymer, who slipped into the lounge on her own with the clear intention of speaking to him. Dillman excused himself and went across to meet her.

"It's so nice to see you again, Miss Rymer!" he said, indicating the chair he has just vacated. "Would you care to join us?"

"I can't stay, Mr. Dillman."

"Are your parents coming into the lounge?"

"No, they're going back to our suite."

"I'm so glad you all ventured out this evening. It was a veritable banquet. I'm only sorry that you didn't seem to enjoy it."

She lowered her head. "Was it that obvious?"

"I'm afraid so."

"I did try."

"I'm sure you did. It's not a crime to be shy. Though I don't think it was only a case of shyness, was it?"

She looked up searched his eyes. "No, Mr. Dillman. There was something else. But I musn't keep you from your friends. I only came to ask you a favor."

"Consider it done, Miss Rymer."

"I wondered if you'd dine with us again sometime."

"Of course."

"You're the only friend I have on board this ship. It's an agony for me to be in the dining saloon with all the other passengers. I feel that they're all staring at me. That they all *know*."

"Know what?"

"Nothing," she said evasively. "So you will come?"

"If your parents have no objection."

"None at all. They like you." Affection suddenly welled up in her eyes but she could not put it into words. She bit her lip. "I must go."

"May I ask one question first?"

"If you wish."

"When exactly is your birthday, Miss Rymer?"

"A week tomorrow."

"So you'll celebrate it in New York?"

"There won't be any celebration involved." She sighed.

"But there has to be," he insisted. "Reaching the age of twenty-one is an achievement. A vital turning point in anyone's life. You'll be a fully fledged adult. Able to make your own decisions. Pursue your own ambitions. You may not have voting rights, of course, but everyone will have to treat you differently." He nodded meaningfully. "Everyone, Miss Rymer. Including your parents."

Tears threatened instantly. Squeezing his arm in gratitude, she took out a handkerchief from her purse, then hurried away before she needed to use it. Violent Rymer was in pain and Dillman feared that he had just added to it with his comment. Moved by her plight, he had to resist an urge to go after her. He would have to help her by stealth.

Philip Garrow had to wait until late into the evening before he got the information he wanted. Having smoked a cigarette on the boat deck and maintained a desultory conversation with some chance acquaintances, he was making his way back down to his cabin when he heard a loud whisper behind him.

" 'Arf a mo, sir!"

He turned to see Albert furtively beckoning him back down the corridor. Garrow followed the steward until they came to a storeroom. After checking that nobody could see them, Albert ushered him inside before shutting the door behind them and switching on the light. The steward was panting slightly and there was a light film of perspiration on his brow. He gave a conspiratorial smirk.

"More private in 'ere, sir."

"Have you spoken to your brother?"

"Don't rush me," said the other, holding up a palm. "Been all over the place, looking for you. Give me time to catch my breath."

"I thought you'd forgotten me," said Garrow.

"Not that stupid, sir. Never forget someone as generous as you. Not that I 'aven't earned my money, mind you," he asserted, flicking a speck of dust off his white jacket. "Broke lots of rules on your be'alf. Lots."

"Does that mean you made contact with your brother?"

"Yes. Wasn't easy, though."

"But you managed it."

"Me and Jack is old 'ands at this, sir."

"Did he agree to do it?"

"Only when I gave him your fiver."

"And?" pressed Garrow, twitching with impatience. "What, then?"

"Jack said he'd do what he could. Not as simple as it sounds. Stewards only cover their own cabins. They don't get to see the full list of passengers. Jack 'ad to do a bit of snooping. Took time."

"But he got results?"

"Eventually."

"Wonderful! Which cabin is it?"

"Suite, sir."

"What do you mean?"

"Two bedrooms leading off a shared lounge and dining room. One of the regal suites. 'er parents must have money."

Garrow was dejected. "So she doesn't have a separate cabin?"

"No, sir. You'd 'ave to go past them to get to 'er."

"That's nothing new!"

"Tricky situation."

"Yes," said the other, running a pensive hand across his chin. "I suppose that I should have expected something like this. They never let her out of their sight. No wonder she feels suffocated." He stepped closer to the steward. "Could your brother get a message to her?"

"Depends."

"He won't lose by it. Nor will you, Albert."

The steward grinned. "Expensive young lady!"

"Worth every penny."

"Take your word for it, sir. Jack *might* be able to get a message to her. On the quiet, like. But there's no telling when that might be. If they got a suite, they might be taking their meals in there as well."

"They're bound to let her out at some stage."

"Jack'll be waiting."

"How will he recognize her?"

" 'e knows 'er name. And he'll speak to the steward who looks after their suite. Casual, like. Ask 'im what sort of people these Rymers is. Probe 'im about the daughter. We always gossips about passengers, sir. Don't you worry. Jack will pick 'er out." He gave another smirk. "Don't want my brother slipping a love letter to the wrong young lady, do we? Could be embarrassing, that."

"Actually, it won't *be* a letter."

"Oh?"

"I want your brother to give her this," he said, feeling gingerly in his pocket. "And he must be discreet. Completely discreet."

"Family characteristic of ours, sir."

The steward held out his hand and Garrow placed a small object into his palm. Albert squinted down at it and then wrinkled his brow.

"A tie pin, sir?"

"She'll understand."

Dorothea Erskine began the exodus. After sitting in the lounge with the others for the best part of an hour, she decided it was time to leave.

"I'm ready for bed," she announced, brushing her necklace with a reverential palm. "And I must have this locked up in the safe again."

"Shall I fetch your husband, Mrs. Erskine?" volunteered Dillman.

"No, thank you. Let him smoke on. Mrs. Weekes?"

"I'll come with you," said Ada Weekes, getting up from her chair. "It looks as if Cyril will be in there for some time yet. If you do see him, Mr. Dillman, please tell him that I've gone back to the cabin."

The other two couples also elected to leave and it gave Dillman the opportunity to break away from the stray banker. The lounge was still quite full. As he made his way to the exit, Dillman reflected on how tolerant both Ada Weekes and Dorothea Erskine seemed to be. Neither had complained about their respective husbands' long absence in the smoking room, and they left without recrimination. It was almost as if they had willingly licensed the departure of their spouses. Dillman did not believe that all the wives aboard would be quite so indulgent.

When he first entered the smoking room, he could not find them. It was only when his eyes grew accustomed to the fug that he was able to pick them out, and he saw at once what had detained them. Instead of withdrawing to enjoy a postprandial cigar, Cyril Weekes and Jeremiah Erskine were seated at a table with four other men and playing cards. Evidently they were not novices. Though both were relaxed and urbane, they studied the cards with the intense concentration of men who took the game seriously enough to play for high stakes.

Dillman now understood why they were drawn together. Judging by the amount of money beside him, Erskine was not faring too well but Weekes appeared to be holding his own. There was a whisper of a smile on his lips. Dillman remembered the annual visit that his friend made to the Grand National and surmised that it must be only one of many race meetings attended in the course of a year. Cyril Weekes was an inveterate gambler. It was more than likely that he had first met Erskine across the card table on the previous evening. They were birds of a feather, flying side by side.

After watching them for a few minutes, Dillman let his eye travel around the rest of the table. Two of the other men were smoking cigars and a third was puffing at a cigarette through a long holder.

It was the fourth man who intrigued Dillman. As one game concluded, he shuffled the pack with expert ease, then dealt the cards
out. He was a big sleek man in his early sixties with a silver beard
and a gleaming bald head. A prominent nose separated two small,
watchful blue eyes that glinted in the light of the table lamp. Dillman knew him from Purser Halliday's description. The man who
looked like an art dealer was the notorious Edward Collins.
Weekes and Erskine were up against a professional.

It was an education to watch them in action. Dillman enjoyed
a game of poker himself but it was an article of faith with him
that he never played for money. These men would never play
without it. It was fascinating to watch the nuances of behavior as
they indulged in bluff and counterbluff, or tried to lure their companions into a trap. Edward Collins was supremely in control. He
did not win every round but he usually managed to claim the pot
when it had the most money in it. By comparison, Weekes had
only small successes. Erskine lost heavily.

Collins was careful to apply no undue pressure. He did not
wish to frighten the others away by emptying their wallets too
greedily at one sitting. It was important to leave them with the
feeling that they might recoup their losses on other nights. Accordingly, he lost the last few games, surrendering the final one
to Erskine when his bluff was called.

"My luck's run out," decided Collins. "Time to quit, I think."

"Only until tomorrow," said Weekes.

"Count me in," said Erskine, pocketing his money.

"What about you other gentlemen?" asked Collins.

One shook his head but the other two were eager to rejoin
battle. Edward Collins thanked them before rising to his feet and
reaching for his silver-topped cane. As he went past Dillman, the
latter got a closer look at him. Edward Collins seemed to be so
cultured and dignified. Decency shone out of him. He inspired
trust. Dillman would have bought an Old Master off him without
a tremor but he would never sit at a card table with him.

Weekes spotted the American for the first time and came over.

"Did my wife send you after me?" he said.

"No, sir. Mrs. Weekes decided to go back to the cabin."

"Oh, dear! Is it that late?" He consulted his watch. "By Jove! So it is. I rather lost track of time in here. Why didn't you join us, Mr. Dillman?"

"I have no skill at cards."

"Not a question of skill, old chap."

"You could have fooled me."

"Luck. That's the secret."

"I prefer other pleasures."

Weekes gave him a sly wink. "So did I at your age. And why not? Every dog and all that. What?" He turned to Erskine. "My wife has gone off to bed. So has yours, probably."

"She usually does," said Erskine. "I've got her well trained."

"What did you use? Lumps of sugar?"

"A diamond necklace."

The two men chuckled aloud and ambled out unsteadily together.

Dillman was glad to get out of the smoking room. His eyes were stinging and the fug was catching in his throat. He made his way to the promenade deck and stood at the rail. It was quite chilly and there were few people about. There was enough moonlight to show how choppy the waves were but the ship rode them with impressive grace and stability. Dillman reviewed the evening. It had been instructive. He had met new friends and learned more about the relationships between existing ones. A visit to the smoking room had also introduced him to Edward Collins. A collective pattern of behavior was beginning to emerge among the first-class passengers, but he saw nothing that might cause any real alarm. Jeremiah Erskine had sensed disaster in the air. Dillman smiled as he considered the possibility that the fellow had merely anticipated his own drubbing at the card table.

The cold wind was encouraging the other passengers to return to their cabins, but Dillman strolled the length of the deck before he was ready to leave. He turned a mariner's eye upward to identify the stars and would probably have stayed there for some time had he not been disturbed by a sudden noise. He looked along the deck in time to see the figure of a man, descending some steps at speed. Dillman only saw him in shadowy outline but he recognized him at once. It was Henry Barcroft. Without quite knowing why, Dillman set off in pursuit of him.

It was a long and bewildering chase, though he was not sure if the journalist even realized that he was being followed. At all events, Barcroft managed to stay too far ahead of him to be caught. Each time Dillman got within sight of him, the man seemed to vanish around a corner or plunge down another staircase, showing a remarkable knowledge of the ship's labyrinthine passages. Eventually, Barcroft vanished altogether and Dillman was left staring in dismay up and down a long empty corridor, wondering which direction his quarry had taken. A decision had to be made. Turning to the right, he broke into a trot and headed for some double doors, pushing them firmly open and surging through, only to find himself colliding with someone.

The young woman let out a cry of surprise and stumbled back. Dillman managed to save her from falling by embracing her in penitential arms. He released her at once and took a step back.

"I do beg your pardon! I had no idea anyone was there."

"Nor more did I," she said, still shaken. "But I suppose I should be grateful that, if I had to bump into anyone, I picked a fellow American."

"George Porter Dillman."

"You were in one heck of a rush, Mr. Dillman."

"I was looking for someone."

"But hit me instead. Amidships. Literally."

"Are you all right?" he said with concern.

"I'll live. Just about. But who were you after?" she asked, looking over her shoulder. "Nobody else came this way."

"Are you sure?"

"Quite sure. My name is Ellen Tolley, by the way." They shook hands. "I like to think I'm pretty tough but you're a big guy to stop."

"I can't apologize enough, Miss Tolley."

"Ellen, please. Why stand on ceremonies? We've just been introduced in the most direct way."

"That was my fault. I can't apologize enough."

"Does that mean you'll insist on Mr. Dillman?"

"Not at all," he said with a grin. "Call me George, please. It will be nice to hear my Christian name again after all this time."

"It's a deal, George."

Ellen Tolley was a bright-eyed, fresh-faced woman in her early twenties with short dark hair that curled naturally and full lips that parted to reveal a perfect set of teeth. Her green striped dress was smart without being arresting and there was a noticeable absence of jewelry. There was a girlish ebullience about her that made her seem younger than her years. While he was appraising her, she was taking the measure of him and she liked what she saw.

"You must be the tall, dark, handsome man that the fortune-teller said I would meet. Trouble is, she forgot to mention you'd be traveling at a hundred miles an hour when our paths crossed."

"I didn't expect anyone else to be there."

"I gathered that."

"Most people have gone off to bed."

"That's where I'd be, George, if only I could find my cabin. I'm lost. I've been wandering around for ages and getting nowhere. Some of these signs are so confusing."

"Allow me to guide you back, Ellen."

"Just point me in the direction of the dining saloon and I'll be okay. That's where I went wrong. I turned left instead of right. All that Champagne. My father would go crazy, if he knew."

"Your father?"

"Yes," she explained. "We're traveling together. He had a headache and went off to his cabin early. I assured him I'd be able to find my own way back. I daren't tell him I went astray. Daddy has always been very protective. It's got worse since Mom died." She adjusted her dress. "You traveling alone, George?"

"Completely alone."

"Where you from?"

"Boston."

"Civilization! We live in New Jersey. I hate it."

"Why?"

"I'll tell you about it another time," she promised. "Right now, I'd appreciate a few directions to the dining saloon."

"I insist on escorting you there."

"What about the person you were chasing?"

"Forget him."

"Who was he, anyway?"

"Nobody."

He walked back down the corridor and she fell in beside him. It was refreshing to be with someone so friendly and unrestrained by convention. Ellen Tolley had great charm and an easy confidence. He could almost feel the zest buzzing out of her. He found himself comparing her with Violet Rymer and wishing that the latter had some of her vitality, but he knew it was a forlorn hope.

"Have you been on vacation, Ellen?"

"Six weeks."

"What did you see?"

"Real history for once. England is dripping with it."

"Sorry to leave?"

"Yes and no," she admitted. "I wanted to stay but, then again, I was not going to pass up the chance of sailing on the maiden voyage of the *Lusitania*. It really is everything it's cracked up to be." She gave a rueful laugh. "If only they'd supply us with a route map."

"Even the stewards haven't got all their bearings yet."

"You seem to be doing pretty well, though."

"Mixture of guesswork and luck."

But he knew exactly where he was going now. Dillman took her up a flight of steps and along a corridor before turning a corner. Ahead of them lay the first-class dining saloon, its lights now largely extinguished.

"At least let me see you to your cabin," he said.

"Kind of you, George, but I guess not."

"Another time, maybe."

A long pause. "Maybe," she said at length. "Aren't you going off to your own bed?"

"I'm on the deck above this."

"Then this is where we separate." She offered her hand again. "Thanks for being my pathfinder. I could have been lost for hours."

"Good night, Ellen," he said, shaking her hand.

"Sweet dreams."

"I hope the bruises don't show in the morning."

"If they do," she joked, "I may sue."

She gave him a cheery wave and Dillman set off up the staircase. He might have lost Henry Barcroft but he had found Ellen Tolley. It was a fair exchange. It was only when he got back to his cabin that it occurred to him to ask himself where the journalist had been going at that time of night and why he had taken such pains to cover his tracks. Barcroft replaced Edward Collins at the top of his mental list for surveillance.

Ellen Tolley edged her way into first position on a different list.

SIX

He had just finished shaving when he received the call. Dillman opened his cabin door to find a junior officer standing outside in the corridor.

"Mr. Halliday's compliments, sir—would you please join him in his cabin as soon as possible?"

"I'll be with him directly," said Dillman, starting to undo the belt around his dressing gown. "Tell him I'm on the way."

"Thank you, sir."

Minutes later, Dillman was inspecting himself in the mirror as he hauled on his jacket. He straightened his tie and ran a hand through his hair. Normally he would dress at a more leisurely pace but the summons betokened urgency. He was soon hurrying off down the passageway toward the staircase, making the last few adjustments to his clothing as he did so and wondering what emergency had prompted the purser to send for him.

Charles Halliday had left the door of the cabin open for him.

"Thanks for coming so quickly, Mr. Dillman."

"It sounded important."

"It is," said Halliday, indicating his other visitor. "I believe you've met our chief engineer before."

"Yes," said Dillman. "Good morning, Mr. Rourke."

Fergus Rourke gave him a noncommittal grunt. He was clearly simmering with anger. The purser closed the cabin door and kept his back to it when he spoke.

"We have a thief aboard the ship," he disclosed.

"Not what I'd call the bleeder!" said Rourke vengefully.

"He may just be a souvenir hunter but somehow I don't think so. We could be up against something rather more serious. I'll let Mr. Rourke explain. He's the injured party."

"Yes," said the chief engineer, bristling. "But my injuries are nothing to the ones he'll suffer when I catch up with the bugger!"

"What exactly happened?" asked Dillman.

"Some items were taken from my cabin."

"Items?"

"Diagrams. Charts. Highly confidential."

"When was this, Mr. Rourke?"

"Who knows? I only discovered the theft this morning when I had to check something on one of the diagrams. It just wasn't there in the folder. Nor were some of the others."

"But they were there yesterday?"

"Definitely."

"Someone must have got into the cabin last night," decided Halliday. "What time did you turn in, Mr. Rourke?"

"Late."

"How late?"

"Late," repeated the other. "Can't put an exact time on it."

"And the cabin was locked while you were away?" said Dillman.

"Of course. It's always locked."

"Who else has a key?"

"Nobody."

"There must be a master key somewhere."

"There is," said Halliday. "First thing I checked. It was locked away in a cupboard all night. The thief got in by some other means."

"I want him caught," demanded Rourke. "Quick!"

"That may not be easy," admitted Dillman, "with the vast number of people aboard. We don't even know if we're looking for a light-fingered passenger or a member of the crew."

"No member of the crew would dare go near my cabin, Mr. Dillman. They know me too well to risk it. No," said the chief engineer, stroking the red beard, "I'm sure this burglar's name is on our passenger list."

"That's why I sent for you, Mr. Dillman," said Halliday seriously. "We can institute inquiries among the crew. The rest is up to you."

"The first thing to establish is motive. From what Mr. Rourke says, I gather that these are highly sensitive documents. Relating to the engine room, presumably? I think that rules out the theory about the souvenir hunter," he concluded. "Since the Cunard emblem has been put on just about everything on the *Lusitania,* you might lose a few towels and bath mats. Even the odd blanket. And the ashtrays will be an obvious target. But not technical diagrams. They'd be meaningless to the vast majority of passengers. No, gentleman, I have an uneasy feeling that this man is rather more than a thief. He's also a spy of some sort."

"Wait till I get my hands on the bastard!" said Rourke with a menacing gesture. "I'll tear his heart and liver out and sling 'em into one of the furnaces! Nobody steals from me!"

"Calm down, Fergus," advised the purser.

"I'll slaughter him, so help me!"

"Making wild threats will get us nowhere. We have to catch him first and, as Mr. Dillman says, that could be tricky."

"Are there any possible suspects?" asked the American.

"Not as far as we know."

"What about you, Mr. Rourke? Anyone spring to mind?"

"No. I been too busy doing my job to notice."

"But you must have had lots of visitors to the engine room. Some people love the thrill of peeping in there to see those pistons clanking away. All part of the experience. Then there's the press, of course," he said. "I daresay you had to give them the guided tour."

"Pain in the arse, they were!"

"Did any of them show an exceptional interest in what went on?"

"No," said Rourke. "Most of them couldn't stand the noise and the heat. Once they'd got the basic details from me, they scarpered. They're more concerned with enjoying their free trip across the Atlantic to worry too much about the men who actually get them there." His chest inflated as a memory nudged. "Wait a minute, though! There was one journalist who came back on his own. Inquisitive little sod!"

"What did he want?"

"To wander around, talk to the men. Ha!" snorted the chief engineer. "Wish I'd let him now. Stokers work hard. They don't like to be put on show like animals in a zoo. They'd have sent him packing with a flea in his ear." He scratched his head. "Now, what was his name?"

Dillman supplied it. "Henry Barcroft, by any chance?"

"That was him! Nosy devil! You know him?"

"Yes." Halliday sighed. "Mr. Barcroft has come to our notice already."

"Fetch him here!" suggested Rourke. "I'll beat the truth out of him!"

"Take it easy, Fergus."

"But he's the obvious person, Mr. Halliday."

"That doesn't mean he's the culprit," argued Dillman. "Obvious suspects often turn out to be completely innocent. And we can hardly have you assaulting a member of the British press. That would lead to the most adverse publicity, Mr. Rourke. I can't imagine you'd get any thanks from the Cunard Line. We must proceed with caution."

"I agree," said Halliday, turning to the chief engineer. "Leave this to us, Mr. Rourke. I know that you're anxious to get back to your post. We'll keep you fully informed of any developments."

"If it does turn out to be this turd Barcroft—"

"Then we'll take the appropriate action," the purser assured him, opening the door to let him out. "Thanks for your help. At least we know where to start now."

The chief engineer looked grimly from one to the other, then ducked his head as he took his huge frame out. Closing the door behind him, Charles Halliday gave an apologetic shrug.

"You'll have to forgive him sounding off like that. Fergus is a proud man. Guards his territory very carefully. This has been a real blow to him. He takes it personally"

"I can see that."

"Not unnaturally, the captain is disturbed as well. He wants the matter cleared up quickly but discreetly. So, where do we begin?"

"With Mr. Barcroft. I didn't want to say this in front of the chief engineer because he's inflamed enough already, but I fancy that I saw our journalist behaving rather suspiciously last night. On the prowl after everyone else had gone off to bed."

"Oh?"

"I can't be certain that it was him, mark you, and I never got close enough to confirm it. But if it was not Barcroft, it was his double."

"Where did you see him?"

"On the promenade deck," said Dillman. "I tried to follow him but he led me all over the ship and eventually shook me off when we got to the main deck."

"Why go down there? His cabin is on the shelter deck."

"He didn't stop to tell me, Mr. Halliday."

"Did he know he was being stalked?"

"I'm not sure."

Halliday pondered. "What do you suggest we do?"

"Firstly, we must search his cabin. Thoroughly. Whoever you assign to the task must leave the place exactly as he found it."

"Unless they actually find the stolen documents."

"Slim chance of that," said Dillman. "We have to be realistic. A man who's clever enough to steal the documents will know where to hide them. I doubt very much if he'd leave them hanging around his own cabin. He might already have passed them on to an accomplice."

"It's still worth a try."

"Definitely. We may not reclaim what was taken but we might

find other clues to Mr. Barcroft's real purpose for being on board. But let's not rush to judgment. He could still be innocent."

"What happens then, Mr. Dillman?"

"We start looking elsewhere."

"Right."

"Will you organize the search of his cabin?"

"Yes. Do you wish to be involved?"

"No," said Dillman. "I'd prefer to speak to Henry Barcroft myself and sound him out. It will also keep him occupied while your men go through his things. I take it that Barcroft is *on* your list of accredited journalists?"

"No doubt about that."

"Yet he's not representing any specific newspaper."

"He's a freelance."

Dillman lifted a sardonic eyebrow. "A freelance what, though?"

Genevieve Masefield agreed to meet him, more out of gratitude than out of any desire to spend time alone in his company. Henry Barcroft had introduced her to Lord Carradine, who in turn had introduced her to his circle of friends. Genevieve had made progress. Unfortunately it was in spite of Abigail and Carlotta Hubermann rather than because of them. Kind and well meaning though the two sisters were, they had been something of a hindrance during the visit to Lord Carradine's private lounge on the previous evening. Genevieve needed to distance herself from them. When she headed for the Veranda Café that morning, she made sure that the Hubermanns did not know where she was going or with whom she intended to pass an idle hour.

Henry Barcroft was in an expansive mood, behaving more like a first-class passenger than a journalist on an assignment. The bright sunshine encouraged him to wear a striped blazer, white trousers, and a straw boater. He lacked only a cricket bat to turn him into a symbol of the English summer. For her part, Genevieve chose a two-piece dress carefully cut to display her figure. The long, narrow patterned skirt reached to her ankles and was matched by a Zoave jacket, which covered her white silk blouse.

Her hat, trimmed with velvet bows, had a low crown and wide brim, and was set at just the right angle to show off her face to its best effect.

Elsewhere in the café, Norfolk jackets were popular among the men though there were a few lounge coats among the more elderly travelers who still seemed to feel that they were relaxing at their London clubs. It was left to the ladies to supply any color, style, or variety. One woman, in a mustard dress and a voluminous hat, sat alone and caressed the tiny dog lying somnolently in her lap. Another, anticipating much colder weather, was huddled in a fur-trimmed coat with a muff at the ready.

Henry Barcroft summoned the waiter and ordered a pot of tea.

"How did you get on with Lord Carradine?" he asked Genevieve.

"He was extremely nice."

"One of the old school. Odd thing is, although he's made millions out of tobacco, he doesn't smoke himself." He gave a laugh. "Not exactly a good advertisement for his cigarettes, is it?"

"I hadn't realized he was such a sportsman."

"Oh, yes. He's a regular on the house party circuit. Quite a shot, by all accounts. And a celebrated horseman. Of course, there's another reason why he gets so many invitations for weekends in the country."

"Is there?"

"Come, Miss Masefield. I don't believe you're that naive."

"Ah," she said, understanding. "Lord Carradine is a bachelor."

"A highly eligible bachelor. I daresay he has an endless array of pretty daughters pushed at him for inspection but none have managed to ensnare him yet. He's too fond of his freedom."

"Yet he did talk about wanting to father children."

"My guess is that he's probably done that already!" said Barcroft with a smirk. "Without even knowing it. Well, if he wants the Carradine dynasty to continue, he'll have to walk down the aisle with someone sooner or later. Do you think he'd make good husband material?"

"I have no idea, Mr. Barcroft," she said, resenting his familiar tone and not wishing to be drawn into speculation. "Lord Carradine is a real gentleman, that's all I know. But what happened to you last night?" she went on, moving the conversation in another direction. "You seemed to disappear from the dining saloon."

"I had to, Miss Masefield. I have no dining privileges in first class. We minions of the press are second-class citizens. We have access to the whole ship during the day but the toffs draw the line at actually breaking bread with us." He beamed at her. "Present company excepted, that is. I only turned up yesterday because I'd promised to make that introduction and I always honor my promises."

"Thank you, Mr. Barcroft. It was appreciated."

The journalist was about to pay her some fulsome compliments on her appearance when he caught sight of a familiar face coming into the café. He rose to his feet and extended his arms in a welcome.

"Here comes our mystery man again!"

"Good morning, Mr. Barcroft. How are you today?"

"Very well, thank you, Mr. Dillman."

Dillman was checked. "You know my name?"

"I told you that I was well informed. Oh," he said, indicating his companion. "Allow me to introduce Miss Genevieve Masefield."

Dillman took the proffered hand and gave her a little bow.

"George Dillman. Delighted to meet you, Miss Masefield."

She gave a polite smile of acknowledgment but it lacked warmth.

"Would you care to join us?" invited Barcroft.

"I don't wish to intrude on a private conversation," said Dillman.

"But you might be able to help us." He turned to Genevieve. "Mr. Dillman has a maritime background. He designs and builds yachts. A true sailor in every way."

"Do join us, Mr. Dillman," she said, endorsing the invitation in order to escape being alone with Barcroft. "Where do you build these yachts?"

"In Boston," he explained, sitting beside her and catching a first whiff of her delicate perfume. "It's a family firm. Over fifty years old now. We have an established reputation."

"Is it a lucrative business?" asked Barcroft, resuming his seat.

"We don't starve."

"Only the rich can afford private yachts."

"The firm has a long waiting list."

"That shows how successful it is. But what I wanted to ask you was this, Mr. Dillman. In your opinion, will the *Lucy* manage to regain it?"

"Regain what?"

"The Blue Riband, of course."

"Your guess is as good as mine, Mr. Barcroft."

"Nonsense. I know very little about oceanic travel. You're a veteran. That means you must have developed instincts. What do they tell you?"

"To beware of foolish predictions."

"The *Lusitania* is bound to regain the Blue Riband," said Genevieve. "That's what everyone was saying over dinner last night."

Barcroft grinned. "One of my colleagues is taking bets to that effect. I need your advice, Dillman. Should I put my money on a record?"

"No. Not yet."

"Why not?"

"Because there are too many imponderables," warned Dillman. "It's far too early to judge. Bad weather might slow us down. Or we might be hampered by ice. It drifts down on the Labrador current and can be a real hazard. Then there's the possibility of technical problems in the engine room, of course. And an outside chance of navigational error."

"Not from Captain Watt, surely?"

"Highly unlikely, I agree, but it's possible. The *Lusitania* is a superb ship but it would be unfair to expect too much of her on her maiden voyage. If you really want to know how to wager your money, Mr. Barcroft," he suggested, "the person to talk to is the chief engineer."

"I've already interviewed Mr. Rourke."

"Have you?" said Dillman artlessly.

"He and I didn't exactly get on."

"Why not?"

"Long story. Ah!" he said, as a waiter approached. "Our tea. We're going to need a third cup. If Americans drink tea, that is."

"Have you never heard of the Boston Tea Party?" said Genevieve.

It was a swift riposte to Barcroft's gibe, and Dillman shot her a smile of thanks. The tray was unloaded by the waiter and a third cup ordered. The man went off to get it. Dillman turned to Genevieve.

"You seem to be without your sentries today, Miss Masefield."

"Sentries?"

"The two ladies I keep seeing with you."

"I didn't realize I'd caught your attention, sir."

"I couldn't help noticing the three of you together."

"They're the Hubermann sisters," explained Barcroft. "I wouldn't care to go three rounds with either of them. But I wouldn't really call them sentries." His oily smile warned Genevieve that a compliment was coming. "Miss Masefield is the *Lusitania* and they are her tugboats."

"They are dear friends of mine," said Genevieve sharply, "and I will not have them mocked."

"I only spoke in jest," said the journalist, semaphoring regret.

"And in rather poor taste."

"I'm sorry."

"Let's go back to the chief engineer," suggested Dillman. "You say that the two of you did not get on. What exactly was the problem?"

But there was no time for Barcroft to answer. Abigail and Carlotta Hubermann suddenly came into the room and swooped down on them. Two more cups and a second pot of tea were ordered and conversation turned to more neutral subjects. Dillman concentrated on winning them over with a combination of charm and deference but he kept one eye on Henry Barcroft. The man was an enigma. His bonhomie was apparently inexhaustible. He was completely at ease in the company of Genevieve Masefield and the Hubermann sisters, even though none of them seemed to have any particular liking for him. Indeed, he was given a stern rebuke by Abigail at one point and a warning stare by Carlotta, but his broad smile survived intact. The more reproaches he was given, the happier he seemed to be. Dillman wondered how exuberant he would remain if he knew that his cabin was being searched at that very moment.

It was almost noon before the chance finally presented itself. While going about his own duties, the steward made sure that he went past the Rymers' suite at regular intervals. Like his brother, Jack was short, stout, and well groomed but with a paler complexion and rather fewer teeth. A chat with a colleague elicited the fact that the Rymers were still in their suite, and he began to think they would be entombed there for the entirety of the voyage, making it impossible for Jack and his brother to earn another reward from a grateful second-class passenger.

Violet Rymer finally broke cover. Tired of being trapped with her parents, she excused herself to go for a walk on deck in order to work up an appetite for luncheon. Sylvia Rymer was too engrossed in her novel to wish to put it aside and her husband also sanctioned their daughter's outing. They took it as a hopeful sign. Being locked in their lounge with a moping girl brought neither of them any pleasure. By giving Violet a degree of freedom, they might lift her spirits. Matthew Rymer went back to the study of his Bartholomew atlas and Marie Corelli weaved her spell anew for his wife.

Jack was lucky enough to see her actually coming out of the suite. That made the identification certain. Violet Rymer glanced over her shoulder, heaved a sigh, then set off down the corridor toward the stairs. The steward hurried after her, looking around to ensure that nobody else would see or hear them.

" 'Scuse me, miss!" he called.

Violet stopped and turned. "Yes?"

"Got something for you," he said, coming up to her and feeling in his pocket. "I am talking to Miss Violet Rymer, am I?"

"That's right."

"Then I'm to give you this."

He offered something to her and she held out a palm to receive it. Mystified at first, she responded with a mild shriek when she saw what she was holding. Her hand closed on the tie pin and her legs buckled. The steward reached out to support her.

"Steady on, miss!" he said in alarm. "You all right?"

"Yes, yes," she mumbled.

"You don't look like it. Shall I fetch a glass of water?"

Violet slowly recovered. "No, thank you. I'll be fine in a minute."

"You sure?" She nodded. "Then I'll be off, miss."

"Wait!" she implored.

"I got my duties."

"Who gave you this?" she asked, opening her palm. "I must know."

"My brother, miss."

"Brother?"

"Albert's a steward in second class."

"And who gave it to him?"

"A gentleman who wanted you to have it."

"Can you describe him?"

"Never even met him, miss."

"Did he give no name?"

"Who knows? I only did what Albert told me."

"But he's a second-class passenger, you say?"

Jack nodded, then scurried off down the corridor. Violet was in turmoil, not knowing whether to be anxious or elated. Philip Garrow was there, after all. She had given him the tie pin as a present. He had sent it back to her as a sign. Violet almost swooned with excitement. Putting a hand against the wall to steady herself, she debated whether she should try to make contact

78

with him or wait for a further message. Whatever happened, his presence on the ship had to be kept secret from her parents. There would be ructions if they discovered that he was aboard. As she looked at the tie pin again, she remembered the moment when she gave it to him and the kiss with which he expressed his gratitude. All hesitation fled. The miracle had happened and Philip somehow contrived to get aboard. Violet had to try to reach him at once. She would find her way to the second-class quarters and begin her search. But her resolve was short-lived. Before she could even get to the steps, a cabin door opened ahead of her and Ada Weekes stepped out. When she saw Violet, her face lit up.

"Going for a walk on deck?" she asked cheerily.

"Yes, Mrs. Weekes."

"Then I'll come with you, if I may."

Charles Halliday was still in his cabin when Dillman returned there. The expression on the purser's face told him that the search had been in vain. Dillman was disappointed but not surprised.

"Did they search the cabin thoroughly?" he asked.

"They turned it inside out."

"And they found nothing?"

"Nothing that would point to Barcroft as our man. Apart from his clothing, all that was in there were his writing materials and a few articles which he'd drafted." Halliday shook his head wearily. "No sign of any diagrams of the ship."

"That doesn't mean he's off the hook."

"No, Mr. Dillman. But it does mean that he's one jump ahead of us. If he really *is* the thief, that is. He's far too cunning to be caught with stolen goods in his possession. Did you manage to speak to him?"

"Yes," said Dillman. "I've just come from him. We had a rather strained tea party with three ladies. Barcroft is a cool customer, I have to admit that. Until this voyage, he'd never met any of them, but he was chatting away as if they were lifelong friends."

"What's your guess?"

"I wouldn't trust him an inch, Mr. Halliday."

"Then he could be the culprit?"

"I'd rather give him the benefit of the doubt until we have proof. That means probing a little deeper," he said, brushing his mustache with a finger as he thought it through. "I want to know much more about Henry Barcroft's reason for being on this cruise. Which newspaper is he selling his articles to? What angle is he taking in them? Why doesn't he move around with the rest of the press contingent? Who is he trying so hard to impress? In short, what's his game?"

"Do you get the feeling he may have an accomplice?"

"No, I think he's very much on his own."

"Just when everything was going so well!" said the other, clicking his tongue. "We expect some petty pilfering, especially in third class, but not theft from the chief engineer's cabin."

"The Cunard Line has fierce rivals."

"It's a cutthroat business, Mr. Dillman."

"They want to know what makes the *Lusitania* tick."

"Men like Fergus Rourke. Technical advances are one thing. It takes blood, sweat, and tears to get the best out of them. That means you need a chief engineer who can hold the whip hand over his men. Stokers are a law unto themselves," he said. "They work hard, drink hard, and fight like demons when they've a mind to, but they'll break their backs for someone like Fergus Rourke. That's why I'm so keen to get those stolen documents back. They're his personal possessions. Upset him and the ripples will spread right through the engine room."

"We'll find them, Mr. Halliday. Somehow."

"What's the next step?"

"I'll chat to some of the other journalists. See what they know about Henry Barcroft. Get some more background on him."

"And then?"

"I'll check the wireless room. If he's been drafting articles, he may already have sent some off. That will at least tell us who's paying him."

"Good thinking!"

"Meanwhile, you continue your own inquiries among the crew."

"We will, Mr. Dillman."

"I'll leave you to it, sir. I know how busy a purser always is."

Halliday gave a hollow laugh. "I've had one of those mornings. Complaint after complaint! The best was from a lady in one of the regal suites. Did you know that we had Itzak Weiss aboard?"

"Yes. I saw his name on the passenger list."

"Most people would be delighted to have a cabin next to one of the world's great violinists. They get a free concert every time he practices. Not this particular lady! She was outraged."

"Don't tell me she complained about the noise?"

"Oh, no," said Halliday with a grimace. "Her objection was that he kept practicing the Brahms Violin Concerto, which she hates. Tried to make me force him to play the Beethoven instead because she loves that. Imagine! Giving orders to a musician of Weiss's caliber!"

"What did you say to the lady?"

"I told her to buy some earplugs."

Dillman smiled. "You're a true diplomat, Mr. Halliday."

"That's why I didn't tell her where to put them."

Violet Rymer was in a quandary. She was uncertain whether she should detach herself from Ada Weekes to begin her search or confide in the older woman and ask her for help. Both courses of action had obvious pitfalls. If she went charging off, she risked upsetting the older woman and there was no guarantee that she would find the man she sought in the melee of second-class passengers. Philip Garrow might be anywhere and her prolonged absence would arouse suspicion. At the same time, she drew back from sharing her secret with her companion. Ada Weekes was a sweet and understanding woman, but Violet doubted if she would take her side against her parents. She was much more likely to report the conversation to Sylvia Rymer, and that would be fatal.

In the end, Violet rejected both options and continued to pace meekly along the deck beside the other woman. What she needed was a friend whom she could trust to act as a go-between, someone who would appreciate her dilemma and refrain from passing any moral judgment. Since she knew so few people aboard, finding such a person would not be easy. She recalled the man who had given her the tie pin but balked at the notion of employing him. The message she wished to send was far too important to be entrusted to a mere steward. A far more reliable intercessor was required.

Violet was still wrestling with the problem when a solution rose up before her. Striding along the deck toward them was George Dillman. He had already offered her tacit support and she sensed that he was a man of discretion. It was an outside chance, but it had to be taken. Acting on impulse, she excused herself from Ada Weekes and hurried off along the deck to confront Dillman. He touched the brim of his hat.

"Good day, Miss Rymer."

"I must speak to you!" she gasped.

"Now?"

"Later. Could you meet me in the lounge?"

"When?"

"This afternoon," she gabbled. "Four o'clock."

"Well . . ."

"*Please*, Mr. Dillman."

Her plea was irresistible. "I'll be there," he agreed.

Ada Weekes came strolling up to them with a warm smile.

"What are you two young people talking about?" she asked.

"The Blue Riband, Mrs. Weekes," said Dillman, taking control. "It seems to be the main topic of conversation. Bets are being taken everywhere on whether or not we'll make the fastest crossing."

"My husband is certain that we will."

"There's your answer, Miss Rymer." He turned to the older woman. "Because I made the mistake of confessing that I know something about yachts, everyone looks upon me as the fount of all maritime wisdom. The truth is that I don't *know* if we'll break the record." He licked his finger and held it up. "We might, though. We have a following wind."

Ada Weekes laughed and Violet gave a sudden giggle. Dillman waved a farewell and moved off, puzzled by the sudden demand from Violet and wishing that it could have come at a more opportune time. Catching a thief took priority over everything else, but he could not ignore her entreaty. He would just put it temporarily to the back of his mind.

Violet Rymer could not do that. The brief exchange with Dillman had left her tingling. It was not simply because he had agreed to meet her. There was something else, deeply felt but not yet fully understood. It was almost as if she had come out of mourning and it enabled her to look at him properly for the first time. Dillman was a kind and caring young man. He also cut an elegant figure. Her father might mock his nationality with heavy-handed humor but it lent him a glow in Violet's eyes. It was bewildering. Clasped in her hand was something that told her the man she loved was aboard the same ship, yet she had felt a wave of affection for someone else wash over her when she spoke to Dillman. She was in more of a quandary than ever.

SEVEN

Having spent longer than she had anticipated in the Veranda
Café, Genevieve Masefield had a stroll around the deck, then
returned to her cabin in order to freshen up before luncheon. She
was delighted to find a handwritten invitation from Lord Carradine to join him for dinner that evening at the captain's table, an
invitation, she hoped, that would not be extended to include to
Abigail and Carlotta Hubermann and that would therefore liberate
her from their well-intentioned but wholly unnecessary protection. She did not wish to lose them as friends, and might, at a
later stage, need to take advantage of their hospitality in Virginia,
but there were some games that she could only play alone. Sitting
at her table, Genevieve reached for a sheet of headed notepaper
and dashed off a reply to Lord Carradine. As soon as she had
sealed it in an envelope, she rang the bell for a steward.

Moments later, there was a tap on her cabin door. She had not
expected so prompt a response to her call. When she opened the
door, however, it was not the steward who was standing there.
Henry Barcroft was beaming at her. Genevieve's unwelcoming
frown did not deter him.

"Ah, good!" he said. "I was hoping I might catch you in."

"I was just about to go off to luncheon, Mr. Barcroft."

"Isn't it about time I got promoted to Henry, Miss Masefield?"

"I don't think so," she said levelly.

"But I'd like us to be friends."

"You seem to want everyone to be your friend."

"Part of my charm."

She gave a cold smile. "What can I do for you, Mr. Barcroft?"

"Read this for me, please," he said, offering her two sheets of paper. "It's an article I want to send off by wireless. Since I quote you, I wanted to let you see it beforehand to get your clearance." She took the article from him. "As I promised, I haven't mentioned you or the Hubermanns by name. I just wanted you to feel that you weren't be misquoted."

"Why didn't you give this to me earlier?"

"I didn't have it on me then."

"But you knew that you'd be seeing me this morning."

"It's something I'd rather give you in private."

"Have you shown this to the Hubermanns yet?"

"No, but I will do. I wanted your response first."

"I see."

"Couldn't I step in while you glance through it?" he said easily. "It will only take a minute. I feel like a steward, standing out here. Invite me in, then give the article the once-over."

"I don't have the time to read it now, Mr. Barcroft."

"Henry."

"Mr. *Henry* Barcroft."

He laughed. "You have quite a sense of humor, Miss Masefield."

"I'm glad you appreciate it," she said, starting to close the door. He reached out a hand to hold it open. "Excuse me, please."

"I've never seen the inside of a first-class cabin."

"Indeed?"

"Not properly, that is. When they gave us the tour, they simply opened a door, let us look inside, then shunted us on to the next thing. Is it as comfortable and well appointed as they claim it is?"

"When one is not bothered by unwanted visitors."

He gave a shrug. "I'm so sorry. I hadn't realized that I was being quite such a nuisance." He let go of the door. "Read the article at your leisure, Miss Masefield. I'll have it back when it's convenient. I won't trespass on your valuable time anymore."

Barcroft turned on his heel and marched away. Genevieve was about to shut the door when she saw the steward approaching. She handed him the envelope, gave him his instructions, then went back into the cabin, locking it after her. She had been grateful to the journalist for introducing her to Lord Carradine and, indirectly, elevating her to the captain's table, but her gratitude extended only so far. It did certainly not go to the lengths that Barcroft seemed to imagine. When she recalled that knowing look in his eye, she gave a mild shudder.

He could easily have shown her the article in the Veranda Café but used it instead as an excuse to call on her when she was alone in her cabin. She remembered the moment when he happened to meet her in the corridor as she set off toward the dining saloon on the previous evening. It had been no chance encounter. That was certain. Barcroft was stalking her. He would need to be forcibly shaken off. Tossing his article unread onto the table, she went into the bathroom to wash her hands.

Dillman made little headway. After leaving Violet Rymer and Ada Weekes, he chatted informally to some of the other journalists and learned that Henry Barcroft was openly disliked by most of them by virtue of his arrogance and his determination to wrest exclusive stories whenever on assignment. What they really seemed to resent was his success, achieved by a combination of hard work and single-mindedness rather than by any literary skills. Barcroft, it transpired, had a genius for getting his foot in the door and did not mind when he got the occasional stamp on the toes; indeed, he nurtured the bruises as mementos of his bravery under fire. At all events, the man's credentials were genuine and Dillman could find no hint of any link with a rival shipping line.

A call on the wireless operators produced the information that the journalist has sent off two articles, both to the *Times,* since the voyage had begun. Dillman read them both and was amused to see himself referred to as "a surly American boatbuilder" in one of them. He was less pleased to see the comments he had made about the *Lusitania* twisted out of all recognition. Instead of praising the vessel, he was portrayed as its sternest critic. Yet he could hardly confront the journalist with the way that he had been reported or he would have revealed that he was on the man's tail.

Barcroft was as ubiquitous as ever, but Dillman eventually caught up with him again on the promenade deck where the journalist somehow contrived an impromptu interview with Itzak Weiss when the violinist and his wife were enjoying a bracing walk in the keen air. Intensely private, Weiss, a short, squat man with a large head surmounted by an even larger homburg hat, gave time to Barcroft that he had denied to everyone else. The musician's comments on the *Lusitania* would no doubt appear in a forthcoming article in the *Times*, leaving Barcroft's journalistic competitors to froth impotently in his wake and to invent new expletives for him.

Time for luncheon came. Dillman shared the same table as Cyril and Ada Weekes, and he was reminded that the theft from the chief engineer's cabin was not the only item on his agenda. The activities of a professional gambler had to be monitored as well. Dillman waited until the rest of the table was immured in a discussion of the quality of the cuisine before he probed Cyril Weekes.

"You did quite well at the card table last night," he observed.

"Beginner's luck!" said Weekes.

"The stakes were quite high."

"That adds a bit of spice to the game, Mr. Dillman."

"Only if you win, surely? When you lose as heavily as Mr. Erskine appeared to do, the spice is far too unpalatable."

"Oh, Erskine can afford it."

"Can he?"

"Yes. He admits he played poorly. Tonight may be very different."

"Unless that other chap is in the same form."

"Other chap? Do you mean Collins?"

"The gentleman with the silver-topped cane."

"That's him. Edward Collins. Decent sort."

"Is he?"

"Pleasure to play against."

"Even when he dominates the game?" said Dillman casually. "How did you meet Mr. Collins?"

"In the smoking room. Where I meet all the people of consequence. He saw me playing with Erskine and a few others and asked if he might join in. We were delighted to have him on board, so to speak." He chortled happily. "The more, the merrier. What more civilized way to bring a pleasant evening to a close than by playing cards with friends?"

The waiters arrived to clear the plates before serving the next course. It provoked a fresh burst of approval from Ada Weekes and the others. Her husband glanced around the dining saloon.

"No sign of the Rymers today."

"They must be having luncheon served in their suite," said Dillman.

"What do you make of that daughter of theirs?"

"Violet Rymer is a very nice young lady."

"But more of a shrinking violet, unfortunately. She doesn't seem to have had a moment's pleasure since she stepped aboard. Ada could hardly get a word out of her when they had a stroll on deck together earlier. What on earth is wrong with the girl?"

"I've no idea, Mr. Weekes."

"Is she ill or something?"

"I don't think so."

"Then what? She'd be such a pretty creature if she could only learn to relax. Someone should take pity on her." He nudged Dillman's arm. "In your position, I must admit, I'd be tempted to try to put a smile on her face. A walk on deck in the moonlight can be so romantic."

"Not if her parents are there as well."

Weekes grinned. "No, they're enough to dampen anyone's ardor." He turned to met Dillman's eye. "But you take my point?

The girl ought to have *something* to remember this voyage by."

"I agree, Mr. Weekes."

"Heavens, Violet is almost twenty-one. The perfect age."

Dillman replied with a neutral smile. Though he was ready to answer Violet Rymer's plea for help, he had no wish to be drawn into anything even approaching an intimate relationship with her. To do his job properly, he needed to keep clear of emotional commitments to other passengers, though that did not prevent him from casting an occasional admiring glance at Genevieve Masefield, who was seated between Abigail and Carlotta Hubermann at a nearby table.

Another person Dillman watched out of the corner of his eye was Ellen Tolley, the young lady into whom he had unwittingly cannoned while in pursuit of Barcroft. She was sitting at a table in the corner next to a man he assumed was her father, a rather gaunt individual in his late forties with close-cropped iron gray hair. Dillman had elicited a warm smile of recognition from her when he first came into the saloon but Ellen and her father were too caught up in the conversation at their table to look in his direction again. As he stole another peep at Ellen, he noticed how striking her face was in profile and how uninhibited her manner seemed. When a joke was made by one of her companions, she put back her head and gave a full-throated laugh.

A booming voice drew Dillman back into his own circle. Jeremiah Erskine's pessism was in full flow again. Even the presence of his wife did not restrain him from another dark prophecy.

"I feel it in my bones!" he announced.

"Rheumatism, old chap," suggested Weekes.

"And I'm never wrong about these things, am I, Dorothea?"

"Oh, don't be so gloomy!" chided his wife.

"A disaster is imminent."

"Jeremiah!"

"I have a sixth sense."

"Stop it, man. You're putting everyone off their food."

"I can't help it, Dorothea," he said, dabbing at his mouth with a napkin. "I felt it yesterday and I feel it even more strongly today. There is catastrophe in the air. Be warned."

"Yes, be warned," echoed Weekes with a wry chuckle. "Mr. Jeremiah Erskine is on the loose again. He'll terrify us all with his dire predictions."

"Truth will out, sir."

"Hear that, everyone? Eat, drink, and be merry—for tomorrow, he may tell us that the end of the world is nigh. Jeremiah by name, and by nature!"

Dillman joined in the laughter but Erskine was not deflected.

"Mock me, if you wish," he said grimly. "Disaster will still come."

"Did he see her? Did he give her the tie pin? What did she say to him?"

"Steady on, sir."

"And where have you been all morning?"

"Busy, sir."

"I needed to speak to you, Albert."

"No point till I 'ad a word with Jack."

"And did you?"

"This afternoon."

"Well? Well? What happened?"

Philip Garrow was as impatient as ever and the steward had to calm him down before a proper conversation could take place. They were standing at the bottom of a staircase close to Garrow's cabin. Albert was determined not to be rushed. He rolled his bloodshot eyes.

"I took a real chance for you, sir."

"What do you mean?"

"Sneaking into first class like that. If I'd been caught, I'd 'ave been for the 'igh jump, and no mistake. Rules is rules."

"But you weren't caught."

"No, sir."

"And you did see your brother."

The steward nodded. "Jack 'ad to 'ang about for 'ours before 'e got 'is chance. The young lady eventually come out of 'iding and Jack pounced. Made sure it was 'er, of course, then gave 'er the message."

"And?"

"She all but keeled over."

"Was she surprised? Pleased? Frightened?"

"Jack says she was sort of dazed."

"What did she say?"

"Nothing, sir."

"She must have said something, man."

"All she wanted to know was where 'e'd got the tie pin from."

"No message for me?"

"None, sir."

"But she obviously recognized what I'd sent."

"No question about that," agreed Albert with a smirk. "Jack says she went weak at the knees. Never known any woman react like that to a tie pin. To a diamond necklace, maybe. Or an engagement ring. I once saw a young lady faint on the boat deck when a gentleman proposed to 'er and opened a box to show 'er the ring." His brow furrowed in bewilderment. "But a little tie pin like that? Not quite the same thing, is it, sir?"

"The main point is that Miss Rymer now has it."

"Oh, yes. Jack did 'is duty."

"She'll find some other way to reply."

Albert looked hurt. "I 'ope she uses me and my brother. I mean, we're part of this now. We got a stake in it. All she 'as to do is to give Jack a note and it'll find its way safely into your 'ands."

Garrow nodded but he sensed that the two brothers had outlived their usefulness. After making the steward go through his story once more, he sent him on his way and adjourned to the second-class lounge to reflect on the latest development. Violet now knew that he was on board, so his primary purpose had been achieved. She would need time to adjust to the situation before she decided what to do. Meanwhile, he could relax and begin to enjoy himself. The *Lusitania* was a seductive vessel, yet he had still to yield himself fully to her charms. While waiting for word from Violet Rymer, he did not have to pine alone. With so many other passengers in second class, he was bound to find some friends.

No sooner had the thought entered his mind than it became a reality. A tall, elegant woman in her early thirties came over to him.

"Good afternoon."

"Oh," he said, looking up. "Hello."

"Do you mind if I join you?" she said, indicating the empty armchair beside him. "I've been twice around the entire ship and my legs simply refuse to take me an inch further."

Garrow rose gallantly from his seat and pointed to the chair.

"Be my guest," he invited with a smile.

Henry Barcroft was indefatigable. In the hour and a half during which Dillman kept track of him, the journalist mingled effortlessly with first-class passengers on the promenade deck before going up to the boat deck to chat to those in second and third class. It was still dry but the wind was cold enough to require hats and coats on even the hardiest travelers. The mood aboard had altered somewhat. When they first struck out into the Atlantic, passengers had been lulled into security by the *Lusitania*'s unprecedented scale and stability. It was like being on a small island. Perceptions had now been adjusted. It was not the size of the ship that they noticed but the sheer vastness of the ocean surrounding it. The North Atlantic was one of the most dangerous bodies of water in the world. Its raw power could be seen and felt. Though it was maintaining good speed, the *Lusitania* had somehow shrunk in size. To some on the boat deck, it felt less like a giant liner than a miniature raft.

Dillman was interested to see that Ellen Tolley and her father were also up on the boat deck, standing at the rail and gazing out across the heaving surface of the ocean. He observed, for the first time, that the father used a stout walking stick when he moved, swinging one stiff leg ahead of him and leaning on his daughter's shoulder to negotiate any stairs. Wanting to speak with Ellen again, Dillman could not break off his surveillance. Time drifted past. When the journalist eventually began to make his way up to the bridge, Dillman started to follow him but another duty called. It was almost four o'clock and someone would be waiting for him in the first-class lounge. Reluctantly he let Henry Barcroft off the hook and went off to meet Violet Rymer. She was torn between fear and excitement.

"I was afraid that you wouldn't come, Mr. Dillman," she said.

"You had my promise."

"That's what I was counting on."

"Who don't we find a quiet corner?" he suggested.

Dillman led her to some armchairs partly obscured by a pillar and a couple of potted palms, thus ensuring the measure of privacy that was vital if Violet was to be drawn out. Her cheeks were flushed and her eyes were dancing. He had never seen her so animated.

"Do your parents know that you're here?" he asked.

"Oh, yes. Honesty is the best policy."

"And they had no objection?"

"None, Mr. Dillman. I told them I was meeting you. What I didn't dare to tell them, of course, was why. Mummy has an appointment in the hairdressing salon and Daddy wanted to do some work, so he's stayed in the suite." She gave a girlish laugh. "I'm free at last!"

"I'm pleased to hear it."

"I've got so much to tell you."

"Have you, Miss Rymer?"

She looked across at him and felt another surge of affection for him, lowering her head at once in embarrassment and biting her lip in dismay. Violet needed a couple of minutes to recover her composure. Dillman waited quietly, a noncommittal smile on his face. Violet looked up and blurted out her question.

"Can I trust you, Mr. Dillman?"

"I hope so."

"You wouldn't report any of this to my parents?"

"Not if you ask me to keep it from them."

"Do you promise?"

"Of course."

"I'd die if I thought you'd betray us," she said earnestly.

"Us?"

Violet blushed as she realized she had already divulged part of her secret, but Dillman's smile reassured her. Having once started, she now plunged in and told him the full story in a low, urgent voice.

"I didn't want to come on this voyage at all," she admitted. "It isn't really to celebrate my twenty-first birthday. It's to get me out of England. Mummy and Daddy planned to come on their own at first, but then they discovered that . . . that there was someone in my life that I cared about. Someone very important to me. I knew they'd never approve of Philip and that's why we kept it a secret, but we were seen together by Mildred."

"Mildred?"

"One of our servants. She's traveling with us on the ship. Anyway, Mildred told my parents and that was that. Daddy was enraged. He called me the most terrible names. He refused even to meet Philip. Daddy said that it was an unsuitable attachment and that it had to stop at once. When I tried to argue back, he just yelled at me."

"But you stuck by your guns."

"Of course. I *love* Philip." Her cheeks crimsoned again at the boldness of her confession. "Nothing will make me give him up. We've sworn to marry one day. Philip is the most wonderful man in the world."

"But not the choice of your parents?" said Dillman discreetly.

"Mummy and Daddy are such snobs."

"What do they have against the young man?"

"Philip's half-Irish, to begin with," she explained, "and he has no money at the moment. But he will have some when he gets another position. He'd still be working at the same office if the senior partner hadn't had a grudge against him. Philip is a brilliant man. He'll succeed at whatever he takes up. He's just going through a bad patch at the moment."

Dillman was sympathetic. "A dreadful patch, by the sound of it, if he's just been deprived of the woman he loves. It must be awful to think that she's three thousand miles away."

"But I'm not, Mr. Dillman. That's what I want to tell you."

"I don't understand."

"Philip is here. On board the *Lusitania*."

"How do you know?"

"He sent a message. One of the stewards brought it."

"That's swell news!" said Dillman with a grin. "You must be thrilled."

"Part of me is thrilled," she confided, "but another part of me is scared stiff. If Mummy and Daddy find out . . ." She brought both hands up to her face in a gesture of despair. "That's why we have to be so careful." Violet sat back and let out a sigh of joy. "I never dreamed that this could happen. The most I hoped was that Philip might come to Euston to wave me off. When he wasn't at the station, I hoped against hope that he might somehow get to Liverpool, but there was no sign of him."

"Yet he was aboard all the time."

"No, Mr. Dillman. I don't think so, or he'd have tried to contact me sooner. My guess is that he joined the ship at Queenstown. He told me that he often went back to Ireland to see his family. He's so clever, don't you see?" she said, almost giggling. "Mummy and Daddy thought I'd be safe once the ship sailed. It never occurred to them that Philip might get aboard, least of all in Queenstown."

"Is he traveling in first class?"

"Second. Just imagine. He's actually *here*. On the ship."

"Who don't you go and find him?"

"That was my first thought," she said, "but it's not as easy as that. I'm frightened that we might be seen. Even if Mummy and Daddy are not watching me, there's always Mildred. Not to mention other people on the ship who know us. It's too big a risk to take."

"So what do you intend to do?"

"Arrange a time and place to meet Philip in secret."

"His cabin is the obvious choice."

She nodded guiltily. "That's what I've suggested. Mr. Dillman, I hope you won't think this is improper behavior. I love my parents, but I can't let them stand in the way of my happiness, you do see that. Philip is everything to me, and you can see from the effort he made to get aboard how important our friendship is to him."

"This goes above and beyond friendship, doesn't it?" he said with a grin. "Good luck to both of you! I'm flattered that you felt able to confide in me, and I hope that everything works out for the best."

"That depends on you, Mr. Dillman."

"Me?"

"Yes," she said, producing a letter from her inside her purse. "I want you to find where Philip is and give this to him. I know it's a lot to ask and I know it's beastly of me to involve you in my private life, but there's nobody else I can ask. Will you, Mr. Dillman? Please."

It was not an assignment he wanted and he could foresee all sorts of complications resulting but it was impossible to turn down Violet Rymer's request. Her earlier behavior was now explained and his guesses about the family secret were confirmed. There was little consolation to be gleaned from all that if he was to be employed as a messenger boy. He had far more pressing things to do than to become part of someone else's clandestine affair. At the same time, he spied a potential bonus. Violet Rymer's growing fondness for him had been imperfectly concealed and could never be requited. In pairing her up with her true love, Dillman would at least be moving her attention completely off him.

"I'll give him the letter, Miss Rymer, but that's all I will do."

"You have to bring me back his reply."

"Well, yes, I suppose that I could do that as well."

"Oh, thank you!" she said, clutching his arm with both hands. "I knew that you'd help us. You've saved my life, Mr. Dillman!"

It was happening at last. Philip Garrow was realizing how invigorating it was to be on board a famous ship on its maiden voyage. Feelings of joy and pride blocked out until now came through with greater intensity. He was happy, even elated. Wearing his new suit and oozing confidence, he was taking tea in the company of a woman who was growing more beautiful and interesting by the minute. What made the conversation even more enjoyable was the fact that Rosemary Hilliard was evidently deriving equal pleasure from it. She was a well-traveled woman with an air of unforced sophistication about her. Garrow found her charming. It was her wedding ring that cast a slight shadow.

"Are you traveling alone, Mrs. Hilliard?" he wondered.

"I'm afraid so. For the first time."

"The first time?"

"Yes, it's something of an adventure for me, Mr. Garrow." She gave a sad smile and lowered her head. "My husband died almost a year ago. I knew that I should get away and have a change of scene, but I could not pluck up enough courage until now."

"You strike me as a person of great courage."

"Do I?" she asked, lifting her eyes.

"Very much so, Mrs. Hilliard. I'm very sorry to hear about your husband. It must have been a dreadful blow to you. But you seem to be bearing up remarkably well now and that's to your credit."

"Thank you."

"Did your have any children?"

"I'm afraid not. It was something that just never happened. In the circumstances, it is perhaps just as well. Children need a father."

"Oh, I can vouch for that," he said with feeling. "I lost mine when I was only six years old and it was as if the whole world went dark all of a sudden. It was a terrible handicap, not having a father."

"Did your mother remarry?"

"Not until we had grown up and left home."

"Is that when you came to England?"

"Yes, Mrs. Hilliard."

"And you took up a position with this company you mentioned."

"That's right. We import goods from all over the world."

"You did extremely well to be promoted to management so soon."

"I was fortunate, Mrs. Hilliard," he said airily, concealing the fact that he was still a lowly clerk when he was dismissed. "The company valued and rewarded enterprise. When they saw that I was full of bright ideas, they decided to give me a chance to prove myself."

"A sensible decision, by the look of it."

"Yes, their faith in me has been justified. They were also generous enough to give me time off to come on this voyage. I've always wanted to visit America, especially as we do a lot of our business there. And the notion of sailing on the *Lusitania* was, well, almost intoxicating."

"That's what I felt, Mr. Garrow."

She gave him a long, searching look, which he answered with a smile. Rosemary Hilliard was an attractive woman whose good looks had largely fought off the ravages of time. The quality of her attire suggested wealth as well as taste, yet she was wholly free from the vanities and prejudices that had their true home in first class. They chatted on for half an hour, probing gently to explore each other's character and to gather more background information. Both were satisfied with what they learned. A friendship was slowly emerging.

The arrival of a steward cut short their conversation.

"Excuse me, sir," he said. "Forgive this interruption, but there is someone who wished to see you on a matter of urgency."

"Who is he?"

"The gentleman did not give a name, sir."

"Gentleman? Then it was not Albert, one of your colleagues."

"No, sir."

Garrow quailed inwardly, fearing that Matthew Rymer might somehow have learned of his presence on the ship and come in pursuit of him. "An older gentleman with side whiskers, by any chance?" he asked, trying to sound offhand.

"An American gentleman, sir. He said it was important."

"How intriguing!" said Rosemary Hilliard. "Off you go, Mr. Garrow."

"I hate to leave you like this."

"Not at all, sir. I'm agog to know what this little mystery is all about. I won't budge from this seat until you return."

Philip Garrow gave her a smile of farewell before going out with the steward. Ensconced with his new acquaintance, he had forgotten all about Violet Rymer but sensed that she had now come back into his ken.

"What's going on?" he said to the waiter. "Where is the man?"

"Waiting outside your cabin, sir."

"Why there?"

"You'll have to ask him."

The steward melted away and Garrow hurried off to his cabin. When he saw Dillman, he became wary and approached slowly.

"Are you looking for me, sir?" he asked.

"Mr. Philip Garrow?"

"That's right."

"I have a message for you," said Dillman, taking the envelope from his inside pocket. "The young lady who sent it was insistent that it should be opened in private."

"It's from Violet?" He snatched it from him. "Give it to me."

"I was told to wait for an answer."

Philip Garrow nodded, unlocked his cabin door, and ushered his visitor inside before closing the door behind them. He tore open the missive and read it with his back to Dillman. The latter could see the tension slowly ease out of the man's shoulders. Garrow spun round.

"Tell her that I'll be here tomorrow at the time suggested."

"Nothing else?"

"Violet already knows that I love her," said the other irritably. "But you can tell her that, if you wish. By the way, what's your name?"

"George Dillman."

"How do you know Violet?"

"We met on the train to Liverpool."

"She must trust you to let you bring this."

"I was happy to oblige, Mr. Garrow."

"How much has Violet told you?"

"Very little," said Dillman reassuringly. "I'll get back to her at once. She'll be anxious to know that her letter was delivered safely."

He gave a nod and left the cabin before Garrow could ask any more questions. On his journey back to first-class, there were questions of his own now nagging at him. Why was Philip Garrow quite unlike the person Violet had described to him? How could a man with no money afford to travel on the *Lusitania* and buy a new suit for the occasion? And, more to the point, where was the romantic ardor that had impelled him to get aboard the ship in the first place?

An afternoon in the hairdressing saloon had been followed by tea with the Hubermann sisters and then a relaxing bath in the privacy of her cabin. Genevieve Masefield wanted to look her best when she joined Lord Carradine for dinner at the captain's table that evening. She spent an hour in front of the mirror, experimenting with different dresses and various pieces of jewelry until she found the ones that matched the best and satisfied her the most. Still in her underwear, she then applied her cosmetics sparingly, taking due account of the lighting in the dining saloon. When she put on her dress, she added the velvet choker and the emerald brooch, standing back to admire the finished result and to assess how she would look beneath the grand dome.

Genevieve was on the brink of leaving when she noticed Henry Barcroft's article on the table. If it remained there, he would have an excuse to come to the cabin in search of it. Though he had no dining privileges in first class, there was every chance that he would be hanging around the saloon before dinner, if only to ingratiate himself with those he had befriended or wished to interview. Genevieve decided to take the article with her, and slipped it into her purse. When she returned it, she promised herself, she would sever all contact with the journalist. Henry Barcroft could look elsewhere for invitations to a lady's cabin.

On the walk to the dining saloon, she passed several mirrors and checked her appearance each time. She was content. Genevieve soon had independent confirmation. Carlotta Hubermann came out of a cabin ahead of her and turned to her appraise her.

"My!" she exclaimed. "Don't you look just great!"

"Thank you, Carlotta."

"Who's the lucky man?"

"Captain Watt."

"Far too old for you, dear," said the other with a playful nudge. "He's much more my vintage. And if Abigail were not with me, I might just do something about it. I've always liked seafaring men."

Genevieve grinned. "Shall I mention it to him?"

"Don't you dare, you wicked girl! Besides, you'll be too busy fending off Lord Carradine. I saw the look in his eye—the one with the monocle, that is. Unless I'm mistaken, you've made a conquest."

"I hardly know him, Carlotta."

"What has that got to do with it?"

"Everything, in my book."

"Abigail thinks he's rather sinister."

"Lord Carradine? He's not sinister at all. He's extremely nice."

"That's my feeling, but Abigail is very critical of men. So few of them meet her standards, I fear. Look at that young man we met in the café this morning. Mr. Dillman. I have to admit that he grew on me, yet Abigail had no time for him. There's a touch of the sailor about George Porter Dillman," she recalled, winking at Genevieve. "Perhaps that's what attracted me. What I do know is this. He was a paragon beside that dreadful journalist. What was his name again?"

"Henry Barcroft."

"Both of us loathed *him*. So damned sure of himself."

"I can't say that I found him very appealing either."

The older woman fell in beside her and they walked on to-gether.

"Stick with Lord Carradine, honey. More your class. So gra-cious. I just can't agree with Abigail's opinion. What's so sinister about having a large amount of money?" She gave a cackle of delight. "I'd call that the most attractive quality in a man."

"Why did you never marry, Carlotta?"

"How do you know that I didn't?"

"Well?" asked Genevieve. "Did you or didn't you?"

A louder cackle. "That would be telling!"

When they reached the saloon, they came to an involuntary halt. Just inside the room, chatting familiarly to Jeremiah Erskine as if they were close friends, was Henry Barcroft, wearing evening dress in order to blend with his surroundings even though he would leave as soon as the meal was actually served. Genevieve forgot about the article in her purse and simply wanted to avoid the man. Carlotta read her mind. Keeping herself between Gene-vieve and the journalist, she shielded her friend from the latter's attention and escorted her all the way to the captain's table. Lord Carradine was waiting to welcome her and to introduce her to Captain Watt himself, resplendent in his uniform and accompa-nied by a few senior officers.

Genevieve was able to relax at last. Male attention helped her to blossom and she was soon fielding compliments from all sides. By the time she finally glanced around the room, she saw that Barcroft had vanished. A sense of relief flooded through her. His presence unsettled her. Now that he was gone, she could really enjoy herself. She had a coveted seat at the captain's table and intended to take the fullest advantage of it. When the Champagne arrived, she joined in the first toast with enthusiasm. All thought of Henry Barcroft had disappeared.

She did not know that she would never see him alive again.

EIGHT

A gainst his better judgment, Dillman agreed to share a table
with the Rymers that evening. They ventured out of their
suite to sample the fare in the dining saloon and to allow Sylvia
Rymer to display her new hairstyle, a mass of tight curls devoid
of any parting and reminiscent of the style favored by Queen Al-
exandra. When he arrived at the saloon, Dillman got his first real
sighting of Mildred, the Rymers' maidservant, a plump woman in
her forties with dark brown hair brushed back severely into a bun
to reveal a pleasant, homely face. During the supper in their suite
on the first night, Dillman had caught only the merest glimpse of
the maidservant, so he was interested to see her more clearly,
especially as she was one of the designated watchers of Violet
Rymer.

Mildred wore a white apron over a light gray dress. A small
white cap sat on her head. She had been dispatched to the hairdressing salon to retrieve an item that Sylvia Rymer had inadvertently left there during her visit that afternoon. Dillman could not
quite make out what it was but he saw Mildred hand it over and
collect a nod of thanks before heading back to the regal suite. He
followed the Rymers into the dining saloon and joined a table that

included a honeymoon couple, a Spanish artist, a rural dean with his wife, a retired barrister, and an elderly couple from Scotland. Dillman found himself seated between the female members of the Rymer family, both of whom seemed to be in excellent spirits, Sylvia, because of the compliments that her hairstyle and dress were eliciting, and Violet, for a reason that Dillman alone knew about.

Matthew Rymer was the revelation. He was positively buoyant, initiating conversation, retailing anecdotes, and generally acting as the focal point of the table. Gone was his earlier pomposity and, in spite of the presence of an American and a Spaniard, he refrained from any disparaging remarks about their respective countries. In appearance and manner, he still embodied British superiority but he no longer trumpeted it so loudly. Dillman was astounded by the improvement in the man and put it down to his daughter's apparent change of heart. Now that Violet had started to enjoy the voyage, both parents were filled with relief, confident that she had at last accepted the banishment of Philip Garrow and was ready to face a future without him.

Dillman wondered how jovial Matthew Rymer would be if he knew that their daughter's unwanted suitor was on board the same ship, and he doubted whether a new hairstyle and a silk evening gown would be enough to sustain Sylvia Rymer through the discovery. Violet herself was bubbling with suppressed excitement, taking an interest in each subject under discussion while savoring the thought that a tryst with her lover had been arranged for the following day. When relaying Garrow's reply to her, Dillman had tactfully omitted any mention of his own reservations about the man. Messengers carried messages. Comment was outside their remit. He just hoped that Garrow was truly worthy of her.

The menu was printed on a beautifully embossed card with an elaborate design framing the actual bill of fare, turning the card itself into a cherished souvenir. The main course consisted of sirloin and ribs of beef served with green peas; rice; cauliflower à la crème; boiled, mashed, and château potatoes. They were in the middle of eating it when Sylvia Rymer finally found a moment to explain how the table had been put together. Adjusting her silver tiara, she leaned across to him.

"I sat next to Mrs. Mackintosh in the hairdressing salon," she said, indicating the elderly Scotswoman. "Her husband owns five thousand acres in the Highlands. I knew that they'd be our sort. They bought some of Miguel's paintings when they visited Spain last year and became good friends of his. He's taking some of his work to New York in the hope of selling it there. In his own country, Mrs. Mackintosh tells me, Miguel is very famous." Her eyes moved to the rural dean's wife. "I also met Janet Palgrave in the salon. A delightful person. Her husband's diocese is in War- wickshire somewhere. Ordinarily, of course, a man of the cloth like him would not be able to afford to travel first-class but it turns out that he has private wealth. He also owns a number of prop- erties in the Midlands, so I simply had to get him together with Matthew." She gave a complacent smile. "Don't you think it's a splendid table, Mr. Dillman?"

"Yes, Mrs. Rymer," he agreed, looking around. "Your visit to the hairdressing salon was productive."

"I met two other charming ladies there as well and put their names in my notebook for another time. And then—silly me!—I went and left my notebook in the salon by mistake."

"Is that what your maidservant gave to you earlier?"

"Yes, thank heaven for Mildred! I'm always forgetting some- thing or other. Mildred is my faithful retriever."

"What about the Latimers?" he asked, glancing at the honey- moon couple. "I don't imagine that you met the two of them in the salon."

"Oh, no. They're friends of the Palgraves. Stuart Latimer comes from a landed family in Warwickshire, I'm told. His young bride is so pretty, isn't she? There's such a bloom on her. This is the first time they've been coaxed into the dining saloon. Shyness, I expect. Being on honeymoon makes you so self-conscious. It did in my case, anyway." She gave a breathy laugh. "But they seem to be getting on well with everybody. There's nothing quite so romantic as a society wedding. When I look at someone like Anna Latimer, I see Violet in a year or two's time."

"That only leaves our barrister."

"My husband collected him this morning when he went for a stroll on the promenade deck. Geoffrey Unsworth and he got into conversation. My husband took to him. That so rarely happens."

"Does it?" said Dillman, keeping sarcasm out of his voice.

The rural dean suddenly took control of the conversation and adopted his pulpit manner as he described an unfortunate incident with a warming pan during his own honeymoon. The memoir stayed well within the bounds of decency but it still brought a blush from his wife. While the clergyman held the rest of them in thrall, Dillman surveyed the room with more than usual curiosity. His gaze went first to Genevieve Masefield, seated at the captain's table between Lord Carradine and Itzak Weiss, clearly entrancing the aristocrat and the violinist simultaneously and making the other ladies in the group fade into invisibility. Dillman noted how much Genevieve was enjoying her position as cynosure.

Her erstwhile companions, the Hubermanns, were at a nearby table so top-heavy with elderly diners that it made Carlotta Hubermann seem relatively young. Dillman searched for Cyril and Ada Weekes and eventually spotted them among the potted palms, sharing a table with, among others, the Erskines. Not far away, at another table, was Edward Collins, looking supremely distinguished in his evening dress and chatting affably to his neighbor. Dillman was certain that another poker game would later reunite the card-playing fraternity and he reminded himself to look in on it when it was fully established.

There were dozens of other passengers whom Dillman recognized but the one on whom his eye finally settled was Ellen Tolley. Even though she was on the far side of the room, he could see enough of her to be impressed once again by the winning simplicity of her beauty. She wore little makeup, no jewelry, and had felt no need of a visit to the hairdressing salon in order to prepare herself for dinner. She was dressed in a plain but well-cut gown made of a cream-colored material that caught the lights and gave off a muted glow. Dillman surmised that her figure needed none of the corsetry so vital to most of the women present as they sought to reduce bulging midriffs into a fashionable slimness around the waist.

Ellen Tolley's natural vivacity made her a lively dinner companion but her father also appeared to have come out of his shell. As Dillman watched, it was the latter who was holding forth and drawing laughter from everyone else at the table. He cut an almost dashing figure in his evening dress, looking very different from the man who had hobbled along the deck with the aid of a walking stick. There was a faintly military air about him now and Dillman wondered if his disability had been the result of a war wound. His real interest, however, was not in the father but in the daughter, and his gaze soon returned to Ellen Tolley.

To his surprise, she was now looking in his direction and their eyes locked for an instant. Ellen gave him a broad smile. Dillman answered with a grin of pleasure as he felt a bargain being sealed. There was a tacit agreement to meet later. He turned back to his dinner companions.

"Who were you smiling at?" wondered Violet Rymer.

"Oh, a friend, that's all," he said.

"Anyone I know?"

"No, Miss Rymer."

"You seem to have made so many friends on board."

"Acquaintances more than friends," he corrected quietly, "but I do like to mingle with my fellow passengers. It's one of the joys of travel."

"You do it so well. I noticed that on the train."

"Thank you."

She became serious. "I was thinking about what you told us on that first night. Did you really leave the family business?"

"Oh, yes."

"It must have been a big decision for you."

"It was. I turned my back on security and tradition."

"Was your father very upset?"

"That's an understatement, Miss Rymer. He almost went berserk. It was what was expected of me, you see. To be the next in line as keeper of the flame. The politest things my father accused me of were desertion and betrayal. After that, his language became a little more hysterical."

"Yet you still held out against him?"

Dillman shrugged. "It was a case of acting for myself rather than against him. It may look strange from the outside, but the truth is that I wanted to strike out on my own. To forge my own destiny. Not to have it decided in advance by inheritance."

"You're so brave!" she said.

"It didn't feel like bravery at the time," he admitted. "And I had several qualms about it, believe me. But I stuck by my decision. The fact of the matter is that it was time to outgrow my family. Be myself."

Violet nodded solemnly, then brooded in silence. Dillman sensed that she was contemplating a break with her own parents. It was odd that she should choose a moment when they were revealing themselves to be normal human beings. Sylvia Rymer emerged from her chrysalis as an engaging social butterfly and her husband, affable to a fault, was showing a gregariousness hitherto hidden beneath his stern Victorian exterior. At a time when they were more amenable, Violet Rymer was trying to advance her own interests. Dillman hoped that she would not involve him again in her private act of rebellion.

"And what do you intend to do when you get to New York?" she asked.

"Make contact with our business associates."

"Where will you be staying?"

"At a hotel in Manhattan. It's all been arranged for me."

"It must be wonderful to have minions who'll do that sort of thing for you. My husband always took care of accommodation whenever we traveled. Now I have to arrange everything myself."

"Well, I'm so glad that you chose to sail on the *Lusitania*."

"Do you mean that, Philip?"

"Of course. Meeting you has been the highlight of this voyage."

"Thank you."

"No," he said, raising his glass in tribute, "Thank *you*, Rosemary."

They were sharing a table in the second-class dining saloon with eight other people but spent most of the time conversing with each other. Philip Garrow felt no guilt about befriending another woman. Rosemary Hilliard helped the time to pass in the most pleasurable way. He found it easy to impress her and was led on from one lie to another as he built up a false picture of himself for her benefit. For all her worldliness, there was a gullible streak in her and he instinctively exploited it. Violet Rymer was the person who brought him aboard in the first place but Rosemary Hilliard was the one who was turning a long voyage into a real treat.

"Do you have any plans to settle down?" she probed.

"I'm far too young for that, Rosemary."

"So there's no young lady on the immediate horizon?"

"None in particular," he said dismissively.

"But plenty in general, I daresay." She gave him a smile and spoke in a whisper. "And why not? Every young man is entitled to sow a few wild oats. I just wish that privilege had been extended in my day to young women. We were so fettered by convention."

"I can't imagine you being fettered by anything."

"It's true."

"People should be able to do exactly what they want."

"That's something I'm only just learning, Philip."

"Never too late."

"I hope you're right."

"I am," he said, gently squeezing her arm. "I know that I am."

"How long will you be in New York?" she asked.

"Two or three weeks, probably. It depends."

"On what?"

"How much there is to detain me."

"I'll be in Manhattan for a little while myself," she said

tentatively. "Perhaps we can get together at some point, Philip."

"Perhaps."

"You sound uncertain."

"I'm not completely sure what my plans are, Rosemary."

"If they rule me out, I won't be offended."

Garrow was suddenly put on the spot, being asked to make a commitment that was quite out of the question. Violet Rymer took priority and eliminated Rosemary Hilliard. Yet he was loath to discard his new friend and did not wish to hurt her feelings in any way. The relationship with Violet brought nothing but tension and frustration whereas he could be completely at ease with Rosemary. His mind was racing as he searched for a way to appease his companion without making a commitment that he knew he could not honor. Violet had to be pushed firmly to the back of his mind until the next day. A more immediate pleasure beckoned.

"Be honest," she prodded. "You don't wish to see me in New York."

"That isn't true at all."

"Then why did you look so doubtful just now?"

"Listen," he said, his confidence surging once more. "Why talk about New York when it's still such a long way away? America will wait. I think you're a marvelous woman and I'm so glad we met. And yes, maybe we will get together in Manhattan. Who knows? Fact is, Rosemary, I don't want to look too far ahead. I'd rather take it one day at a time." It was his turn to whisper. "One day at a time, one night at a time."

She hesitated for a full minute, playing nostalgically with her wedding ring under the table while she did so and keeping him on tenterhooks. He could not believe he had made such a bold suggestion, but he did not regret it. When she reached a decision, Rosemary gave a little nod of approval. Philip Garrow was utterly delighted. It had all been so easy. As he sipped his Champagne once more, the thrill of conquest shot through his whole body.

Violet Rymer might have been a thousand miles away.

*   *   *

Dinner was an occasion of unrelieved joy for Genevieve Masefield. The meal was delicious, the company interesting, and her impact on them was undeniable. Itzak Weiss insisted on kissing her gloved hand before he retired to his cabin with his wife and Lord Carradine was now besotted with her, encouraging Genevieve to ignore his title and call him by his Christian name. The crowning moment of the dinner was when the captain invited her and a few others to join him on a tour of the bridge.

It was only when she picked up her purse that Genevieve recalled the article she had stuffed into it. Since she wanted to avoid Henry Barcroft, she cast around for a means of returning his article without actually having to meet him in person, and her eye alighted on Dillman. As she walked across the saloon in the wake of the captain, the idea that had formed became ever more appealing. Genevieve acted on it.

"Good evening, Mr. Dillman!" she said pleasantly.

"Oh, hello there, Miss Masefield."

"I'm glad I bumped into you. I wonder if I might ask a favor?"

"By all means," he said, spreading his hands.

Dillman had just risen from his seat with the rest of his table. A chance meeting with Genevieve was an unexpected treat. She looked even more ravishing at close quarters and was wearing that beguiling perfume. She held out some sheets of paper, folded over.

"That journalist we met this morning," she began.

"Henry Barcroft?"

"I'm sure you'll run into him again at some point. He seems to have a thing about you, Mr. Dillman. You're his mystery man." She thrust the papers into his hand. "Could you possibly give this article back to him for me, please? Tell him that I have no objection to the way he's quoted me even though I don't actually remember saying that. Thank you so much."

"I'll see that he gets it, Miss Masefield."

"You don't mind, do you?"

"Not at all."

"To tell the truth, I'd rather not have to speak to the man again.

I find him rather obnoxious." She gave him a token smile. "Do excuse me. Captain Watt is going to take us up to the bridge."

Dillman waved her off, then glanced at the article in his hand. He was a little peeved to be used as a messenger boy once more, but saw an immediate advantage, quite apart from incurring Genevieve's gratitude. The article gave him an excuse to track down Barcroft and find out how the journalist had spent the evening. Though no proof of guilt had yet been found, the man was still the prime suspect concerning the theft from the chief engineer's cabin. Dillman stowed the article away in his pocket and joined the general exodus.

The Rymers tried to shepherd everyone from their table into the lounge but the Latimers felt that their honeymoon was best continued alone and they excused themselves. The rural dean was inebriated enough to start voicing some trenchant opinions about the future of the Anglican Church, and Nairn Mackintosh countered by waving the banner of Presbyterianism at him. Their respective wives joined in the good-humored discussion and Matthew Rymer was not excluded for long. His appetite for debate sharpened by brandy, he took a delight in provoking both the rural dean and the elderly Scotsman. Sylvia and Violet Rymer were amused spectators.

Before he could take a seat beside them, Dillman felt a tug at his elbow and swung round to see the friendly face of Ellen Tolley.

"I just came over to say hello," she began.

"I'm glad you did, Ellen. Lovely to see you."

"What a meal!"

"The food gets better and better."

"Did you try the gateau Mexicaine?"

"No, I opted for the petits fours."

"You missed a treat, George."

"I'll remember that next time the gateau is on the menu," he said, looking around. "But I was hoping for a chance to meet your father."

"He's just limped off, I'm afraid. That leg of his gives him so much pain. Daddy went off to change the dressing."

"It's a recent wound, then?"

"Yes," she explained. "Daddy had an accident in England. All his own fault. He does tend to be a bit clumsy at times. But he's a real stoic. Hates to show any discomfort in public. That's why he's slipped off quietly to the cabin."

"Does that mean you're free to join us?" he invited.

"No, thanks, George. Not this evening. I'm very tired. If I sit down, I'll probably go straight off to sleep." Her tone became confidential. "Made a pig of myself in the dining saloon and rich food always makes me feel drowsy." She touched his arm. "Go back to your friends."

"Unless you need a pathfinder again."

"What?" She laughed. "Oh, last night. No, I think I've mastered the way back to the cabin now. Just about."

"If you get lost, send up a distress flare and I'll come running."

"I bet you would at that!"

"I'm always ready to help a lady."

"You're a sweet guy," she said fondly. "See you around, George."

Ellen touched his arm again and gave him a farewell grin. Dillman watched until she was out of sight. He then realized that Violet Rymer was standing beside him.

"That was she, wasn't it?" she asked.

"Who?"

"The person you were looking at during dinner. Who is she?"

"A friend."

"She seemed to be more than that, Mr. Dillman."

"I'm afraid that you're jumping to conclusions, Miss Rymer. We only met yesterday. And that was only for a matter of minutes."

"But you're both Americans!" said Violet as if it were conclusive proof of a deep relationship. "I just caught that drawl in her accent."

Dillman was amused. "Believe it or not, we Americans are just as conservative as you when it comes to certain social conventions. The young lady is a friend and I was pleased to see her. But that's where the story ends. Sorry to disappoint you."

"I'm sorry on your behalf, Mr. Dillman. I sort of hoped that—"

"Forget about me," he said firmly, cutting her off. "All you need to think about is yourself, Miss Rymer. My advice is that you should have an early night. There's an important day ahead of you tomorrow."

She trembled visibly. "I know! I can't wait!"

Second thoughts had set in well before the end of the meal, but they did not find expression until she was walking along the corridor with him. Rosemary Hilliard came to an abrupt halt then waited for another couple to go past before she spoke.

"I'm not at all sure about this, Philip," she said uneasily.

"What's the problem?"

"I don't know that I should be going into a man's cabin."

"We can go to your cabin, if you prefer."

"That's not the answer."

"Then what is?" he said, starting to get cold feet himself. "All we need do is to have a drink together and chat. Get to know each other a little better. I thought that's what you wanted to do."

"It is."

"Then why hold back now?"

"I don't know."

There was a long pause during which Philip Garrow's own doubts began to make themselves felt. He foresaw complications. His readiness to betray Violet had surprised him and he did not feel the slightest twinge of guilt but had agreed to meet her in the very cabin into which he was trying to entice Rosemary Hilliard. Whatever happened, the two women had to be kept far apart. If he took Rosemary into his cabin, he would be taking a dangerous step, setting up expectations that might rebound on him. What if she called on him when he was alone in the cabin with Violet? The very thought of it made him shudder.

"Are you cold?" asked Rosemary, seeing him shake.

"A little."

"So am I, Philip. I should have brought a wrap."

"Shall we go to your cabin to fetch one?" he suggested, seeing a way to shift the location from his own territory. "Where exactly is it?"

"Never you mind!" she teased.

"Is it a state secret?"

"As far as you're concerned, yes."

"Is it an inside cabin?"

"Mind your own business, Mr. Garrow," she said playfully.

"I've got a porthole in mine. I can see the ocean through it."

"I've seen enough ocean to last me a lifetime. There's a limit to the amount of pleasure you can get simply from watching waves."

"Much more fun to create your own waves," he said with more bravado than he felt. "What would you like to do, Rosemary?"

"I'm not sure."

"You've come this far. Why turn back?"

"Instinct, I suppose."

"About me?"

"Oh, no, Philip. About me. I don't think I'm quite ready for this yet."

Garrow saw the hesitation in her face. At the same time, he sensed that it would not take much persuasion to dispel her fears. All that she wanted was reassurance and flattery. If he made the effort, he was sure that the words would trip off his tongue as easily as they had done so far. But his own reservations were gaining in strength. He looked down the corridor toward his cabin and turned back to Rosemary. Potential problems loomed ahead larger than ever. He became tongue-tied.

"I've never done this sort of thing before," she confessed quietly. "To tell you the truth, I've rather shocked myself. That's not meant as a criticism of you, Philip," she added quickly. "I don't blame you in any way. I'm old enough to take responsibility for my own actions. But the truth is that I've never looked at a man since my husband died, let alone spoken to one in the way that you and I have spoken. It's all happened so fast. That frightens me. On the other hand," she continued, brushing her hair back from her face, "I don't want to let you down. I'd hate you to think of me as a . . . well, as a woman who leads men on, because I'm not like that at all. And, as you say, having come this far . . ." She took a deep breath. "Tell me what to do, Philip. I'll leave the decision to you."

Philip Garrow was caught on the horns of a dilemma. Before he could extricate himself, someone came along the corridor and walked between them, forcing them to step guiltily apart. It was Albert. As he passed Garrow, the steward shot him a look that made him squirm with embarrassment. It robbed him of the last few shards of his confidence.

"Well?" asked Rosemary. "What are we going to do?"

"Go up on deck for a walk," he said. "I need some fresh air."

"Six longcloth nightdresses trimmed and embroidered with tucks, four silk chemises with trimmed edging and four with insertion tucks, six slipped bodices with trimmed edging, six flannel petticoats embroidered with silk, two silk petticoats, two plain skirts, one pair of white corsets, three evening gowns, two fancy underskirts, one twill dressing gown . . ."

Janet Palgrave's memory was phenomenal. Allowed a privileged glimpse at Anna Latimer's bridal trousseau, the rural dean's wife had memorized each item and was retailing them in turn to Sylvia Rymer and her daughter. Without wanting to, Dillman also heard the droning recital while trying at the same time to contribute to a debate among the men about salmon fishing. There were limits even to his civility and Dillman felt that they might be reached if he remained trapped in the lounge indefinitely with the Rymer party. Issuing thanks and apologies, he rose from his chair and moved away in time to escape the Palgrave litany about knickers, handkerchiefs, and black hose. At that point in the evening, he suspected, the bride was probably dispensing with every item in her trousseau.

Retreating to the smoking room, he found two games of cards in progress. Edward Collins had found new victims for his nimble fingers. Cyril Weekes and Jeremiah Erskine were at a separate table with four other men, both faring better without the professional skills of Collins to hamper them. Weekes peered at his cards through his pince-nez as if puzzling over a conundrum. Erskine, by contrast, glared fiercely at his hand, breathing heavily through his nose as if working up his anger for a charge across the room. Dillman watched them for a while until the cigar smoke became too troublesome. As soon as he left, he was confronted by Charles Halliday. The purser gave him a nod of recognition and drew him behind some potted palms so that they could talk in private.

"Well met, Mr. Dillman!"

"Were you looking for me, Mr. Halliday?"

"Not especially," said the other, "but now that I've bumped into you, I might be able to use your help. Before I do that, of course, I'd like to hear how your inquiries have been going."

"Slowly," admitted the other.

"No glimmer of light in the darkness yet?"

"I'm afraid not."

"What have you found out?"

Dillman described his research among the other journalists and his visit to the wireless room. He also mentioned his surveillance of Edward Collins, who was winning too consistently to be relying entirely on luck but who somehow convinced his playing partners that he was a relative novice at the poker table.

"Anyone losing a large amount of money to him?" said Halliday.

"Not yet. He's too cunning for that."

"Taking a bit from here and a bit from there."

"He won't make a real killing until the last night on board," guessed Dillman. "Otherwise, he'll scare everyone off. What would you like me to do, Mr. Halliday? Spread the warning?"

"No, just keep a friendly eye on him. If he cheats, of course, that's another matter. We simply can't have that sort of thing on board."

"Collins doesn't need to cheat. He outplays the rest of them with ease. He was collecting IOUs from three of them when I left." Dillman gave a sigh. "Lambs to the slaughter. But you said a minute ago that you might be able to use my help."

"That's right. More complaints have been coming in."

"Henry Barcroft again?"

"How did you guess?"

"He's managing to upset almost everybody."

"Barcroft really went too far this time," said the purser. "Apparently, he cornered Itzak Weiss and his wife on deck today. They thought they were just exchanging a few pleasant words with a fellow passenger. Mr. Weiss was mortified when Barcroft had the gall to go to his cabin later to show him the text of an article he'd written. 'Music on the Lucy', I think it was called, or something equally abhorrent to Mr. Weiss. He's notorious for *not* giving interviews. You can imagine what his reaction was."

"Did he slam the cabin door in Barcroft's face?"

"He's far too civilized to do that. He came to me instead. I was in the middle of another chat with Fergus Rourke so it wasn't the best time to hear a complaint from Itzak Weiss. It would be such a pleasant change if someone actually brought me good news for once instead of endless protests and whinges."

"I'll bring you good news soon," vowed Dillman.

"Can I hold you to that?"

"It's only a question of time, Mr. Halliday."

"Coming back to Barcroft . . ."

"Have you rapped him over the knuckles yet?"

"I was going to but he's been a bit elusive this evening. Besides, I'm not quite sure that I'm the ideal person to wag a finger at him. It makes it too official and that might be used against us. Journalists always have more ink than we do. I can't have him traducing Cunard in print to get his own back because a purser gave him a roasting."

"What's the alternative?"

"You can have a word with him."

"In what capacity? I don't want to lose my cover."

"You won't have to, Mr. Dillman. Make it sound casual. Say that you met Itzak Weiss in the dining saloon and heard him complaining about an inquisitive British journalist. Give Barcroft a friendly warning," he urged. "A nod is as good as a wink."

"Not where Henry Barcroft is concerned."

"I just think it might be better coming from you. After all, you know the rogue. You can get in under his guard."

Dillman thought it over. "Very well, sir. If that's what you want." He checked his watch. "It's not too late to find him now. My guess is that Barcroft will be in the lounge bar, crowing over the other journalists. I might just take a stroll along there."

"Do that. And thanks."

"As it happens, I have another reason to see him," said Dillman, patting the pocket containing the article. "I can kill two birds with one stone. I'll report back to you first thing in the morning."

"I'll be there. As for that good news you promised . . ."

"Be patient, Mr. Halliday."

"Make it sooner rather than later, old chap. It's no fun having the chief engineer breathing fire down my neck. Anyone would think that *I* stole those things from his cabin."

"I'll do my best."

Dillman nodded a farewell, then headed for the second-class lounge. It was still quite full, but there was no sign of Henry Barcroft. Other members of the press were enjoying complimentary drinks from the bar, but none of them could tell him where their colleague was. Barcroft had left the second-class dining saloon fairly early and had not been seen since. Someone suggested that he might be unwell and that produced a spontaneous cheer from the others.

A tour of the other public rooms yielded nothing, so Dillman began to explore the various decks, working upward until he reached the boat deck. A blustery wind was raking the ship and making the tarpaulins flap on the lifeboats. Only a couple of people braved the elements and they were swaddled in greatcoats, hats, and scarves. Dillman gave a shiver and went below again, venturing this time into the third-class areas and feeling rather conspicuous in his evening dress. Those who lolled on wooden benches in the public rooms looked up with a mixture of curiosity and resentment. Once again the search was fruitless.

Only one possibility now remained. Dillman consulted his watch again and saw that it was getting late, but he could not believe that the journalist would have gone to bed. The likelihood was that the man was in his cabin, drafting one of his articles, pulling together comments gleaned from the dozens of interviews he had done among passengers and crew. The press had been assigned to a block of cabins in second class but Dillman did not have to guess which one belonged to Barcroft. When he took out the article given to him by Genevieve Masefield, he saw that the number of the cabin was written in large numerals at the top of the first sheet. That was obviously for her benefit. He was not surprised that Genevieve had felt able to resist the covert invitation.

The cabin was on the shelter deck at the end of a long corridor. Dillman moved silently over the thick carpet and glanced at the series of nautical paintings adorning the walls. Though it lacked the unstinting luxury of first class, there was still an appreciable degree of comfort and taste. Dillman reached the door, then paused to rehearse what he would say. It was not only Itzak Weiss who found the journalist so objectionable. Genevieve Masefield's complaint could also be passed on and that would probably carry more weight even than the protests of a celebrated violinist. All Barcroft wanted from the latter was an unauthorized interview. Having seen them together, Dillman sensed that he had more serious designs on Genevieve.

He tapped on the door and waited. No sound came from within. He knocked again with more force but there was still no response. Dillman was about to move away when it occurred to him to try the door. It was unlocked. He opened it cautiously and peered into the darkness.

"Mr. Barcroft?" he called. "Are you there?"

There was no answer yet he had a strong feeling that someone was in the cabin. Light from the corridor was spilling into the room, enabling him to see the ornate pattern on the carpet. Dillman stiffened. He saw a figure in shadowy outline. An ugly stain disfigured the carpet. Reaching for the switch, he turned on the light. The cabin was, after all, occupied by the guest assigned to it, but he would not be able to enjoy its facilities again. Henry Barcroft lay facedown on the floor with a gaping wound in the back of his head. Blood had seeped onto the carpet. It took Dillman a matter of seconds to establish that the journalist was dead.

NINE

He was shocked. Dillman had seen murder victims before, but none in such a gory condition. Closing the cabin door, he stood with his back to it while he studied the body and tried to come to terms with what he had found. Henry Barcroft was stretched out on the floor beside the built-in table. He still wore the white tie and tails he had put on to fraternize with the diners in first-class. When Dillman knelt beside the corpse again, he winced at the sight of the hideous wound. It seemed as if Barcroft had been struck viciously and repeatedly from behind. Though he had never liked the man, Dillman felt a profound sympathy for him now. It had been a most brutal attack. Henry Barcroft had not stood a chance.

Dillman stood up and looked for clues. Taking care not to walk on the bloodstained patch, he moved slowly around the cabin and took a mental inventory of its contents. Writing materials lay on the desk beside a small pile of books, a bottle of Champagne standing unopened in an ice bucket, and two glasses. A pair of slippers poked out from beneath the bed. The wardrobe was half-open, displaying a couple of suits and the striped blazer that Barcroft had worn earlier. Nothing appeared to be out of place.

Whoever killed the man had carefully removed all traces of his visit before he left. Dillman was dealing with a professional.

Eager to begin a more detailed search of the room, he knew that he must report the murder first. Everything had to be left exactly as he found it. As he gazed down at the prone figure, the words of Jeremiah Erskine echoed in his ears. The bearded prophet of doom had warned that disaster was at hand. His premonition seemed to have come true. Dillman crouched beside the body for the last time and offered up a silent prayer for the soul of the dead man. He was about to rise to his feet when he saw something out of the corner of his eye. Attached in some way to the underside of the desk was a large brown envelope. It was so cunningly placed that it eluded his scrutiny when he was standing up and, he suspected, evaded those who searched the cabin earlier on. Only someone at floor level would possibly find it.

Dillman reached under the desk and slowly detached the drawing pins holding the envelope in place. It was not sealed. Guessing what it contained, he needed the merest glance to confirm his theory. The key was still in the lock. Dillman removed it, switched off the light, then let himself out and locked the cabin door. The scene of the crime was secured. Nobody else would stumble in on the horror that had confronted him.

Charles Halliday climbed into bed and reached for his book. At the end of a long day, he liked to read himself asleep, escaping into a fictional world far removed from his onerous round of duties. The purser had only reached the end of the first paragraph when there was a firm knock on his door. He put the book aside and sat up.

"Who is it?" he said.

"George Dillman," came the reply.

Hopping out of bed, the purser crossed swiftly to the door and unlocked it to admit his visitor. Dillman handed him the envelope.

"What's this?" said the other.

"That good news you wanted."

"Good news?"

"One crime has been solved," said Dillman. "We've recovered the missing items from the chief engineer's cabin."

"Wonderful!"

"Let me finish, Mr. Halliday. One crime may have been accounted for, but a far more serious one has been committed. I'm afraid that I must ask you to get dressed again. Henry Barcroft has been murdered."

The purser gaped. "Are you serious, man?"

"Never more so. We'll need the surgeon. Who's on duty?"

"It doesn't matter. Lionel Osborne is the man we need, even if he's fast asleep. Barcroft murdered? How? When? Where?"

Dillman gave him the details as the other man scrambled into his uniform then the two of them went off to rouse Lionel Osborne from his slumbers. When the surgeon had put on his clothes, all three of them repaired at speed to Barcroft's cabin, grateful that they met nobody else on the way. Dillman used the key to let them in, then locked the door once again. Even though they had been forewarned, both Halliday and Osborne were badly shaken by what they saw. The surgeon was the first to recover, kneeling beside the body to examine it for vital signs but soon emitting a long sigh of regret.

"Dead as a dodo," he said, standing up. "I think Mr. Dillman was right in his estimate of the time of death. I'll need to give it a more thorough examination, of course, but my guess would be recently, perhaps even less than an hour ago." He pointed to the wounds. "Blunt instrument. Used repeatedly, by the look of it. Dreadful way to die."

Halliday was less concerned about the nature of the death than its implications. His already gaunt features acquired new crevices of anxiety.

"The captain will have to be told at once," he said ruefully. "He's not going to like this. He so wanted the maiden voyage to go off without a hitch. This is a calamity. It'll ruin everything."

"Only if it gets out," argued Dillman.

"What do you mean?"

"Just this, Mr. Halliday. At the moment, only four of us actually

know that this murder has taken place. The three of us in here—
and the killer himself, of course. Obviously the captain must be
informed, but I'm sure he'll agree that the fewer people who learn
about this, the better."

"I'd go along with that," said Osborne.

"So would I," decided the purser, mulling it over. "Broadcast
this news and we'll spread terror throughout the whole ship. How
could anyone enjoy a voyage when they know there's a savage
murderer on the loose? On the other hand, it won't be easy to
keep this under wraps." He gazed down at the body. "Mr. Barcroft
was highly conspicuous. If he vanishes completely from sight,
people are bound to ask what happened to him. His colleagues in
the press, most of all."

"They're the last ones who must find out," insisted Dillman.
"Or the story will be all over the newspapers in London and New
York. We must avoid that at all costs. Besides, Henry Barcroft
didn't run with the pack. That's what they resented about him.
He was a lone wolf, always trotting off in search of fresh meat and
keeping it to himself when he found it. I fancy that some of the
other journalists will be glad if he's not around. It'll be a bonus
for them. They'll assume he's on the ship somewhere, which—
technically—he still is."

"That raises another problem," said Halliday with a grimace.
"Where do we keep him in the meantime?"

"Certainly not in here," declared Osborne.

"You must have had fatalities aboard Cunard ships before," said
Dillman.

"Yes, but not like this. Most of our passengers have the decency
to pass away by natural means. Apart from anything else, it absolves us of any blame from grieving relatives. Mr. Barcroft is our
first murder victim." The surgeon glanced down at him. "He needs
to be put in cold storage."

"Do you have refrigerator space?"

"Ask Charles."

"It can be arranged," said the purser.

"Do it discreetly, old chap," said Osborne chirpily. "We don't want him hanging among the sides of beef or the chefs will have the shock of their lives. Before we wrap him up and put him on ice, of course, I'll want to do a proper autopsy. That means bringing Roland in." He turned to Dillman. "Roland Tomkins is my assistant. Bright spark. Worked for a coroner at one point, so he knows his stuff."

"Roland also knows how to keep his mouth shut," said Halliday. "And we could hardly keep a thing like this from the assistant surgeon. Will the two of you take responsibility for moving of the body?"

"Yes, Charles."

"Count on me, if you need help," volunteered Dillman.

"Thanks—and we probably will. What about the cabin?"

"I'll have it cleaned up and sealed off," said the purser, blanching as he studied the ugly stain on the carpet. "When we've had a thorough search in here, that is. Have you moved anything, Mr. Dillman?"

"No. What you see is exactly what I saw."

"Except that we had some idea what to expect."

"There is that," said Dillman softly.

"Poor devil! Nobody deserves to die like that."

"No, sir. With your permission, I'd like to search the body."

"Fine by me. Lionel?"

"Go ahead," encouraged the surgeon. "I'll slope off to fetch Roland. He's got a stronger stomach for this kind of thing than I do. And I'll leave you to break the bad tidings to the captain, shall I, Charles?"

The purser nodded, let his colleague out, and locked the door again. Dillman was already feeling gently in the pockets of the dead man.

"Was there any sign of forced entry?" asked Halliday.

"No, the door was unlocked."

"Do you think the killer had a key?"

"I think that he was probably invited in here," said Dillman, slowly extracting a wallet. "Look at that bottle. Two glasses. My hunch is that Mr. Barcroft knew and trusted the man. He was caught completely off guard. That's why there are no signs of a struggle."

"That eliminates Fergus Rourke, then."

"Why? Did you suspect him?"

"His name did cross my mind," confessed the other. "When you told me that Barcroft had been battered to death, I wondered if Fergus had come after him, thirsting for blood. Our chief engineer has a violent temper at times. I was relieved to see that it couldn't have been him."

"What makes you so sure?"

"The Champagne. Fergus would certainly have taken it with him. Show me an Irishman who'd walk away from a free drink."

"That bottle is a vital clue. If we find out when the steward brought it to the cabin, we can get a clearer idea of the time of death. As you can see, the ice in the bucket has melted. How long would that take?"

Dillman laid the contents of the wallet on the table for inspection. There was a small amount of money, a membership card of a London club, a sepia photograph of a young woman, and several visiting cards. The item that interested Dillman most was a letter folded twice in order to fit into the wallet. It was from a well-known publisher. Dillman read it, then handed it over to Halliday.

"Doesn't tell us much, does it?" complained the other. "Two short sentences, that's all. 'Further to our recent meeting, we look forward to receiving the manuscript at the earliest opportunity. I trust that you will have a most interesting and productive voyage.' What's all that about?"

"We'll find out in time."

"Do you think this could be a coded message?"

"I don't know," said Dillman, taking it from him and setting it down beside the other things. "But it's a valuable clue. I think it may lead us to the real reason that Henry Barcroft was aboard the *Lusitania*."

"To steal those charts, obviously."

"For whose benefit?"

"One of our rivals."

"I wonder, Mr. Halliday."

"But you found them hidden in his cabin."

"True."

"Someone paid him to get hold of them."

"Not the publisher, surely? What use would technical diagrams be to George Newnes Limited? Don't they specialize in fiction?" He pointed to the books. "These all seem to be published by Newnes. They're novels." A thought struck him. "Will you give the envelope to Mr. Rourke?"

"Of course. It'll get him off my back."

"What will you tell him?"

There was a pause. "Ah, I see what you mean."

"Say as little as possible," advised Dillman.

"I'll have to tell him something."

"We don't want to bring the chief engineer in on this as well. Why not tell him that they came to light during our search? Say that we found them hidden away in one of the storerooms."

"What if he presses for details?"

"Invent them, sir. You know Mr. Rourke better than I do, but my guess is that he'll be so pleased to get his property returned that he won't be too bothered about exactly how it came into our possession."

"I'm not sure about that. He can be an awkward cuss."

"Do you want to help me search the cabin?"

"No. I need to pay a call on the captain. He won't thank me for being kept in the dark about this any longer than is necessary. Will you be all right in here on your own?"

Dillman smiled sadly. "I'm not on my own."

"I wasn't counting Barcroft," he said. "Well, I suppose we're in your hands now, Mr. Dillman. I thought your work would be confined to thieves, pickpockets, and the odd confidence trickster. I never envisaged anything like this. Do you really think you can solve a murder?"

"I'm certain of it."

"Why?"

"To start with, I know exactly where the killer is. On this ship.

He can't escape. It's largely a question of eliminating suspects one by one."

"But everyone on board is a suspect."

"Oh, no," corrected Dillman. "Look at the way that skull was cracked open. That's the work of a strong man. No woman, child, or elderly person could inflict that kind of damage so we can remove over two-thirds of the people from the list of suspects. But we can narrow it down even further. Mr. Barcroft invited someone here for a late-night drink. I don't think he'd have ordered Champagne for anyone traveling in third-class, do you? Look what he's wearing. It suggests he was expecting someone in similar attire. An able-bodied man from first-class. It's an expensive bottle. He must have liked his visitor, to have spent that much on him. Who was it? A special friend? Someone he wished to interview? Unless, of course, the killer got here before the invited guest. There's no sign of a struggle. He must have attacked Mr. Barcroft while his back was turned. Yet it seems he was allowed into the cabin. You see, Mr. Halliday? That list gets smaller and smaller. By the time I've finished in here, it will have shrunk even further. Go and wake up the captain," he said. "And assure him that we'll have this problem sorted out long before we reach New York."

"Do I have your word on that?"

"My solemn promise."

"I admire your confidence. I wouldn't even know where to start."

Dillman remembered the article from Genevieve Masefield.

"I do," he said.

Philip Garrow had bungled his opportunity. He saw that now. As he lay on his bed in the darkness, he reviewed the catalog of missed chances. Rosemary Hilliard was an attractive and desirable woman. She was his for the taking. After a long period of mourning, she was finally ready to allow some romance back into her life again, to replace sad memories of her dead husband with a new and exciting experience. Garrow had been tempted to supply that experience, to enjoy the feel of a mature woman in his arms and, if he was persuasive enough, to bring her enforced celibacy to a joyful end. But he tried to rush her. Instead of taking more time over the preliminaries, he sought to hustle her off to his cabin in a way that made her hesitate.

The evening had ended abruptly as soon as they went out on deck. Cold wind had made Rosemary shiver and she retreated to her cabin for the night before he could even steal a farewell kiss. Yet the situation was not beyond redemption, he felt sure of that. She was as drawn to him as he was to her and the magic of the setting had done the rest. On land, such a relationship could never exist because she would see Garrow for what he really was, an unemployed clerk with no prospects. In the middle of an ocean, trading on his appearance, he could pass himself off as someone else, an ambitious young man with an important position in his company, able to pay his way on a costly voyage and entitled to take his pleasures where he found them. For a few hours that evening, he saw the Philip Garrow of his dreams reflected in her admiring gaze. Then he stumbled. Badly.

It was so refreshing to be with a person like Rosemary Hilliard. She was honest, endearing, and compassionate. She had a becoming air of independence about her. The difference in their ages was an attraction rather than a deterrent, her married status hinting at someone seasoned in the delights of the bedchamber. Compared with her, Violet Rymer seemed gauche and unsophisticated, a child beside an adult. A timorous virgin beside a real flesh-and-blood woman. Violet's attractions were of a different nature and he reminded himself that it was they that had prompted him to take the impulsive step of joining the ship when it docked at Queenstown Harbor.

After his own fashion, he loved Violet Rymer but she aroused none of the urgent desires that his new friend set off. In a single day, he had achieved a deeper intimacy with Rosemary Hilliard than he had in six months of wooing Violet, and there would be none of the obstacles that attended his relationship with the latter. He did not have to circumvent two hostile parents whenever he wanted to speak to Rosemary or feed on morsels of affection. Set against each other, both women could be seen in their true light, and Violet unquestionably had prior claim on him. She could offer him uncritical devotion. The older woman was a temporary pleasure. Only Violet could give him the financial security he sought.

What made him cringe was the memory of that look on the face of the steward. Albert had registered mild disgust. Having spoken to his brother, he would have been given a description of Violet Rymer and realized that she was not the woman he saw in the corridor. In the bloodshot eyes of the diminutive steward, Philip Garrow was transformed from a pining lover into a shameless predator. He would get no further help from Albert and his brother. Their sympathy would shift to Violet.

For the first time, he began to feel genuine remorse. He had to make amends to her. The thrill of being on the same vessel as she had faded slightly, but he hoped to recapture it once he actually saw Violet again. Courtship could be renewed in earnest and the beauty of it was that it would take place right under the noses of her parents. That was where the real satisfaction lay, in outwitting and punishing Sylvia and Matthew Rymer. They were the enemy and their daughter was the prize to be snatched away from them. Garrow addressed his mind to the problem of how it could best be done.

But he still fell asleep thinking of Rosemary Hilliard.

After an exhaustive search of the cabin, Dillman learned a great deal about the character of Henry Barcroft but rather less about that of his killer. He was still working his way systematically around the bathroom when Lionel Osborne returned with the assistant surgeon. Dillman let them in and was introduced to Roland Tomkins, a dour individual in his thirties with a long face and bulbous eyes. Tomkins immediately knelt beside the corpse to carry out his own examination and he speculated at some length about the type of weapon used in the assault. When their language became too medical, Dillman stopped listening to them.

The purser was the next to arrive, escorting the captain, who had insisted on seeing for himself what had happened. Captain Watt, a well-built man with a craggy face, was a veteran seaman due for retirement in the following year. Delighted to be given command of a vessel as illustrious as the *Lusitania*, he was horrified at the thought of having his maiden voyage smeared by the blood of a murder victim and was as keen as any of them to keep the tragedy secret from all but a select few.

"We are in international waters," he told them sonorously, "and thus free from the jurisdiction of either English or American courts. We have to be our own police force, our own judge and jury. Or, to put it another way, gentlemen, we are in limbo. We make up our own rules. Let us begin by building a wall of silence around this gruesome incident." His voice darkened. "And let's catch this vicious killer as soon as possible."

"Yes, Captain," said Dillman. "We shall. But it will be easier to do if life aboard the ship carries on as normal. It's very difficult to conduct a murder investigation in an atmosphere of hysteria."

"You sound as if you speak from experience, Mr. Dillman."

"I do, sir."

"It's good to know that we have a trained detective on board."

"Mr. Dillman worked for the Pinkerton Agency," said Halliday. "Their record is second to none in the United States. Over the next couple of days, we will have to rely heavily on Mr. Dillman's expertise."

"I hope it's not found wanting," said Watt crisply. "Mr. Halliday?"

"Captain?"

"Find a refrigerator where the body can be stored.

"Aye, aye, sir."

"Report back to me when it's arranged."

"Aye, aye, sir."

As the purser left the room, Watt turned to the surgeon.

"Mr. Osborne?"

"Captain?"

"Where will you conduct the autopsy?"

"In the surgery, sir. All our instruments are there."

"Speed is of the essence."

"Aye, aye, sir."

"I want the body safely tidied away in cold storage where it can provoke no curiosity. Be brief, gentlemen. Brief but thorough."

"Aye, aye, sir."

"As for you, Mr. Dillman . . ."

"Yes, Captain?"

"You've just taken a huge load on your shoulders, young man. Are they strong enough to bear the weight?"

"I believe so."

"Mr. Halliday will be able to help, of course, and so will our other purser, Mr. Voysey. I'll put him in the picture as soon as I leave."

"Thank you, sir."

"Pursers already have their hands full on a vessel as large as this," warned Captain Watt. "They can only offer limited assistance. Besides, this is a case when officers are at a disadvantage. Uniforms define us. They represent authority and are designed to offer reassurance to the passengers." A throaty laugh. "Even the biggest damn fool of a seaman can look like a potential Nelson in a smart uniform! It imparts faith. Do you hear what I'm saying?"

"I think so, Captain Watt," said Dillman. "This is a task for someone in plainclothes who can move easily among the passengers as one of them. Someone whom the killer won't recognize as a threat."

"Precisely."

"I work best that way."

"Do you carry a weapon, Mr. Dillman?"

"None beyond an agile brain and an able body, sir."

"They may not be enough against this villain. He's dangerous. Anyone can see that. If you need a revolver, I'll authorize the master-at-arms to provide you with one."

"I'll remember that, sir."

The captain nodded, then appraised him shrewdly. "The *Lusitania* is my pride and joy, Mr. Dillman. I've sailed on many ships in my time but none can touch this one. She's an absolute daisy.

We've hit rough water. Steer us through it," he said earnestly. "Keep us afloat and you'll win the undying gratitude of the Cunard Line. Do I make myself clear?"

"Aye, aye, sir," said Dillman.

A night that ended for the second time in Lord Carradine's private lounge had left Genevieve Masefield feeling stimulated rather than tired. She needed little sleep and awoke not long after dawn. A long, lazy bath gave her time to reflect on the many pleasures of the previous evening. Genevieve was on her way to breakfast when she was intercepted by another early riser. George Porter Dillman had snatched only a couple of hours' sleep but there was no hint of weariness in his body or manner.

"Good morning, Miss Masefield."

"Hello, Mr. Dillman. I didn't expect anyone else to be up yet."

"No more did I," he said, "so it's all the more gratifying to see you. I wonder if I might have a word with you, please?"

She was guarded. "What about?"

"That article you gave me last night."

"Oh, that," she said, relaxing slightly. "I'm so sorry to have dumped it on you like that but I couldn't think of any other way of dodging that Mr. Barcroft. I didn't want him knocking on my cabin door again."

"Again?"

"Yes, he called earlier to give me the article and tried to talk his way into my cabin while I read it. I drew the line at that. And when I did read the article, I couldn't see what all the fuss was about. He asked for my approval, but I wasn't mentioned by name and the opinions that he ascribed to me were, in any case, quite wrong. The truth is that he didn't need to show me the article at all."

"Perhaps he had another motive," suggested Dillman.

"No question about that!"

"What time did he give you the article?"

"Just before luncheon."

"I see."

"Why do you ask?"

"Because I took the trouble to read it," he explained. "You're right, Miss Masefield. There was no point at all in trying to get your approval before he sent it off because it would have been too late."

"Too late?"

"That article was dispatched from the wireless room hours earlier."

"How do you know?"

"Because I happened to be getting a message of my own sent when Mr. Barcroft came in," he said, amending the truth to cover the fact that he had deliberately gone there in search of anything presented to the wireless operators by Henry Barcroft. "He insisted on reading the article and sniggering when he came to the reference to me. What he gave you was an exact copy of something already beyond recall."

"The deceit of it!"

"I felt that you should know."

"Thank you, Mr. Dillman. I'm most grateful. I'll lodge a complaint against him with the purser."

"You may have to join a queue in order to do that."

"So I understand," she said. "I had the privilege of sitting beside Mr. Weiss last night and he was deeply offended by a trick which Mr. Barcroft played on him. He's managed to annoy us all, even Percy."

"Percy?"

"Lord Carradine."

"I see."

"Did you return the article to him?"

Dillman nodded. "It's back in Mr. Barcroft's cabin."

"I hope that you conveyed my feelings about him."

"He will not trouble you again on this voyage, Miss Masefield. I can guarantee that. He finally understood the weight of hostility against him."

"I've never met anyone so thick-skinned."

"Yet you seemed to like him at first," he said artlessly. "To be honest, I took him for a friend of yours. That was the impression he gave me, at all events."

"Well, it was a wholly false impression!" she asserted. Genevieve gave an apologetic smile. "I'm sorry to speak so sharply, especially when you've been kind enough to uncover a deception for me. Do we have to stand out here in the corridor? Couldn't we continue this discussion over breakfast?"

"By all means," he said, walking beside her, glad of the opportunity to probe at leisure. "It's strange, isn't it? I mean, I would have thought that it was part of the stock-in-trade of any journalist to be affable. To go out of his way to be *liked*. Yet he seemed to take delight in antagonizing people. As you just pointed out, he upset just about everybody. I doubt if there's anyone aboard with a kind word to say about him."

"Oh, there is one person, I think."

"Who's that?"

"The man I saw him chatting to when I went into dinner last night. Actually," she admitted with a girlish grin, "I sneaked in past him under the cover of Carlotta Hubermann but I did notice how intensely he and Mr. Barcroft were talking together. Not for the first time, either. I spotted the pair of them together a couple of times throughout the day. So perhaps he did have one real friend, after all."

"Who was it?"

"A rather odd-looking fellow. Quite grotesque, in fact. He had a large black beard and dreadful warts all over his forehead. You must have seen him. He's quite unmistakable."

"I know, Miss Masefield. I've crossed swords with him."

"Does he have a name?"

"Erskine," said Dillman meditatively. "Mr. Jeremiah Erskine."

Fergus Rourke had lived far too long and sailed in too many ships to believe everything a purser told him. Pleased to get his property back, he was less than convinced by the story that came with them. He stood in the middle of his cabin and glowered at Charles Halliday.

"Now try telling me the truth," he ordered.

"That is the truth, Fergus."

"Pull the other one!"

"We searched, we found, we returned. What more do you want?"

"The full story. Stop trying to pull the wool over my eyes, Charlie. Who took these diagrams and where did you really find them?"

"I told you," repeated Halliday. "In one of the storerooms."

"Just lying harmlessly about on the floor."

"No, they were hidden in a cupboard."

"What sort of cupboard?"

"A linen cupboard."

"Ah, we're getting down to details now, are we?" said the chief engineer with cheerful cynicism. "Important material is stolen from me and where is it found? Under a pile of bedsheets, in a cupboard, in a storeroom, somewhere up my arse! Who do you think you're fooling?"

"There's no need to yell, Fergus."

"Then stop treating me like a child."

Halliday gritted his teeth. "I've told you all that I'm in a position to tell you. And that is the truth."

"In other words, you're hiding something."

"No, I'm not."

"I can see it in your face, man. I can smell it on you."

"You'll have to excuse me," said the other, moving away.

"Hold on!" said Rourke, blocking his way. "You're not leaving until this is sorted out." He held up the brown envelope. "These were my diagrams that were stolen. Surely that entitles me to an explanation?"

"I've given it to you."

"What you've given me is a pack of lies that wouldn't deceive a blind dromedary, let alone a chief engineer. Doesn't my rank stand for anything on this ship? Now, will you tell me the truth or would you rather I referred the whole matter to Captain Watt?"

"He'll give you the same answer as I would."

"What do you mean?"

"I mean," said Halliday, irritable from lack of sleep, "that we're dealing with restricted information here. You've been told all I'm allowed to tell you. Press me any further and you'll have Captain Watt to answer to. I can't put it any plainer than that, Fergus."

The chief engineer blinked and tugged vigorously at his beard. Taking the diagrams from inside the envelope, he unfolded them and put them side by side on the desk. He shook his head in bewilderment.

"Beats me." He sighed. "I can understand someone wanting to steal this cross section of the boiler room or even detailed layout of the whole ship." His stubby finger pointed at another diagram. "But what use is this to them? It's a wiring diagram. Only a trained electrician could make sense of it. Is that who you found under that linen in the cupboard in the storeroom? Some mad electrician?"

"We don't know who stole the diagrams."

"And you wouldn't tell me, even if you did. Is that it?"

"Fergus—"

"I thought we were shipmates, Charlie."

"We are."

"Then let me in on the secret!"

"I have to go."

"It was him, wasn't it?"

"Who?"

"That bleeding reporter. Whatsisname? Barcroft. He stole them."

"There's no proof of that."

"Bring the sod here and I'll get the proof."

"This is nothing to do with Henry Barcroft."

"No?"

"No," said Halliday with emphasis. "He doesn't come into contention at all here. I know he got on your nerves and you won't be surprised to learn that he's upset half the ship one way or another, but it's no use pointing the finger at him. Henry Barcroft

139

is out of this. Forget him. He won't come anywhere near you in future. You have my word on that, Fergus." He straightened his tie. "Now, will you let me out, please?"

"You're a rotten liar, Charlie."

"You'll have to give me lessons sometime."

Rourke shook with mirth, then stood aside from the door.

"Off you go," he said sarcastically. "Back to that storeroom."

Charles Halliday was relieved to escape so lightly.

Though he ate very little and relied largely on cups of black coffee, it was the most pleasurable meal Dillman had enjoyed on the *Lusitania*. An hour in Genevieve's company seemed to fly past yet an enormous amount of useful information was dredged up in the course of it. She was an observant young woman with a keen insight into character, and her analysis of some of their fellow passengers was chillingly accurate. His admiration for her steadily increased and, by the same token, he improved his standing markedly with her. Genevieve found him relaxed and undemanding, well versed in maritime lore, entertaining on the subject of the foibles of the English, and quite unlike any of the other Americans whom she had met. Given the chance to talk properly to each other at last, they realized how much in common they had.

Dillman had no need to ply her with questions. The conversation twisted and turned naturally in the direction he would have wanted it to go. She described each meeting she had with Henry Barcroft and listed all the other passengers on whom she had seen him pouncing. Her eyes flashed when she recalled the article he had thrust at her for approval.

"The effrontery of the man!"

"Did you observe that he'd put the number of his cabin on it?"

"I chose *not* to observe it, Mr Dillman."

"Very wise."

"The fellow is beneath contempt!"

"Who are we talking about now, honey?" asked Abigail Hubermann, scenting a touch of scandal. "Which men are we tearing to pieces this morning, eh? Mind if we join you?"

"We want to hear how you got on last night," said Carlotta.

"Sounds like my cue to go," said Dillman with a grin. "Good morning, ladies. Do excuse me." He rose to his feet. "I'll leave the field clear for you to take out your anger on the entire male sex." He gave Genevieve a slight bow. "Thank you, Miss Masefield. It's been a treat."

"The pleasure was mine, Mr. Dillman."

She waved him off, then turned to look into the inquistive faces of the Hubermann sisters as they settled down opposite her. Abigail was signaling disapproval of Dillman but Carlotta was beaming maternally.

"I was hoping you two might get together one day," she said.

"Well, I wasn't," said Abigail with the light of contradiction on her eye. "The American gentleman is a far more dangerous animal than the English variety. Let me tell you why, Genevieve."

Unaware that he was the subject of discussion, Dillman was heading for the exit when he saw Cyril Weekes seated alone at a table in the corner. He waved a greeting and went across.

"My wife is having a sleep-in this morning," explained Weekes. "We didn't get to bed until rather late, I fear."

"I noticed you at the card table. You seemed to be in luck again."

"One of those things."

"Skill must come into it as well."

"A little, perhaps."

"Mr. Erskine wasn't faring quite so well."

"No, poor chap. Jeremiah lost a bundle again. He soon got fed up with it and stalked off. He said that he was going to walk around the entire ship and give himself a good talking-to." Weekes put on his pince-nez and reached for the menu. "Glad I didn't bump into him out there."

"What do you mean?"

"He was in such a foul mood when he charged out. It would have been a case of ill-met by moonlight! No, Mr. Dillman, when Jeremiah Erskine is angry with himself, it's best to give him a wide berth." He looked up. "Do you think I should risk the prunes?"

TEN

Violet Rymer found it difficult to contain her joy. Knowing that she would be seeing Philip Garrow that afternoon, she was in a state of continuous excitement from the moment she awoke. Over breakfast in their suite, her parents both remarked on the welcome change in her manner.

"You seem to be in a good mood today, Violet," said Rymer.

"Do I?"

"Starting to enjoy the voyage at last?"

"It's impossible not to enjoy it, Father."

"That's why we brought you with us, dear," said Sylvia Rymer. "It's a unique experience and we wanted you to share in it."

"It's one of the reasons we brought you," added Rymer. "But not the main one, of course. We all know what that was."

"Matthew," murmured his wife warningly.

"There's no point in hiding it, Sylvia."

"But do we need to discuss it now?"

"I can't think of a better time. Now that we're in the privacy of our own suite." He began to butter some toast. "Violet formed an unfortunate attachment and it was our duty to put a stop to it.

Which we did. The day will come when she's profoundly grateful to us."

Biting back a retort, Violet lowered her head and brooded. Sylvia Rymer gestured to her husband that he might change the topic of conversation but he ignored her advice. After chewing a piece of toast, he sipped his coffee, then returned to the attack.

"Appalling fellow!" he snapped. "God knows how a daughter of mine could get involved with a such a person. No breeding, no manners, no prospects, no nothing! Just one more Irish layabout!"

"That's not true!" defended Violet, looking up.

"I met the rogue."

"Philip is not a rogue, Father."

"Don't argue with me."

"Need we argue at all?" said his wife with a pacifying smile. "It's all in the past now, so why don't we leave it there?"

"Because I'm not sure that it is in the past, Sylvia. We sent him packing but Violet clearly hasn't forgotten him. Have you, Violet?"

"No, I haven't."

"She will, Matthew," said Sylvia Rymer. "In time. It was all rather sudden. Violet had strong feelings for the young man. You can't expect those to fade away."

"Whose side are you on here?" he demanded.

"Yours, of course."

"We're her parents, Sylvia. Our job is to protect our daughter."

"And we did that."

"Then let's hear no more nonsense about 'strong feelings' for that disgraceful individual. Garrow was an absolute bounder!"

"No!" protested Violet.

"You should never have let him within a mile of you."

"He was kind to me."

"Well, of course, he was." Rymer sneered with heavy sarcasm. "And we all know why. He turned that Irish charm on like a tap. But it didn't work on me, young lady. I've seen too many of his type to be taken in by them for a moment. That's why I had to step in the way I did."

"Violet understands that," said Sylvia Rymer, jumping in swiftly before her daughter could reply. "Nothing can be served by bringing it all up again now. Especially as Violet is beginning to take some interest."

"Not before time!"

"Let the matter rest, shall we?"

"As long as Violet appreciates what we're doing for her."

"I'm sure that she does."

"How many girls of her age have an adventure like this? The maiden voyage of the most famous liner in the world. Any other daughter would give her eyeteeth for such an experience."

"Violet knows that. Don't you, dear?"

"Yes, Mother," said the other, taking the line of least resistance.

"You didn't mean to contradict your father, did you?"

A conscious effort was needed. "No, I didn't. I'm sorry, Father."

"I should think so, too!" he said.

"More coffee?" asked his wife, lifting the pot.

"I've finished, thank you."

"Violet?"

"Not for me, Mother."

"Then all we have to do is to decide how we're going to spend the morning," said the older woman, replacing the coffeepot on the table. "I promised to meet Janet Palgrave at ten. She's such an extraordinary woman. Not at all what you'd expect from the wife of a clergyman."

"No," said Rymer. "Clergymen's wives are usually mousy little women with buck teeth and that awful stink of poverty. Makes a change to find one who actually dresses with some taste. Well," he continued, putting his napkin aside. "You go off with Mrs. Palgrave. I need to spend some time with Mackintosh. From what I hear, I don't think he's getting value for money from that land agent of his."

"What about you, Violet?" asked her mother.

"I'm going to explore the ship a little more," said the other. "I still haven't been up on the boat deck yet. And it's such a nice day."

Her parents traded glances and had a silent conversation.

"You need some company," decided Rymer at length.

"I made a sort of tentative arrangement with the Latimers," lied Violet, fearing supervision. "I liked them enormously."

"There's only room for two people in a honeymoon, dear," said her mother. "I think it might be more tactful to let them be on their own."

"Violet can take Mildred with her," decreed Rymer.

"Mildred!" gasped the girl.

"She's been cooped up down here ever since we embarked. Unfair on her. We must give the woman some freedom. Can't ask a maidservant to be on duty twenty-four hours a day. No," he said with finality. "Explore the ship with Mildred. It will be a little bonus for her. Something to tell the rest of the staff about when we get back to London."

Violet quaked. She knew why she was being told to take the maidservant with her. Mildred was her chaperon. Her parents still wanted to keep their daughter under close surveillance.

"What did the postmortem reveal?" asked Dillman.

"Little more than we already knew," said Halliday. "Especially as they were having to hurry. It wasn't a full postmortem, but Roland Tomkins was able to make some useful comments."

"Oh?"

"From the nature of the injuries, he's certain that Barcroft was struck from behind by a right-handed man. As for the weapon, he thinks it must have been made of wood. Metal would have done even more damage, if that's possible, ripping the skin open. Lionel Osborne agreed. A metal implement would have left different lacerations."

"What else did they find?"

"That the killer took no chances. Belt-and-braces man."

"Belt and braces?"

"He wanted to make absolutely sure that his victim was dead. When he battered him senseless, he turned him over and stabbed him through the heart. There was a puncture wound in his chest."

The purser heaved a sign. "We only saw him lying facedown so we didn't know there was a second wound."

"No," said Dillman. "And there was so much blood about, it never occurred to me that some of it was coming from a stab wound. I don't suppose the killer was obliging enough to leave a weapon behind?"

"Not a hope of that!"

"What did Mr. Tomkins think?"

"That the wound was inflicted by a long, narrow-bladed knife. He was surprised how neat and precise the incision was." He gave a mirthless laugh. "Roland said that any surgeon would have been proud of it."

"It gives us something to go on, anyway."

"Yes, Mr. Dillman, but it also reinforces what we already knew. This man is highly dangerous. He carries a knife. I think you should consider Captain Watt's offer of a firearm."

"At a later stage, perhaps. I certainly don't want to walk around with a loaded pistol on me just yet." He indicated his suit. "Can't have that bulging under my jacket. It would spoil my appearance."

"I know that you like to be something of a dandy but safety must come first. You need a means of defense, Mr. Dillman."

"Only when I close in on the killer."

"Did you ever carry a gun when you were a Pinkerton man?"

"Occasionally, Mr. Halliday. Like most operatives, I had to know how to use a firearm. When I was in pursuit of desperate criminals, I knew they'd be armed."

"So is this man."

"Only with a knife."

"He knows how to use it."

"I know how to take it off him," said Dillman calmly. "What about the body? Has that been safely stowed away?"

"It's in cold storage. Under lock and key."

"And the cabin?"

"Cleaned up and sealed off."

"What about the steward responsible for it?"

"I told him there were problems with the plumbing and that we'd had to move Mr. Barcroft to another cabin. He didn't complain. One less passenger to worry about."

"Did he remember delivering that Champagne to the cabin?"

"Yes, Mr. Dillman. Not long after ten last night, he reckons."

"And he saw Mr. Barcroft alive?"

"Alive and alone."

"That gives us a more accurate of idea of time, anyway."

Dillman was talking to the purser in the latter's cabin and he could see that the events of the night had taken their toll on his companion. He also knew how busy Charles Halliday was going to be.

"I won't hold you up much longer," he said. "And I have several lines of inquiry I need to pursue but I wondered if I might make a suggestion?"

"Please do, Mr. Dillman."

"We're all anxious that none of this will get out."

"That would be fatal."

"Then you might employ some diversionary tactics. The best way to ensure that none of the passengers start asking questions about Henry Barcroft is to keep them fully occupied. Lay on some special events to focus their minds."

"Special events?"

"The obvious one is a dog show. Dozens of first- and second-class passengers seem to have brought dogs with them. Organize a contest of some sort and I'm sure it will arouse enormous interest. Dog owners are fiercely competitive and there must be somebody on board competent enough to act as a judge."

"There may be something in that."

"It's only one of many ideas. You can probably come up with a dozen better ones yourself. But don't forget the third-class passengers. They're entitled to some entertainment as well."

"There are precious few dogs in third class, Mr. Dillman."

"But a large number of children. What about a fancy-dress contest for them? I know that most of their parents have little money and a only few belongings with them but it's amazing what they can achieve with a some imagination." He saw Halliday's deep frown. "Am I making sense?"

"Oh, yes. Great sense. Vital to keep a happy ship and we could lay on plenty of extra attractions. Problem is finding the time to do it." He forced a grin. "But we'll manage it somehow, Mr. Dillman. And thanks."

"I know what would be the best attraction of all."

"What's that?"

"A recital by Itzak Weiss. How often do most people get a chance to hear someone as distinguished as him? The music room would be bursting to the seams. I don't suppose you could persuade Mr. Weiss to honor us, could you?"

"I wouldn't even try. Itzak Weiss is traveling as a passenger. We can't impose on him. Besides, we have our own orchestra. They don't include any virtuosos, maybe, but they provide excellent music."

"Just a thought." Dillman paused at the door. "I almost forgot."

"Yes?"

"Have you spoken to the chief engineer yet?" Halliday let out a long groan. "I take it that he didn't believe your story."

"Called me a rotten liar to my face."

"But he must have been glad to get his property back."

"He was, Mr. Dillman. Only one thing puzzled him."

"What was that, sir?"

"Well, the thief had been very selective. When he broke into Fergus Rourke's cabin, he took some drawings and left others. Yet one of them was an elaborate wiring diagram of the whole vessel. It would have been incomprehensible to anyone but a trained electrician."

"I don't think Henry Barcroft could claim to be that."

"So why did he steal that particular diagram?"

Dillman shrugged. "I'm afraid it's too late to ask him."

The *Lusitania* maintained its impressive speed, cleaving through the water with ease and leaving it churned up into white foam by its four massive screw propellers. It was a bright day though an occasional cloud drifted across the sun to block out its rays and deprive it of some of its warmth. Most passengers wore hats and long coats as they promenaded. Those who reclined in deck chairs also took the precaution of wrapping themselves up. Some of the novelty of the voyage had worn off and the buzz of enjoyment had mellowed into a quiet satisfaction as people settled into routines, punctuated at regular intervals by their meals.

Ellen Tolley was only one of a number of artists on deck. With her back against the rail, she used a pencil to draw a sketch of the bridge and upper section of the vessel. As she checked another detail, her head went down to her sketch pad again. When she looked up, the smiling face of Dillman loomed over her.

"Good morning!" he said.

"Hello, there!"

"I didn't know you were an artist, Ellen."

"I'm not really. It's just something to pass the time, George. Main thing is, it gets me out in the fresh air."

"May I see?"

"Sure," she said, offering him the sketch pad. "Not that there's much to see as yet. I've only been out here for a short while."

"Then you must work fast," he said, studying the drawing and noting its clear indication of talent. "This is terrific. You've got a great sense of perspective."

"Is that what it's called? I just draw what I see."

"Do you do portraits as well?" he asked, returning the pad.

"Why?" she teased. "Would you like to sit for me?"

"Anytime, Ellen."

She laughed. "It's a nice offer but I guess you'll be too busy sitting for someone else, so I'll defer to her."

"What do you mean?"

"I saw the pair of you at the breakfast table this morning. You were so engrossed in each other, you didn't notice anyone else. Who is she?"

"Miss Masefield?"

"Is that her name? Beautiful lady!"

"Very beautiful."

"Trouble is, you're not the only guy to spot that. Miss Masefield has quite a following. She dined at the captain's table last night, seated between Itzak Weiss and that English lord with the monocle."

"Lord Carradine."

"That's him. Both men were hanging on her every word."

"You're very observant."

"I was so jealous of her, George. How does she do it? I'd love to dine at the captain's table like that. Do you have any pull with her? Reckon she could wangle *me* an invitation to join the elite?"

"You're already one of the elite," he said gallantly.

"Thank you, kind sir."

"But the truthful answer is no. I have no pull at all with Miss Masefield. It was pure coincidence that we had breakfast together."

"That's not how it looked to me."

"Appearances can deceive," he said easily, looking around. "Is your father not with you this morning?"

"No, he wanted to rest his bad leg. I left him reading in his cabin. This voyage hasn't been much fun for him so far."

"But you're enjoying it, aren't you?"

"Every moment. Apart from the time when I had to stop a runaway American at full speed the other night." She grinned amiably. "And even that had its pleasanter side. I got to make a new friend."

"That cuts both ways."

She looked at him quizzically, and a wistful look came into her eye.

"New Jersey will sure seem dull after all this."

"You'll liven it up, Ellen."

"I daresay I will at that!"

"I'll let you get on with your drawing. Good-bye."

"Nice to see you again, George."

She returned to her sketch and Dillman walked away, pondering the differences between Genevieve Masefield and Ellen Tolley and deciding that his ideal woman would be a subtle blend of the two. It was not a thought on which he allowed himself to dwell.

Private pleasures had to be subdued beneath the call of duty. Wearing only a suit, he became aware how cold it was now that the sun had been smothered by another cloud, but he was glad that he had taken an exploratory walk around the boat deck. The brief meeting with Ellen Tolley had been a delight, following on, as it did, from breakfast with Genevieve Masefield. He hoped that he had not used up all of his good fortune for the day.

When he went down to the promenade deck, he was in search of Jeremiah Erskine but it was the man's wife whom he first encountered. Clad in a fur-collared coat, Dorothea was standing at the rail with Ada Weekes, whose wide-brimmed hat was flapping gently in the breeze. Both women gave him a cordial welcome.

"You must be very hardy, Mr. Dillman," said Ada Weekes. "No coat, no hat, no scarf. We're in northern latitudes."

"I've always had warm blood, Mrs. Weekes," he said.

"We suspected that," commented the other woman with a twinkle. "Jeremiah is the same. He refuses to wear thick vests or anything of that sort. He thinks it's a sign of weakness."

"Cyril is the opposite," confided Ada Weekes. "He never stirs out without proper underwear. When we went to the Grand National last year, it was so cold that he wore three vests and two pairs of socks. You'd have thought we were going to Siberia."

"Does he hope to see any racing in America?" asked Dillman.

"Oh, yes. He loves it. We both do."

"So does Jeremiah," explained Dorothea Erskine. "He's a great fan of all sports. You may not think it to look at him but he was quite an athlete in his day. And a skillful boxer."

Dillman was interested. "Boxer? Mr. Erskine?"

"Yes, in fact—" She broke off with a laugh. "No, I won't tell you that. You'll think that it's so ridiculous. Yet it did happen. I can't deny it."

"Deny what?" pressed Ada Weekes.

"It seemed so unromantic when he first asked me."

"Go on."

"Oh, no. It will sound so absurd to anyone else." She turned to Dillman. "Have you ever made a proposal of marriage, Mr. Dillman?"

"Not exactly."

"But I expect that you will one day."

"I'm counting on it."

"And where would you like it to take place?"

"That depends on the lady," he said, "though I can't think of a better setting than the *Lusitania* by moonlight. It's so evocative. Given the opportunity, I reckon I could propose at least three times a week on a ship like is." The women laughed. "Without any effort."

"You have a wicked side to you, Mr. Dillman," said Ada Weekes. "But I have to admit that I'd find it hard to resist a man who proposed to me on board an ocean liner. As it was, I had to settle for the potting shed. It was the only place where Cyril and I could be sure of being alone."

"At least it was somewhere private," said Dorothea Erskine with a smile. "Jeremiah proposed to me in public. At a boxing match."

"Heavens!" shrieked the other woman. "What were you doing there?"

"I can't really remember except that he was so keen for me to go there with him. Jeremiah hates opera, you see. And he'd sat through so many just to please me that I felt I owed it to him. The curious thing was that I rather enjoyed it. Strong young men, fighting each other like demons. Not that I'd wish to go again, of course," she said quickly, anxious to dispel any possible misunderstanding. "It's not an experience one cares to repeat. But it did produce a proposal of marriage. During a heavyweight bout, actually. I think that Jeremiah felt he was on home ground, so to speak. He would have lost his nerve in a box at the opera."

"But not in the middle of a boxing match," said Ada Weekes.

"It could have been worse, I suppose. He proposed to his first wife on a crowded railway platform in Birmingham."

"Oh, Mr. Erskine was married before, was he?"

"Yes. His first wife died some years ago."

"I see."

"I understand that your husband was involved in a card game last night," said Dillman, starting to fish. "How did he get on?"

"Very badly, I think."

"Didn't he tell you?"

"No, he wouldn't talk about it when he got back."

"Was he too upset?"

"He was still so angry with himself."

"I wouldn't mind them playing cards if they didn't go on so late," said Ada Weekes, clicking her tongue. "It was well past midnight when Cyril came back to our cabin."

"Jeremiah was a little earlier than that. But he hadn't come straight from the card game. He'd been for a walk on deck. I could see that by the look of him."

"In what way?" said Dillman.

"His face was pinched, as if he'd been out in a cold wind. And his clothing was soiled. I think he must have brushed against something dirty in the gloom out here." She smiled loyally. "He loves playing cards. It's such a pity that's he's not very good at it."

It was an awkward meeting. Rosemary Hilliard was just about to leave the second-class lounge when Philip Garrow walked into it. They all but collided. The unexpected encounter compounded their embarrassment.

"I'm so sorry," he apologized.

"It was my fault."

"Mine. I should have looked where I was going."

"Yes," said Rosemary quietly. "Perhaps we've both been rather guilty of doing that." She manufactured a smile. "Good morning, anyway."

"Hello. I didn't see you over breakfast."

"I stayed in my cabin."

"I had half a mind to come in search of you."

"Perhaps it's just as well you didn't."

"Why?"

She moved aside as four people came into the lounge.

154

"We're blocking the entrance. And I must go."

"But I want to talk to you, Rosemary."

"After last night?"

"Can't we forget that?" he said earnestly. "I was to blame and I apologize." Two more people brushed past them. "Look, can we sit down and have a proper conversation?"

"I'd rather not, Philip."

"Then at least come for a walk on deck with me."

She considered the offer. "Five minutes," she said at length.

"Am I being rationed now?"

"It's all I'm prepared to give you."

"Then I won't waste a second of it. Let's go."

Repeating his apology all the way, Philip Garrow escorted her to the boat deck and found a quiet place beside the rail. He could tell that her pride had been injured and he did his best to assuage her wounded feelings. Rosemary Hilliard slowly relaxed but she still kept him at a distance. In the bright morning light, she looked older and more tired.

"It was a mistake, Philip," she said bluntly.

"No, it wasn't."

"We should never have let it get that far."

"But it was what we both wanted Rosemary. You know that. Be honest with yourself."

"I've spent hours being honest with myself. Long, painful hours. They've left me feeling rather silly and very ashamed."

"What is there to be ashamed about?"

"We met, we had a pleasant time together, and that should have been that. Instead of which . . ." She bit her lip. "Instead of which, I let myself behave very foolishly and I'm old enough to know better. I'm a respectable woman, Philip. I just can't imagine how I let myself get into a situation like that."

"It all seemed so natural."

"That was the trouble."

"I kicked myself for letting you down like that. If I'd had any sense, I'd have taken you into my cabin when I had the chance and then we'd both have been happy this morning."

"No, Philip. I'd have felt far worse."

"Worse?"

"I've got enough guilt as it is."

"Why should you feel guilty?"

"I'm a married woman. Or, at least, I was. I have a social position. I can't get involved with a man I hardly know, especially when he's so much younger than I." She held up a hand to rebut the protest he was about to make. "We went too far, too fast. I was shocked."

"Well, I was delighted," he said, stung by her words and going on the attack with a passionate declaration. "You're the best thing that's happened to me in ages, Rosemary. I don't care if I've known you for five minutes or five years. You're a very special lady and it pains me to think I've upset you in any way. Nobody could respect you more than I do. I wasn't making assmptions about you last night. I was just praying that I'd have the courage to go through with it. The courage and the luck."

Touched by his words, Rosemary reached out to clutch his arm but she took a step back when he brought up a hand to brush her cheek. Not yet ready for a proper reconciliation, she was embarrassed by a display of affection in public. Doubt and apprehension still lingered. She looked at him steadily for a long time, then gave a wan smile.

"You've had more than five minutes, Philip."

"Don't go!"

"I need some time on my own."

"Can we meet later?"

"I'll have to think about that.

"In the lounge, perhaps? Over dinner?"

"Make some other friends."

"But you're the one I want, Rosemary."

She fixed him with a cool stare for a moment before turning on her heel and walking away. Philip Garrow was tempted to go after her but common sense held him back. Rosemary was in no state to be talked around. She needed to be given space and time.

Only then would there be a possibility of reeling her back in again.

He gazed idly around the boat deck, surprised at the number of people who were milling about, noting with dismay that almost everyone but he seemed to be part of a group or a family. He recognized some of the passengers who had joined the ship with him at Queenstown. They were not simply visiting America out of curiosity. Necessity was forcing them to emigrate there. Like them, Garrow was facing an uncertain future, traveling between two worlds, searching for a security that had so far eluded him.

His thoughts turned to Violet Rymer but no sooner did she enter his mind than she appeared before his eyes. He was startled. Warmly attired in a coat and hat, she was strolling along the deck with a plump woman whom Garrow remembered seeing at Violet's home. A sense of joy competed with feelings of remorse. Pleased to see her at last, he was detemined not to let her see him, especially as her companion would also observe him. With his head turned away from the two women, he hurried to the nearest staircase and plunged down it, grateful that they had not come on the scene two minutes earlier. It was a narrow escape.

Dillman did not track down Jeremiah Erskine until well after noon. The man was seated alone in the corner of the smoking room, puffing absentmindedly at a cigar and reading a book with halfhearted interest. Erksine looked subdued. He was not in a sociable mood.

"What's the book, Mr. Erskine?" asked Dillman, going over to him.

Erskine looked up. "Nothing that would appeal to you."

"How do you know?"

"It's a book on photography, Mr. Dillman."

"Then you're probably right. It's a subject I know little about." He indicated the chair beside Erskine. "May I join you for a moment?"

"If you must."

"I didn't realize that you were a photographer," said Dillman as he lowered himself down. "You're a man of many parts, Mr. Erskine. Your wife was telling us earlier about your passion for boxing."

"The noble art of self-defense."

"There hasn't been much nobility in the fights I've witnessed. It's been more a case of the ignoble art of attack."

"Then you haven't seen real boxers, sir. They rely on speed, balance, and fast hands. They don't stand toe-to-toe and slug it out like two drunken sailors. Boxers have style. Panache." He closed his book and stubbed out his cigar in the ashtray. "Does the name Byron mean anything to you?"

"Lord Byron? Of course."

"Read his poems, I suppose."

"Some of them."

"Did you know that he took boxing lessons?"

"No, I didn't."

"Well, he did," said Erskine knowledgeably. "From the best possible teacher. A man called Gentleman John Jackson. Champion of England. Jackson had a boxing school on Bond Street. Lord Byron was only one of his famous pupils. What he learned was pugilism of the highest order."

"Mrs. Erskine said that you fought yourself at one time."

"Oh, that was a long time ago, Mr. Dillman. When I was much younger. These days, I fear, my sporting prowess is confined to the golf and tennis."

"Lawn tennis?"

"We have our own court."

"Then I envy you, sir."

"Keeps me fit in summer months." Erskine pulled the watch from his waistcoat pocket. "Almost time for luncheon. My stomach never lies." He shot Dillman a searching glare. "What else did my wife say about me?"

"Very little."

"Is that the truth?"

"She was with Mrs. Weekes when I met her."

"Women will gossip so."

"They see it as taking an interest."

"Sheer nosiness most of the time!" His gesture took in the whole room. "Wonderful to have a safe refuge like this."

"Yes," said Dillman casually. "I believe I saw you talking to that journalist yesterday evening. In the dining saloon."

"Journalist?"

"Henry Barcroft."

"Oh, him? Yes, nice chap. Rather took to him."

"Not many people have said that, Mr. Erskine."

"Eh?"

"They tend to find Mr. Barcroft a little too forward. Too brash."

"That's what I like about him," returned the other. "He's brimming with confidence. Can't stand people who hide their light under a bushel. Barcroft is bright and he knows it. He's ambitious. He'll go far."

"How well do you know him?"

"Not well at all. We've only met, what, two or three times. But that was enough. When you're in business, you learn to size a man up quickly. I could see at once that Barcroft had the spark."

"Spark?"

"That glow inside a man that gets things done. That drive and urgency." He pulled himself out of the armchair. "I must go back to the cabin to fetch my wife," he said, looking shrewdly at Dillman again. "You never done any boxing?"

"Not what you'd would call boxing, Mr. Erskine."

"Pity. You've got the build for it."

"But not the enthusiasm."

"Oh, that's critical. It's the enthusiasm which helps you to absorb the punishment. We all enjoy landing well-aimed punches. But you may have to take a few in the process. It's your enthusiasm for the sport which carries you through. Will you stand up a moment, please?"

"Of course," said Dillman, rising to his feet.

Erskine appraised him. "Yes," he said, "you'd have a longer reach and a decided height advantage but I still think I might pack the stronger punch. I'd have enjoyed a bout with you. In my day, that is. Always liked a challenge." He slapped Dillman playfully on the arm. "Excuse me. My wife will be wondering where I am."

Erskine walked off and left Dillman with his arm still stinging.

Nairn Mackintosh and his wife were luncheon guests in the Rymers' suite and thoroughly approved of the Scotch salmon being served. Wine flowed freely but the men still had room for two glasses apiece of malt whiskey at the conclusion of the meal. Sylvia Rymer went out of her way to be hospitable, realizing that it was not just a pleasant social occasion. Though the Mackintosh estate was not even mentioned, she knew that it had aroused her husband's interest and that he was eager to befriend the wealthy Scotsman in order to win his confidence. Further down the line, perhaps, that friendship might eventually lead to some kind of proposition relating to the Highland property. Luncheon was a first important investment.

While the others at the table talked, laughed, and argued happily, Violet Rymer was largely reduced to the status of an onlooker. She smiled when it was required and answered questions from the guests with studied politeness but her mind was elsewhere. The tryst with Philip Garrow had been set for that afternoon. Fervently hoping that nothing would happen to imperil it, she watched her father's steady consumption of alcohol with some relief, knowing that it would put him in a liberal mood and, at some point, send him quietly to sleep.

It was Sylvia Rymer who noticed how the time had raced past. "Come on, everybody!" she announced. "We must go."

"Must you?" complained Rymer.

"The concert starts in ten minutes, Matthew."

"But we were just about to have another glass of whiskey."

"I've had enough, thanks," said Nairn Mackintosh, holding up a gnarled hand. "If I touch another drop, I'll nod off during the concert."

"That won't do," said his wife. "You snore so loudly."

They all laughed and got up from the table. Violet had agreed to go to the concert with her mother but planned to leave in the interval in order to hurry off to her assignation, secure in the knowledge that one of her parents would be listening to music while the other, most probably, was taking a nap. The plan seemed to be working.

"Why don't you come with us, Matthew?" asked his wife.

"No, thank you, Sylvia."

"But you'll enjoy it. There's some Mozart in the program."

"I'll sit this this one out, dear. Feel a bit drowsy, to be honest."

"I'm not surprised," she chided.

After a flurry of farewells, the four of them left the suite and headed for the music room. By the time they arrived, it was already quite full but they managed to find seats together. Violet made sure that she was sitting on the end of the row. The orchestra was small but they were all talented musicians. When the conductor appeared, he was given a generous round of applause. He took his bow, faced his orchestra and lifted his baton, waited for ten seconds, then led them into the melodious world of Franz Schubert.

Neither Sylvia Rymer nor her daughter had any idea that they were being watched through the glass doors by a plump woman in a light gray dress. As soon as the concert was under way, Mildred left and went straight back to the suite. Matthew Rymer was waiting in the parlor, his coat off, his waistcoat open. He was toying with a glass of whiskey.

"Well?" he said.

"The concert has started, sir."

"That gives us plenty of time, Mildred."

"Yes, sir."

"Did you enjoy your walk this morning?"

"Yes, thank you."

"I promised you a tour of the ship," he said airily. "I told you that there would be treats if you came with us."

"Being here at all is a privilege in itself, sir."

"Is it, Mildred?"

"You know it is, Mr. Rymer."

"Are you grateful that I brought you?"

She gave a submissive smile. "Very grateful."

Matthew Rymer gazed at her with quiet pleasure for a while. Then, he reached into his waistcoat pocket to extract a large gold watch. After checking the time, he replaced the watch and looked up again at Mildred.

"Why don't you lock the door?" he said.

ELEVEN

The orchestra played to an appreciative audience that included Cyril and Ada Weekes, Dorothea Erskine, Genevieve Masefield seated between Abigail and Carlotta Hubermann, the Palgraves, the Latimers holding hands surreptitiously, Edward Collins, and Ellen Tolley, who had come early to ensure seats in the front row so that her father could stretch out his leg. It was a long and varied program. During the first half, Violet Rymer was as taut as the strings on the instruments. Though two of her favorite pieces were played, she hardly heard a note, rehearsing instead her excuse to withdraw during the interval and looking forward to the joyful reunion with Philip Garrow. She was at once exhilarated at the thought of what lay ahead and terrified that something might happen at the last moment to threaten it.

Mozart brought the first half of the concert to an end. Applause was generous. As the orchestra retired for well-earned rest, there was a rustle of dresses and flapping of programs beneath the heavy murmur of voices. Nairn Mackintosh was among several who withdrew to relieve himself. Sylvia Rymer was about to join those heading for the ladies' room when her daughter touched her on the arm.

"If you don't mind, I think I'll slip out now," said Violet.

"But why, dear?"

"I have a slight headache."

"What a shame!"

"You'll have to excuse me."

"But it may pass off soon."

"What I need is some fresh air."

"Do you want me to come with you, Violet?"

"Oh, no!"

"I hate the thought of you being unwell."

"It's only a headache, Mother."

"You are looking a trifle flushed, I must say."

"There's no point in your missing the second half as well," said Violet, detaching herself. "I'll be fine, I'm sure. I just need to . . . go on deck for a while. Good-bye."

Before her mother could say anything else, Violet moved quickly toward the exit and went out, not daring to look back until she was well clear of the music room. Nobody had followed her. She was safe. It would be at least another hour before Sylvia Rymer emerged to look for her, and her father, she was certain, would now be dozing in their suite. As she hurried off, she reflected on the kindness and discretion of George Dillman. The American had tracked down Philip Garrow, delivered her letter, brought a verbal reply, and given her directions to the second-class cabin where she was to meet her lover. She was tripping along as fast as she could, resisting the urge to break into a run and trembling so much that she bunched her fists hard in an effort to control herself.

When she reached the cabin, she first checked her appearance in a nearby mirror and brought a hand up to stroke back her hair. Clearing her throat and wishing that her heart would not pound so violently, she tapped on the cabin door. It opened almost immediately.

"Philip!"

"Come in," he urged.

Drawing her into the cabin, Philip Garrow locked the door,

then turned to gaze at her. Dressed in his new suit, he looked smarter than she had ever seen him before and that added to his luster. She did not see the dark shadows under his eyes or observe how nervous he was. Violet was too overwhelmed by the wonder of what was taking place. It was the first time they had ever been alone in a room with a bed before. As she glanced across at it, she blushed. Garrow gave a sudden laugh, almost a giggle of triumph, then reached out to embrace her. Violet Rymer clung desperately to him as her eyes became fountains of tears.

The first theft took place at the concert. An elderly lady had her purse stolen. The problem was that she could not remember whether she had left it on her seat during the interval or took it with her to the ladies' room. A search of both places was fruitless. A second crime, it seemed, was also committed during the concert. When they got back to their cabin at its conclusion, a retired doctor and his wife discovered that a number of small items were missing, including a valuable French Empire clock, which they were taking to America as a gift for their hosts. Charles Halliday did his best to reassure the victims but all three were deeply upset by what had taken place.

When yet another theft was reported, the purser had to call in Dillman. One of the most priceless items aboard the ship had been stolen and its owner was in a towering rage.

"I will sue the Cunard Line!" threatened Itzak Weiss. "How on earth could this happen? It's monstrous."

"We must have the full details, sir," said Halliday patiently.

"My violin was taken!" yelled the other. "That is the only detail that matters. It is a Stradivarius. Quite irreplaceable. I bought it many years ago in Vienna and it has been a sublime instrument. Do you know what a Stradivarius is? How much it means to a musician to possess one?"

"I assume that the instrument is insured, Mr. Weiss."

"That's immaterial! No amount of money can atone for its loss. We are talking about one of the finest violins ever made."

"The thief appreciates that, sir," said Dillman. "An artiste of your distinction would only play an instrument of the highest quality."

"Find him! Arrest him!"

"One step at the time, Mr. Weiss."

The musician paced up and down the cabin like a caged tiger. His heavy jowls were puce with rage. His broad shoulders were hunched, his eyes blazing. Dillman noticed how small, white, and delicate his hands seemed. Weiss brought them up to his temples in a gesture of despair.

"I am ruined!" he wailed. "Without my violin, I am ruined."

"If you could give us more details, please," the purser began.

"Who could *do* such a thing! It's abominable."

"You have our deepest sympathy."

"What use is that, man? I want my violin!"

He came to a halt and unleashed a stream of abuse. Austrian by birth, he had a guttural accent that gave his words more bite and authority. As his fury built, however, he lost faith in the ability of the English language to express his full disgust and lapsed back into German. Dillman waited until the storm blew itself out, then he took command of the situation.

"Might I suggest that we all sit down, Mr. Weiss?" he said.

"What?" mumbled the other in a daze.

"Sit over here, sir," said Dillman, guiding him to an armchair, "so that we can review the situation more calmly. Before we go any further, let me assure you that we will retrieve your violin as soon as possible."

"How?"

"I will explain." Indicating that Halliday should join him, Dillman lowered himself on to the sofa. "Your violin is still on board this ship. We will search the vessel from top to bottom until we find it. There is no chance whatever that anyone will manage to smuggle it into New York. It is only a question of time before it is safely back in your hands."

Weiss was distraught. "If, as you say, it is still on board. But what if it has been destroyed? Or thrown into the sea?"

"Inconceivable."

"Is it?"

"Nobody would take the risk of stealing it in order to damage it, still less to hurl it overboard. The thief understands its true value. There is an old Turkish proverb, Mr. Weiss. 'He who steals a minaret knows where to hide it.' That is what must have happened here. Only someone who knew how to sell such an instrument at the best price would go to the trouble of stealing it."

"Then why didn't they take the case with it?"

"I can only hazard a guess."

"*Mein Gott!* It's a Stradivarius. It needs to be treated with the utmost care. When I am not practicing, it never leaves its case. What kind of a madman would just grab the violin on its own?"

"Someone who probably has another case waiting for it," said Dillman, speculating quietly. "One that does not have a name inscribed on it as yours does. There's another consideration. This theft took place sometime in the past hour or so. In broad daylight. A violin case is very conspicuous. The thief didn't want to be seen carrying it when he took it back to his cabin. On its own, it might more easily be concealed inside a coat or beneath a garment draped over an arm."

"How long were you absent from the cabin?" asked Halliday.

"I told you. An hour, perhaps a little more. My wife and I had a walk on deck, then she went to the lounge." A fresh surge of despair sent his hands up to his temples again. "Ruth! My dear wife! What is she going to say when she learns about this? She will be heartbroken!"

"Perhaps it is just as well that you made the discovery on your own," said Dillman. "Mrs. Weiss was spared that horror. I know that it's small consolation, but you will have time to prepare her before you break the news to her. That may lessen the pain slightly."

"It will not lessen my pain, Mr. Dillman."

"I understand that, sir."

"I am due to play in New York the day after we land. Brahms. How can I honor my commitment when I have no violin? How can I practice?"

"We can at least solve that problem," said the purser helpfully. "I'm sure that we can borrow a violin from a member of the orchestra." He saw the other's grimace. "Yes, Mr. Weiss, I know it's not the same, but it's better than nothing."

"I want my own instrument."

"You will get it, sir."

"When?"

"When we find it," promised Dillman. "Both the violin and the thief are rarefied specimens. There's only one person aboard this ship who would even dream of committing such a crime."

"He deserves to be shot!" exclaimed Weiss.

"Don't worry," said Halliday. "He'll pay the full penalty."

"He'd better, sir. I hold you responsible."

"You should have kept the violin in my safe, Mr. Weiss."

"What use is it in there when I want to practice?" The virtuoso jumped up from his seat. "Are you telling me that the Cunard Line *expects* to have Stradivarius stolen? Is that why I should have had it locked away? What sort of a ship is this if a man's violin cannot be left safely in his cabin? Are all our possessions in danger? Have other people had things taken from them? What kind of security do you call this?"

Charles Halliday chose not to answer and he was grateful when Dillman again came to his rescue, calming the violinist down sufficiently to be able to extract full details of his whereabouts during his absence and how he made the discovery of the crime. When they were about to depart, Itzak Weiss's misery had got the better of his anger. He looked up dolefully into Dillman's face.

"Tell me the truth, sir. I will get my violin back?"

"Without a shadow of doubt."

"And this vile thief?"

"Leave him to us, sir."

"Where will you look for him?"

"Among the audience at the music concert. We're dealing with a man who loves music, who might even be, or have been, a musician himself. That's where I'll start searching for him."

"But how could he take my Stradivarius if he was at the concert?"

"There was an interval, Mr. Weiss. A long interval."

"But who exactly is he, Violet? Who is this George Porter Dillman?"

"I told you, Philip. He's a friend."

"What sort of friend?"

"One that I can trust," she said. "I needed help from someone."

"But why him?"

"Mr. Dillman was the only person I could ask."

"And what will he expect in return?" asked Philip Garrow.

"Nothing."

"Are you sure?"

"He's such a considerate man. He was glad to help."

"I didn't see any signs of gladness when I met him. He was much too smooth for my liking. Too smooth and too watchful. I began to wonder if this Dillman had designs on you himself."

"That's ridiculous!"

"Is it?"

"I've only known him a few days."

"So?"

Violet Rymer was almost overcome with disappointment. Expecting to fall into his arms and kiss away their long absence, she had spent most of the time with Philip Garrow arguing pointlessly about the man who had indirectly brought them together. When she stepped into the cabin, she had left all thoughts of Dillman behind her but he appeared to have followed her in. Garrow's jealousy was turning the meeting into an ordeal. She had never seen him in such an unpleasant mood before.

"Perhaps I'd better go," she announced.

"No!" he protested. "Not yet. We haven't decided anything."

"You seem to have decided something about Mr. Dillman. And I find it very distressing. How could you even think such a thing? After all that we've been through together, all the risks I've taken on your behalf." Her eyes moistened again. "There isn't a man in the world to touch you. How can you stand there and accuse me like that?"

"I'm not accusing you, Violet," he said soothingly.

"It's very hurtful."

"Then I apologize, I really do, because I'd hate to hurt you in any way. I love you. I've missed you. That's why I'm so on edge. I hardly slept a wink last night."

"Neither did I."

"I've been dying to see you again."

"Thought of nothing else," she said, dabbing at her eyes with a lace handkerchief. "When I realized that you were on board the ship, I nearly fainted with joy. It was the last thing I dared hope for."

"I wanted to surprise you."

"Well, you certainly did that."

"And are you happy now, Violet?"

She nodded. "Are you?"

He took her in his arms again and kissed her on the lips. Violet was willing but too inexperienced to put any real passion into the kiss. Still holding her tight, he moved her slowly across the cabin. When her leg touched the side of the bed, she tensed in alarm.

"No, Philip!"

"Why not?"

"I can't. I daren't."

"Won't you just sit on the bed with me?" She hesitated. "Violet, it's me. We're alone together at last. Isn't that what you wanted?"

"Yes, but I'm not ready for anything else yet."

"We have to seize the chance when we can."

Violet was shocked. "Just like that? With no time to prepare? It's wrong, Philip. I know I couldn't go through with it. Besides, I'll have to get back soon or they'll start wondering where I am."

"Let them wonder." He tried to lower her into a sitting position on the bed but she resisted. "I thought you loved me."

"I do!"

"I thought you wanted me, Violet."

"Yes. But the first time must be special. We always promised each other that it would be. I can't be rushed into it like this. I want it to be perfect. In a hotel room. In a bed. With no pressures. Perfect."

"Wherever it happens, it will be perfect," he said, stroking her hair. "It's me, Violet. You've nothing to be afraid of here. I'm your lover. I'm going to be your husband. Why must we wait?"

He exerted a little more force and she consented to perch on the very edge of the bed. As soon as he started to fondle her with more urgency, however, Violet grew frightened and broke away from him. She stood up and crossed to the other side of the cabin.

"This isn't at all as I hoped it would be," she complained.

"No, it isn't!" he said ruefully.

"We haven't even talked properly yet."

He stood up wearily. "What is there to talk about?"

"In the first place, how on earth you come to be here."

"I bought a ticket, embarked at Queenstown."

"But where did you get the money from, Philip? And how could you afford that new suit? You had nothing when you were in England. I had to lend you some of my own savings."

"And I'll repay every penny of that," he said quickly.

"Have you got a new job or something?"

"Not exactly."

"Did someone loan you the money, then?"

"No, Violet. I'm paying my own way."

"That's wonderful! How are you managing to do it?"

"Don't bother about that."

"But I do bother. You said we were to have no secrets from each other. Three weeks ago, I thought I'd lost you forever. My parents told me that they were taking me on this voyage to get me away from you. Daddy swore that I'd never see you again. He was horrid to me." She quailed at the memory, then looked plaintively across at him. "So tell me, Philip. Where did the money come from?"

"Where do you think?" he said, raising an eyebrow.

"No!" she cried. "I don't believe it."

"Couldn't you work it out for yourself?"

"It never occurred to me."

"Well, that's how it was, Violet."

"But they told me that they'd simply warned you off."

"I don't warn off easily."

"My father actually *paid* you?"

"Handsomely," said Garrow with a smirk. "He's the sort of man who thinks you can solve any problem if you throw enough money at it. So he bought me off. Or tried to, anyway. He gave me a large amount of cash on condition that I stopped bothering you. So I did." Another smirk. "For the time being, at any rate. I went back to Ireland and booked a passage on the *Lusitania*. Had this suit made up by a tailor in Dublin. Bought a whole new wardrobe, in fact. Daddy was very generous."

"That's dreadful!" she said. "Paying you off like that."

"I wasn't going to refuse the money, Violet. Especially as it enabled me to get close to you again. Don't you see? That's the beauty of it. In trying to get rid of me, your father made it possible for us to be together. The joke is on him!"

"I'd hardly call it a joke."

"Would you rather I hadn't come?"

"No, no, of course not," she said, going back to him to take his hands in hers. "I'm just shocked, that's all. It's a terrible thing to do. Giving you money to leave me alone."

"Happens every day, Violet," he said. "All over London, there are anxious fathers trying to get rid of their daughters' unwelcome suitors."

"You're not unwelcome to me!"

"I'm so glad to hear you say that."

"I just wish you'd thrown the money back in my father's face."

"And miss the chance of this voyage?"

She let him kiss her again but it was a perfunctory embrace. Her mind was deeply troubled. Violet was still trying to make sense of what she had just heard. It forced her to revalue her relationship with her parents in the most profound way. When she looked up at him, she was completely bewildered.

"Philip?"

"Yes?"

"All of a sudden, I've lost my bearings."

"What do you mean?"

"I don't know where I am—where *we* are."

"Together, Violet. Where we've always wanted to be."

"Yes," she said. "But whatever are we going to do now?"

When they left Itzak Weiss, they went straight back to the purser's cabin. Charles Halliday closed the door behind them, then snatched off his hat and flung it down on the desk.

"It never rains but it pours!" he wailed. "And I'm the idiot who's caught in the middle of the downpour without an umbrella."

"It's not that bad, Mr. Halliday," said Dillman.

"How could it possibly be worse? We have a serious theft from the chief engineer's cabin. The violent murder of a passenger. A purse is stolen from an elderly lady. A retired couple have their cabin rifled. And a celebrated violinist has just had his Stradivarius taken." He slumped in a chair. "What's next? Mass suicide? Rape and pillage? A typhoon?"

"Every crime will be solved in due course," argued Dillman. "We've already returned those stolen items from Mr. Rourke's cabin. I have every confidence that we'll retrieve everything else that was taken."

"Put the violin at the top of the list!"

"I'm sorry that Mr. Weiss rounded on you like that."

"Everyone seems to be rounding on me today. Honestly, I feel as if I've got a target painted on my back." He ran a hand through his hair, then pulled himself together. "No bleating! I took the job so I have to take the blows that come with it. Now, what do you want me to do?"

"Get me a list of everyone who went to that music concert."

"There is no list. They just rolled up."

"I know," said Dillman, "but you must have had stewards on duty at the door to sell programs and act as ushers."

"Four of them, at least."

173

"Between them, they'll have recognized dozens of the passengers who were there. That gives us a start. And each person who went to the concert will be able to give us additional names."

"Are you certain that the thief was in the audience?"

"I'm certain that he used the concert as his cover. And I'm certain that the thefts are related to each other in some way."

"That doesn't seem possible."

"Oh, it is, Mr. Halliday, believe me."

"What sort of man steals a woman's purse, a French Empire clock, and a Stradivarius in one afternoon?"

"A very cunning man."

"Cunning?"

"Yes," said Dillman. "I didn't want to say this in front of Mr. Weiss because it was important to calm him down before he had a seizure, but there is a possibility which has to be taken into account. In my view, it's a rather strong possibility."

"I don't follow."

"What we have here is another dog show."

"Dog show?"

"Don't you remember why I suggested that you organize one?"

"Of course. To create a diversion."

"Well?"

The purser's face registered bafflement, surprise, then amazement in three separate stages. When he leaped from his chair, it was covered by an expression of mild hysteria.

"Do I understand you aright, Mr. Dillman? Are you suggesting that the killer and the thief are one and the same man?"

"What better way to throw you off the scent than by getting you entangled in a series of thefts? Especially the one from Itzak Weiss's cabin. That's really rung the alarm bells. It's bound to cut into the amount of time you can devote to solving a murder."

"Yet that must remain a priority."

"Don't tell that to Itzak Weiss. Nothing is more important to him than getting his precious violin back. In his opinion, a massacre of the ship's complement would take second place to that. But if your theory is correct, Mr. Dillman—"

"It is only a theory."

"Then the man we're after may not have such an interest in music."

"I still believe that he does, and I'm sure he treated that Stradivarius with great respect. After all, it may help him to escape arrest for murder. That's the plan, anyway." Dillman pondered, then snapped his fingers. "The couple who had that clock stolen. Remind me of their name?"

"Mr. and Mrs. Anstruther."

"Find out who sat at their table for luncheon."

"Luncheon?"

"And dinner last night," said Dillman. "They probably talked about going to that concert this afternoon. That's how the thief may have picked up the information. He planned that break-in. I don't think he waited to see who turned up in the music room before sloping off to their cabin. The Anstruthers were deliberately picked out."

"What about Mr. Weiss and his wife? They weren't at the concert. How could the thief be sure that their cabin would be empty as well?"

"By studying routine."

"Routine?"

"Musicians are usually very methodical. They keep strictly to a set pattern. So many hours of practice a day and so on. Mr. and Mrs. Weiss have had a walk on deck every afternoon since we sailed. They're rather distinctive people. Nobody could miss them."

"I'm more confused than ever," admitted Halliday. "Stealing an old lady's purse would have been relatively easy, particularly as, I suspect, she left it on her chair. She was a rather absentminded old dear. But how did the thief get into two locked cabins? Neither showed signs of forced entry."

"Then he must have had a master key."

"Impossible!"

"Is it? If I'm right, we're talking about a man who can commit a murder, leave no clues behind him, and vanish into the night.

175

He's cool and calculating. My guess is that he can get into any cabin he chooses."

Halliday stiffened. "I'm going to alert every member of the crew and institute patrols. Passengers must be protected from this man."

"Oh, I don't think there'll be any further crimes," decided the American. "Prevention is not the problem. He's already given you more than enough to keep you occupied. He'll just keep his head down now."

"I hope so. We can't cope with anything else."

"You're stretched enough as it is."

"So how do we catch him, Mr. Dillman?"

"You don't, sir. I do. He can see you coming in that uniform, but he can't see me. I've probably rubbed shoulders with him already. Even talked to him, perhaps." He opened the door. "We'll catch him."

"When?"

"When he slips up. They always do."

When the concert was over, Sylvia Rymer adjourned to the lounge for tea in the company of Dorothea Erskine and Ada Weekes. All three lingered there for the best part of an hour as they chatted away.

"I do wish Matthew had come," said Sylvia. "He missed a treat."

"Yes," agreed Ada Weekes. "I can't understand why Cyril left at the interval. I thought he was enjoying it as much as I did. And the second half was even better than the first. I loved the Tchaikovsky."

"Oh, I preferred the Mozart. Mrs. Erskine?"

"Give me Beethoven any day. He's the one who stirs my blood!"

"Does your husband know that?" teased the other.

"Oh, yes. Jeremiah knows everything about me by now!"

"How long have you been married?" asked Ada Weekes.

"Twelve years."

"Cyril and I have been together for thirty-three. Our children have long since flown the nest. Do you have any children, Mrs. Erskine?"

"No," said the other briskly. "Only stepchildren. Two boys. They've also left home to strike out on their own." She turned to Sylvia Rymer. "It will be Violet's turn next. Does she have a young man in view?"

"No," said Sylvia Rymer firmly. "Not at the moment."

"That will soon change. Such an attractive girl!"

"We think so, Mrs. Erskine."

"Is she your only child?"

"Sadly, yes. We wanted more but . . ." She glanced around to make sure that nobody was within earshot. "Well, you see, there were severe complications after Violet's birth. I had an operation but the surgeon told me that I could never have any more children. It was a terrible blow at the time but one gets used to that kind of thing. And there are, after all, certain compensations."

"Compensations?" echoed Ada Weekes.

"For a woman."

"I'm not sure that I follow."

Sylvia Rymer looked from one to the other to see if she could entrust them with a confidence. Both smiled encouragingly. In a short time, they had become good friends. They would be sympathetic.

"To be candid," she continued, lowering her voice, "I never really enjoyed that side of marriage. Not because of Matthew," she added hastily, "I wouldn't want you to think that. He was always considerate. It was just the way that I was brought up. My mother led me to believe that it was something a woman endured in order to bring children into the world. Once that became impossible, there seemed no need anymore. I felt so relieved."

"I'm not sure that I would have done so in your place," confessed Dorothea Erskine. "I think a woman is entitled to take some pleasure from that aspect of married life. In the right way, that is. When all is said and done, it is an act of love."

"Sometimes," murmured Sylvia Rymer.

"I'm not sure that I can remember anymore," said Ada Weekes.

And their laughter dissolved the faint embarrassment that had sprung up. Sylvia Rymer was glad to see her daughter coming into the lounge at that point. She raised a hand to signal to Violet, then frowned as she saw how pale and drawn she looked. Greetings were exchanged all round.

"Where have you been, Violet?" said her mother anxiously.

"Just walking on deck. I watched a game of quoits."

"You must have been out there for hours. How is your headache?"

"It's gone, Mother. I'm fine now."

"You don't look fine. You seem so strained."

"Do I?" said Violet, contriving a smile. "I'm not, really I'm not."

"A nice bath will revive you," said her mother, getting up from the chair. "Will you excuse us, please, ladies? We have to go now."

"We'll be on your tail as soon as we've drained our cups," said Ada Weekes, waving them off. As soon as they had left, she looked over at her companion. "What did you make of all that?"

"It didn't surprise me, Mrs. Weekes."

"No?"

"I wondered why her husband looked so grim at times."

"There seems such a lot of tension in that family."

"I feel sorry for the girl. They watch her like hawks."

"Didn't your parents do the same to you?"

"Of course," said Dorothea Erskine, "but I learned to handle them. I told them just enough of the truth to keep them happy. For instance, they would have been outraged if they'd known that Jeremiah took their daughter to anything as violent and rowdy as a boxing match. I told them we went to a ballet that night." She emptied her cup in one gulp. "No harm was done by a white lie."

"I found that out for myself a long time ago."

Ada Weekes laughed, then drained her own cup. As they were leaving their seats, Dillman strode slowly across to them. He noticed the programs they were holding.

"Ah," he said. "You've been to the concert as well. I just bumped into Mrs. Rymer and her daughter. They were telling me what a success it was. Was it well attended?"

"It was packed, Mr. Dillman," said Ada Weekes.

"Who else was there?"

She rattled off a dozen names and Dorothea Erskine added another ten or so. Dillman made a point of memorizing all the men's names. One name in particular was missing from the list.

"What about *your* husband, Mrs. Erskine?" he asked casually. "Didn't he go to the concert?

"Not at the start," she explained. "He joined us in the interval."

Before dinner that evening, Genevieve Masefield was invited to drinks in Lord Carradine's private suite. Hoping that she might be able to talk to him alone at last, she found him surrounded by his cronies yet again.

"You're a topping host, Percy!" said one of them.

"I've had plenty of practice," replied Lord Carradine, adjusting his monocle. "I like to have my friends around me."

"Provide Champagne like this every day and we'll move *in* with you."

"That would be abusing my hospitality too much, old chap."

Brittle laughter greeted this exchange. Lord Carradine finally found a moment to take Genevieve aside to pour whispered compliments in her ear. Behind the easy charm, she sensed real interest and encouraged it with the subtlest of signals. He spotted each one instantly.

"You're inscrutable, Miss Masefield," he said, studying her closely. "We've talked so much and yet I still know so little about you."

"Is that a complaint, Percy?"

"Far from it. I hate people who wear their hearts on their sleeves. Ruins the fabric. And they're so transparent. Nothing to learn about them. Whereas you have hidden depths," he said over the top of his Champagne glass. "You're the most enchanting kind of young lady."

"And what kind is that?"

"One with a past. Do you have a past, Miss Masefield?"

"Everyone does, Percy."

"Not the kind that I'm referring to. When I look at a creature as gorgeous as you, the first thing I wonder is why someone hasn't already snapped her up. Be frank with me. You must have had packs of suitors baying at your heels."

"One or two, perhaps," she conceded. "But I might say the same of you, Percy. You're the epitome of an eligible bachelor. How have you managed to elude the pack at your heels?"

"That is a well-kept secret."

"Even from me."

He laughed. "The night is young. Ask me again later."

"I know what I'd like to ask you now," she said seriously. "How on earth do you do it? As well as running a large estate and keeping up a busy round of social engagements, you're a successful businessman. Most people in your position would be ground down by responsibility."

"I was at first, Miss Masefield. Taken me years to find my feet." He became solemn for once. "The pater, you see. He was a Trojan. Ran the estate with great vigor and still had energy enough left over to go into business. So many companies wanted him to be a director simply to have a title on their letterhead. Lords still have a snob value, thank God. But the pater wasn't satisfied with being a standing statue at board meetings. He wanted to run a company himself. Picked one out, invested wisely, ended up taking over some of the people who'd made him a director because they thought he was an old buffer who'd lend a bit of tone. Then, of course," he added, sipping his drink, "he died, alas. Before his time. Dumped the whole lot on me. Nobody thought I'd survive more than a year, if that. I certainly didn't."

"You confounded your critics."

"I had to, Miss Masefield. For the sake of the family."

"Who will carry on after you?"

"I've been thinking about that," he said with a slow smile. "You know, I'm so grateful to that journalist for introducing us."

"Henry Barcroft?"

"That his name? They're all the same to me."

"Who are?"

"Men of the press. Necessary evils. I mean, what decent man would want to make a living scribbling nonsense about his fellow human beings? It's so infra dig, don't you know?" He gave a shrug. "On the other hand, they can sometimes be useful and that's why I always show them a little indulgence. Publicity is invaluable when you're in business. A mention in the *Times* does wonders for my tobacco company. I just wish I'd had a few copies of the newspaper before I met that Barcroft fellow."

"Why is that?"

"I'd have put them on the floor in readiness. Know what I mean? There was a mongrel quality about him." He leaned in close. "How did you get on with him?"

"Not at all well."

"Pushy?"

"Worse than that."

"He would keep trailing me around. Do you know, he actually tried to barge in here on one occasion. When I was having a few friends in for drinks. It was unforgivable. Who on earth did he think he was?"

"Henry Barcroft tried to gate-crash a private party?"

"Had some flimsy excuse about an article."

"Article?"

"Quoting me, apparently. Wanted clearance before he sent it off. Clearance, my foot! He was just trying to insinuate himself."

"I had a dose of that myself."

"So did Honora."

"Who?"

"Lady Carlyle's daughter. Pretty thing. Barely seventeen."

"What happened?"

"Barcroft had the gall to invite her to his cabin. Imagine!" said Lord Carradine with polite contempt. "Honora actually fell for that greasy charm of his. Might even have gone to his cabin if her mother hadn't nipped it in the bud." He held out his glass and the waiter topped it up. "The man is a positive menace. Inviting a girl of seventeen to his cabin at night! I felt obliged to have a word with the purser about him. I assume that's why we haven't seen anything of Barcroft since. He's been warned off. Quite rightly. No," he concluded, "Henry Barcroft deserves to be put well and truly in his place."

Wrapped in a shroud, the body of Henry Barcroft lay on a bed of packed ice in one of the refrigeration units. He seemed to have diminished in size, as if all the arrogance and ebullience had been squeezed out of him. He was just one more lifeless carcass in the unit. A key scraped in the lock and the heavy door swung slowly open. The beam of a torch played on the corpse. An amused voice spoke.

"So this is where they've put you, is it?"

TWELVE

George Porter Dillman was troubled by the speed of events. Having been given so little in the way of evidence, he now felt that he had far too much and it was causing confusion. In that confusion, he decided, he had missed something crucial. It was time to go back to the crime that set all the others in motion. Lying in his bath, he reflected on the motives that might have led Henry Barcroft to steal the technical diagrams from the chief engineer's cabin. Was it simply a case of the obsessive curiosity of a journalist or were there more sinister implications? Could the theft be connected in some way with the publisher's letter in Barcroft's wallet? The more Dillman thought about it, the more convinced he became that a vital clue had eluded him and it might be lying a few mere yards away.

Clambering out of the bath, he dried himself with a towel and pulled on a dressing gown. In a drawer in his cabin was an envelope containing the journalist's effects. He took out the wallet and spread its contents on his desk. Money, a photograph, a membership card of a London club, the enigmatic letter, and a series of visiting cards with Barcroft's name and address printed in black type. The young woman in the photograph was beautiful, standing in a garden and smiling happily at the camera. Was it Barcroft's wife? Mistress? Or some stray conquest? The fact that he carried the photograph suggested its importance. And whoever the young woman was, she would be shattered by the news that Henry Barcroft had been murdered in a particularly gruesome way.

That raised the question of next of kin. They were entitled to be informed of his death, yet that would break the blanket of silence in which the dead body was wrapped. The easiest way to identify and make contact with Barcroft's family was to send a wireless to the *Times*, one of his known employers, but that would lead to the most adverse publicity for the *Lusitania* and, eventually, have every journalist aboard hampering the murder inquiry as they competed for the inside story. For the time being, Henry Barcroft had to be kept alive in the minds of his family, friends, and colleagues.

It was when Dillman picked up the visiting cards that he made a new discovery. There were a dozen in all and he had assumed that they all bore the journalist's name and his address in Chelsea. Yet when he sifted idly through them, he saw that there were a number of business cards in the pile, obviously collected from passengers aboard the ship. One came from Lord Carradine, a second from Robert Balfour, MP, a third from a member of the Christian Science delegation. Four other business cards had been kept in the wallet and it was the last one that interested Dillman the most. It was from Jeremiah Erskine, whose business address was in the City. When Dillman turned the card over, however, he saw that the address of a Manhattan hotel had been written on the back. Had the journalist arranged to make contact with Erskine in New York?

A pounding on the door forced him to suspend his meditations. Fearing that it would be the purser with more dire news, he moved swiftly to open the door and found himself staring instead at the bulky frame of the chief engineer. Fergus Rourke had no time for civilities.

"We need to speak," he said, brushing Dillman aside and stepping into the cabin. "Maybe you can give me some straight answers."

Dillman shut the door. "About what, Mr. Rourke?"

"These," explained the other, holding up the brown envelope in which the stolen diagrams had been found. "Where did you get this?"

"Didn't Mr. Halliday tell you?"

"All I heard from Charlie was some cock-and-bull story about a linen cupboard in a storeroom."

"That's more or less right," said Dillman, calm and impassive.

"Can't anyone around here tell me the truth?"

"We carried out a methodical search, Mr. Rourke, and the envelope eventually turned up."

"Just waiting to be found, eh? How very convenient!"

"There was a bit of luck involved, I must admit."

"More than luck, Mr. Dillman." He waved the envelope. "Looking for something this small in a ship this size! It's not just a case of searching for a needle in a haystack but for a needle in a hundred haystacks. A thousand, a million. The whole of British bloody agriculture!"

"There's no need to bellow."

"As long as you take my point."

"I do, Mr. Rourke, but I can't add anything to what the purser told you. Not at this stage, anyway. I'm just grateful we were able to return your property to you."

"So was I—at first."

"What do you mean?"

"Did you see what was inside this envelope?"

"Of course. The missing diagrams."

"All safely back where they belong," said the other, taking them out and unfolding each one to lay them on the desk. "I was so pleased to get them that I didn't notice the difference."

"What difference?"

"These little holes, Mr. Dillman. Look."

A huge finger jabbed at the four corners of each diagram. Every corner was punctuated by a tiny hole. Inside the envelope, the diagrams had been folded over. Dillman saw that the holes could not have been caused by the drawing pins used to secure the envelope beneath Henry Barcroft's desk. Only one conclusion could be drawn.

"Someone pinned these up in order to copy them!" said Rourke.

"That's what it looks like."

"I'd put my life on it. See what it means?"

"Yes, Mr. Rourke."

"We've got a spy aboard. He's taken copies of the diagrams, then allowed the originals to be found again so that we'll call off the chase." The chief engineer was fuming. "I still think that journalist is at the bottom of this. The nosy one, Barcroft! He's probably got copies of these stashed away somewhere. Challenge the bastard! Search his cabin."

"We already have."

Rourke was checked. "Oh! When?"

"When you first reported the theft."

"Search it again."

"There's no point."

"Why not?"

"Because we've eliminated him from our inquiries."

"He's not involved, then?" said Rourke with disappointment.

"There's nothing Mr. Barcroft can tell us, I promise you."

"Then who can?"

"We don't know yet, Mr. Rourke. But I'm very grateful to you for bringing this to my attention. I think you're right. Copies of these diagrams may well be in existence."

"Somebody pinned them up and drew exact copies."

"Don't put your life on it," advised the other.

"Why not?"

"There's a quicker way."

"Quicker?"

"They may have been photographed instead."

Dillman thought about a book he had seen earlier in the lounge.

When the party reached the dining saloon, Genevieve Masefield excused herself so that she could visit the ladies' room to check her appearance and have a moment alone to gather her thoughts. Though she would not be at the captain's table, she would be sitting beside Lord Carradine again and she wanted to reflect on what he had told her over a drink in his suite. Genevieve also wanted to decide whether his interest in her was serious or temporary. His manner toward her was markedly more confidential and he kept asking where she would be staying in New York. Seated beside him again, she might be able to move the relationship along that much further.

She was powdering her nose when a face appeared in the mirror.

"Hello," said Ellen Tolley. "Miss Masefield, isn't it?"

"That's right."

"I'm Ellen Tolley. No need to tell you which side of the Atlantic I live on, is there? Mind if I join you?" she said, lowering herself on to the velvet-topped stool beside Genevieve. "I need a few repairs before I put myself back on show again. No fun being a woman, is it?"

"I wouldn't have thought any repairs were necessary," said Genevieve, noting how little makeup her companion wore. "Could I ask how you happen to know my name?"

"Everybody in that saloon knows it, Miss Masefield. One way or another, you've created quite a stir, but I don't need to tell you that."

"What do you mean?"

"Oh, come on," said Ellen, brushing her hair. "You know how gorgeous you are and you make the most of it. Why not? I'd do the same in your position. Whenever you come into a room, every man under the age of ninety gets a crick in his neck." She laughed. "My father's one of them. Can't take his eyes off you."

"Your father?"

"Don't worry. You're safe from him. He's one of the walking

wounded. Besides, you've got someone a lot more appealing than my father to dance attendance on you. Your beau with the monocle."

"Lord Carradine."

"A real English blue blood, eh?"

"The genuine article."

"Even I could tell that." Putting the brush into her purse, she turned to Genevieve. "But that isn't the reason I followed you in here. Look, Miss Masefield, can I ask you a personal question?"

Genevieve smiled. "Is there any way I can stop you?"

"Probably not."

"Ask away, then."

"Since you and the aristocracy seem to be getting along so well, does that mean Mr. Dillman is free and available?"

"Mr. Dillman?"

"You must remember him. You and he had breakfast together."

"I didn't realize I was being watched," said Genevieve, bridling slightly. "What exactly is your interest in Mr. Dillman?"

"That depends on you."

"I don't understand."

"Oh, come on, Miss Masefield. We're two of a kind. Sisters under the skin. What nicer way is there to brighten up a voyage than by enjoying a little dalliance?" She grinned amiably. "Except that I'm not stupid enough to compete with you. I mean, what English lord would look twice at some nobody from the murky depths of New Jersey? Besides," she added, "Lord Carradine is not my type, but George Porter Dillman most definitely is. I just wanted to make sure that I wasn't treading on your toes, that's all."

"You certainly aren't, Miss Tolley."

"Ellen, please."

"The field is clear, Ellen."

"You're a pal!"

"I'm not sure about that," said Genevieve, warming to her but still having reservations. "And I'd dispute that we're two of a kind.

It seems to me that you're quite unique. I've never met anyone so direct."

"Daddy is always warning me about it."

"It doesn't seem to have made any difference."

"Of course not," said Ellen with a conspiratorial giggle. "Where would any of us girls get if we listened to our fathers?"

As soon as he walked into the room, Dillman realized that word of the thefts had got out. Ada Weekes accosted him to pass on the rumor before intercepting the Rymers to tell them as well. Dillman was glad that only the loss of a purse, a French Empire clock, and a few other items were mentioned. Acting on his advice and in response to the earnest plea from Charles Halliday, the other victim had agreed to keep silent for the time being. Itzak Weiss did not broadcast news of the missing violin. He and his wife were so mortified that they had locked themselves away in their cabin and were taking it in turns to console each other. Dillman was relieved. Minor thefts were almost inevitable on a voyage and would cause no more than a flutter of anxiety among the other passengers. The loss of a Stradivarius was quite another matter. It would make headlines in every way.

"Hello, Mr. Dillman," said a voice at his elbow.

"Good evening, Miss Rymer."

She was standing too close to her parents to risk anything more than a few passing remarks but her face was eloquent. Dillman knew that she had kept her tryst that afternoon but he now saw that it may not have delivered all that Violet Rymer hoped. She was tense and preoccupied as if caught in the grip of ambivalence. Matthew Rymer, by contrast, was in unusually high spirits again and gave Dillman a cordial greeting before ushering his wife and daughter to their table, where they settled down with a group of friends including Nairn Mackintosh and the Latimers.

Dillman had accepted an invitation to join Cyril and Ada Weekes again. On his way to their table, he encountered someone he had already seen a number of times on the voyage. Using his walking stick, Ellen Tolley's father was moving slowly across the room. When he saw Dillman behind him, he stepped aside to wave him on.

"You go on ahead, sir," he suggested. "I'd hate to hold you up."

"Mr. Tolley, isn't it?" said Dillman.

"That's right.

"George Porter Dillman."

"Ah!" said the other, face brightening. "That's a name I've heard before. My daughter keeps mentioning it." They exchanged a firm handshake. "Pleased to meet you, young man. I'm Caleb Tolley."

"Are you enjoying the voyage, sir?"

"Very much. Though I'd enjoy it far more if I was mobile. This bad leg of mine is proving a real handicap."

"You daughter said that you had an accident."

"Yes, Mr. Dillman. Just before we left England. Damn nuisance. Ellen tell you how it happened?"

"No, Mr. Tolley."

"We went riding one afternoon and I got the horse with a grudge against humanity. Crazy animal bolted on me. Charged into some trees," He patted his thigh. "Got this from an old English oak. The horse scraped me against it so hard that it opened up a gash. My riding breeches were soaked with blood."

"Ellen said that you had to keep dressing the wound."

"The knee is the real problem. Doctor thinks I'll need an operation when I get back. Something to do with cartilages." He waved a dismissive hand. "But you don't want to hear all that stuff. Water under the bridge. I'll live. Say, look, why don't you join Ellen and me for a drink later on? Do you have any plans?"

"Yes and no."

"The offer stays on the table."

"If I get the chance, I'll be glad to take it up, Mr. Tolley. Thanks."

"Hope to see you later, then. I'm glad I've put your name to your face at last." He stepped back as a group of people went past. "We're holding up the traffic here. Off you go, Mr. Dillman."

"Right."

"We must look like the tortoise and the hare."

Caleb Tolley gave a ripe chuckle and limped slowly away. Dillman was pleased to have met him at last. He was an interesting man with a face full of character and a deep, melodious voice. He was impeccably dressed and had an air of quiet prosperity. There was none of Ellen's exuberance about him but that might be explained by the injury. A drink with the two of them might give Dillman a brief interval of pleasure. For the rest, he was very much on duty.

When he got to his table, he was given three different versions of the thefts and saw once again the insidious nature of rumor. Doing his best to play down the crimes, he joined in the small talk while letting his gaze traverse the whole room. Dillman knew nobody else at the table apart from Cyril and Ada Weekes. For two people with typical English reserve, they had a remarkable ability for widening the circle of their acquaintances. Dillman was sorry that the Erskines were not there but, when the opportunity arose, he brought them into the conversation.

"I don't see Mr. and Mrs. Erskine here," he said to Cyril Weekes.

"They're dining in a private suite this evening."

"I see."

"Erskine is still licking his wounds over last night."

"How heavily did he lose at cards?"

"Oh, I don't think it was the money that worried him," said Weekes, spearing a potato with his fork. "He could afford to lose ten times that every night for a year. No, what upset Jeremiah Erskine was that he played so recklessly. He's a businessman. Used to winning every time, whatever the stakes. He can't cope with the idea that others have more skill at the poker table."

"More skill and more luck."

"They go together, Mr. Dillman."

"What exactly does he do?"

"Erskine? Just about everything. Imports this, exports that, buys and sells whatever he chooses, by the sound of it. He seems to have a finger in several pies. Certainly moves among the rich and famous."

"Does he?"

"Yes, he was boasting about the fact that he'll be dining with Mr. Morgan when he gets to New York."

Dillman was impressed. "J. P. Morgan?"

"John Pierpont, of that name. Even I've heard of him."

"They don't come any richer than J. P. Morgan."

"I know that," said Weekes, popping the potato into his mouth and chewing. "I teased Erskine about him."

"Teased him?"

"Yes, Mr. Dillman. I warned him that I'd let out his dirty secret. Sailing on the *Lusitania*. The Cunard Line is about the only one that isn't owned, at least in part, by J. P. Morgan. How would he feel if he knew that Erskine didn't sail on one of *his* steamers?"

Dillman said nothing but he found the comment intriguing. The conversation turned to the subject of royalty and it was some time before Cyril Weekes was free for a more private exchange. Dillman picked at his sorbet and leaned in close to him.

"I understand that Mr. Erskine was at the concert this afternoon."

"Only for the second half, according to Ada."

"Didn't you see him arrive?" asked Dillman. "Mrs. Weekes said that you were there yourself."

"I was but I sneaked out at the interval."

"Oh?"

"In effect, Erskine and I changed places."

"Weren't you enjoying the music?"

"Very much, old chap. But I had something on my mind." He made sure that his wife was not listening. "I told Ada that I had an upset tummy but the person who got me out of there was Catullus."

"Catullus?"

"Remember that competition I mentioned on the train? The one that involved a Shakespearean sonnet?"

"Yes. 'When in disgrace with fortune and men's eyes.' Right?"

"Well remembered, sir. The truth is that I'm something of a

dab hand at Latin elegiacs so I've been working on my own version. Not to send in to the *Westminster Gazette*, mark you. Just to keep my hand in."

"I knew that you're a scholar, Mr. Weekes."

"I was." The other sighed. "One loses so much with the passage of time. When I left Oxford, I taught Classics for some years at a public school. In our country, public schools are actually private schools. Don't ask me to explain the idiosyncrasies of the English language or I'll be here all night. Anyway, that was my first job. It was also where I met Ada. Her father was the headmaster." His eyes twinkled. "But that's another story and, besides, the poor chap is dead."

"I thought you said that you were in business, Mr. Weekes?"

"Yes, I was. When I retired from the groves of academe."

"What sort of business?"

"The only sort that appealed to a person who prefers to live in the past rather than the present. I became an antiques dealer. As I'm sure you noticed, England is one huge antique shop, so one is never short of things to sell. I did specialize, of course."

"In what?"

"Clocks and musical instruments."

Dillman masked his surprise between a smile of interest.

"Oh, I meant to ask you," continued Weekes quietly. "How well have you got to know the Rymers?"

"Not well at all, I'm afraid. Why?"

"That tomfoolery I quoted from the *Westminster Gazette*."

"How a young man induces his fiancée to break an engagement?"

"You have got a memory, Mr. Dillman!"

"It amused me."

"But it didn't amuse the Rymers, did it?" said Weekes. "I wonder if I stumbled on something when I read that piece out. Broken engagement, what? Is that why Violet Rymer looks so desperately unhappy? And why her parents watch her so carefully?" He nudged Dillman. "There's a young man in the story somewhere. I'd bet on it. What do you think?"

*   *   *

Philip Garrow was in a rueful mood. As he sat in the corner of the second-class lounge, he nursed a drink and reviewed the events of the afternoon with considerable misgivings. Violet Rymer had actually been alone with him in his cabin yet none of the expected intimacies took place. Instead of advancing their relationship, their meeting had set it back slightly and he could not fully understand why. She had changed. When he first met Violet in an art gallery, he had been struck by her aura of innocence. It had made it difficult to strike up a conversation with her because she immediately went on the defensive. Garrow had been extremely patient. It took three separate meetings to talk his way past her guard. Once that was done, he encountered no further resistance. Until now.

What had changed her attitude toward him? She still loved him but her love was no longer so endearingly uncritical. Violet had raised doubts, expressed fears, put up barriers. The money had done the real damage and he cursed himself for being stupid enough to mention it to her. It would have been much easier to tell her one more lie, to say that he had inherited the money from a relative or earned it in some way. To admit that he had been bought off by her father had been a gross tactical error. In her eyes, the money was tainted. It upset her that Garrow drew so much satisfaction from being able to use it against her parents. What thrilled him had only appalled her.

Draining his glass, he sought for some positives. Violet had, after all, come to him. She had agreed to see him again the next day, albeit under different circumstances. Their relationship was solid enough to overcome the temporary setback. Garrow's mistake was in looking at their reunion from his point of view. He expected to appear before her once again as her savior, a knight in shining armor who had come to rescue his fair damsel in distress. But his new suit was rather tarnished armor and the fair damsel had no wish to be saved in the way he had envisaged. Instead of thinking of his own gratification, he should have to tried to put himself in her position.

Violet Rymer was a shy, nervous, immature young woman who

had been through a domestic crisis. Having met her parents, Garrow knew the kinds of severe pressures they could exert on their daughter. Violet's suffering had been exacerbated by the fact that she thought she had lost her lover altogether. It was unrealistic to expect her to move from despair to ecstasy in one great leap. Garrow conceded that freely. He was to blame. He had tried to take far more from her than she was yet ready to give and that had damaged the trust between them. It would need careful rebuilding in the few days that remained.

His confession about the money had shaken her but it had also had one good effect. It deepened her resentment of her father. Garrow could see the disgust in her eyes. She would never look at either of her parents in quite the same way again. The more she hated them, the more she would turn to him. All he had to do was bide his time and refrain from any more false moves. The future was still bright for him. The mistakes and misjudgments of the afternoon could be retrieved.

"Hello, stranger," said a gentle voice.

He looked up. "Rosemary!"

"I didn't see you in the dining saloon."

"I wasn't hungry."

"Pity. You missed another excellent meal." She regarded him closely. "Are you sure that you're all right, Philip?"

"Fine, fine," he said, rising to his feet.

"You were brooding on something when I came in."

"Was I?"

"Her name didn't happen to be Rosemary Hilliard, did it?"

He rallied at once. "Why? Would you object?"

"I'm not sure."

"Then I won't come clean."

"Not even if I buy you a drink?"

Her manner was pleasant but still a trifle guarded. On the other hand, it was she who had sought him out. Rosemary was offering an olive branch and he reached out to take it.

"Be my guest," he offered.

"I asked you first, Philip. What would you like?"

"Another glass of whiskey, please."

"What kind?"

"The only kind. Irish whiskey."

Once again, a meal in the first-class dining saloon had been an educative experience for Dillman. What he had learned about Jeremiah Erskine had only deepened his suspicions, but he had begun to have doubts about Cyril Weekes as well. The man's proficiency at the card table sat uneasily beside his declared passion for Latin elegiacs. One thing was now certain. There was an antiques dealer aboard who would know the exact price of a French Empire clock and the approximate value of a Stradivarius. By a strange coincidence, that expert walked out of a music concert that he claimed he was enjoying and was absent during the time when both objects were stolen. Dillman wondered if Catullus had really exercised that much attraction for his companion. Weekes was a deep man.

He was also alert and attentive. His comments on the Rymers had been very apt though Dillman did not tell him that, preferring instead to adopt a neutral stance on the subject. When he looked at the Rymer table now, he saw that Violet Rymer was almost as uncomfortable as she had been on the first night. While her father was in a humorous vein and her mother was reveling in the social niceties, Violet sat bolt upright and wrestled with her thoughts.

Genevieve Masefield had no inner torments to spoil her meal. Throughout the evening, Dillman had noticed how happy and relaxed she was, mixing easily with the titled dinner guests who surrounded Lord Carradine and charming her host once again. When he gazed over at her table, he saw that she was in fact watching him this time with an intensity she had never shown before. For a second, he was oddly disconcerted.

When the meal was over, Dillman wanted to slip away to speak to the purser but Ellen Tolley descended on him and took him by the arm. She insisted that he join them in the lounge for a drink and he gave way under her persuasion. The three of them reclined in chairs, Caleb Tolley using a footstool on which to rest his leg. Ellen was bursting with gossip and her father seemed content to let her hog the conversation.

"I don't believe her," she said.

"Who?" asked Dillman.

"Your admirer. Miss Genevieve Masefield."

"I wouldn't call her an admirer."

"You didn't see how often she glanced across at you during the meal. That was more than curiosity, believe me. You fascinate her, George. I think she's fallen for your Bostonian sophistication."

Dillman grinned. "I didn't know that I had any, Ellen. In any case, Miss Masefield is rather more interested in the sophistication of the English aristocracy. My charm can't compete with that. Whenever I looked at her, she was absorbed in a conversation with Lord Carradine."

"That's a smoke screen. She's only toying with him."

"I don't know that I'd agree with you there, Ellen," said Caleb Tolley. "And I don't think you should embarrass Mr. Dillman by raising this subject in the first place. I invited him to a drink, not to listen to an analysis of his private life. Now, you behave yourself, young lady."

"George doesn't mind, do you, George?"

"Not at all."

"There!"

"Back off, Ellen," warned the older man.

"But I haven't told him what Genevieve said."

"Mr. Dillman doesn't want to hear it."

"Every man wants to hear praise of himself." She beamed at Dillman and gabbled the information before she could be stopped. "We were in the ladies' room together and I asked her if she had serious intentions with regard to you because, if she didn't, well, it meant that you were sort of available, whereas if she did, there'd be no point in nursing vain hopes because nobody would stand an earthly chance against her. And Genevieve denied—"

"That's enough!" interrupted her father.

"—that she was interested in you," continued Ellen unchecked. "But I think she was lying. I know admiration when I see it. That lady was all but drooling over you, George."

"English ladies don't drool," said Caleb Tolley, quelling her with a look, "and we're drawing a line under this topic. I'm sorry, Mr. Dillman," he said, turning to him, "but Ellen gets a little excited at times. She's always been rather headstrong. As I'm sure you've noticed."

Dillman gave her a forgiving smile but made no comment.

Tolley appraised him. "What's your line, Mr. Dillman?"

"I don't exactly have one at the moment. I'm on my way home to get my future sorted. I started in the family business in Boston. We design and build luxury yachts. Somehow, I didn't want to spend the rest of my life doing that so I opted out."

"How did your parents feel about that?"

"If my father'd had a rope handy, he'd have lynched me. Dillmans don't give up on the family business. They carry on the tradition."

"You see?" said Ellen. "He's a rebel. Just like me."

"Nobody is just like you," said Tolley with an indulgent smile. "Now, let Mr. Dillman finish."

"That's about it, really. Always wanted to visit England so I took a vacation there and managed to get on the *Lusitania* for the return voyage. Quite what will happen when I get home, I can't say."

"No chance of you going back into the family business?"

"No, Mr. Tolley. Not a hope."

"You have to make a living somehow."

"I'm not entirely without ideas."

Ellen giggled. "I'll bet you're not."

"But what about you, sir?" asked Dillman, reaching for his drink. "What line are you in? Ellen says that you come from New Jersey."

Tolley nodded. "Trenton. And I can't claim to do anything as interesting as building luxury yachts. I chose a dull profession, I fear. Dull, dutiful, but oddly lucrative."

"And what's that?"

"Insurance."

When the other guests began to peel away, Genevieve Masefield knew that they were leaving Lord Carradine's suite by prearranged signals but she pretended not to notice. Nine of them had returned there after dinner to enjoy a postprandial drink. While the men chose brandy, most of the ladies opted for hock and seltzer but none of them dallied too long. When the waiter withdrew as well, Genevieve was left alone with her host. Lord Carradine waved her to the sofa and sat beside her. He let his monocle fall from his eye and hang from its ribbon.

"I don't really need the thing," he confessed. "Bit of an affectation, really. I feel that it makes me look more the part."

"What part?"

"The one out of *Burke's Peerage*."

"That's not a part," she's said, "That's the real you, Percy."

"I wonder sometimes."

"Nobody would mistake you for anything else."

"Kind of you to say so."

"Breeding always shows."

"That's what I think when I look at you," he said, putting his glass down on the side table. "You really are the most bewitching creature, you know. When do I get a view of the real Genevieve Masefield?"

"You're looking at her right now."

"Am I?"

"Don't you believe me?" she teased.

"I'm in a mood to believe anything you say, dear lady."

"How sweet!"

"I'm a very sweet man when I take my monocle out."

She let him kiss her hand and move in closer to her. Genevieve had grown fond of Lord Carradine. He allowed her to remain in control. He seemed content to let her set the pace, sedate as it had been until this point. Genevieve decided to accelerate it a little.

"Did you really mean what you said over dinner?" she asked.

"I said all sorts of wild things. I always do when I'm enjoying myself with friends. Which particular thing did you have in mind?"

"Your invitation, Percy."

"Oh, that."

"You haven't forgotten it, have you?"

"On the contrary, I was waiting for you to put that glass down so that I could issue it again. In stronger terms." She smiled and set her glass aside. "How would you like to stay with me for a while in New York?"

"I'd love to!"

"It will give us a chance to get better acquainted."

"I was hoping you'd say that."

He put a hand on her shoulder. "What else were you hoping I'd say?" he purred, kissing her earlobe. "I'm very amenable to suggestions."

"Don't tempt me."

"If only I could, Genevieve!"

"You already have, believe me."

It was a rather clammy kiss but she endured it easily and came out of it with a smile. Lord Carradine stroked the side of her cheek with a gentle finger and gazed into her eyes.

"There's something I feel bound to tell you, though."

"Can't it wait, Percy?"

"Not really," he said, restoring his monocle. "Never been much of a one for false pretences. Fact is, I happen to know Nigel Wilms-hurst extremely well. I understand that he broke off his engagement to you because he had severe doubts about your motives. Is that true?" He smiled at her obvious discomfort. "The invitation still holds, of course. I just wanted you to understand the terms on which it's based. Well?"

Covering her embarrassment with an excuse, Genevieve left.

Dillman enjoyed the chat with the Tolleys and stayed longer than he intended. When her father excused himself to leave, Ellen hoped that she would have Dillman to herself but he, too, elected to go and she was left looking rather crestfallen. He was sorry to disappoint her, but other priorities loomed. When he reached the purser's cabin, Dillman found him in his shirtsleeves. Fatigue and apprehension had made even deeper inroads into Halliday's already gaunt features.

"I had a visit from your chief engineer," said Dillman.

"So did I. Fergus was rampant."

"I think he may be on to something, Mr. Halliday. Someone may have copied diagrams from the originals. It might be worth having a more thorough search of Henry Barcroft's cabin."

"I'm one step ahead of you, Mr. Dillman. I've just come from there. Nothing. I even unscrewed the light fixtures and took off wall panels. No sign of any copies." He scratched his head. The killer took them. It's the only explanation. That must have been the motive for the murder. To get the diagrams he knew were in Barcroft's possession."

"But he didn't get them," Dillman reminded him. "All he got were the copies. The originals were concealed under the desk in that envelope. That's what's been puzzling me all evening, Mr. Halliday.

"What?"

"Why make copies when he already had one set of diagrams?"

"You tell me."

"Barcroft never intended that envelope to be found."

"Perhaps he was making doubly sure of his prize," guessed the other. "Having a second set as backup. Like spares."

"There was no camera in the room."

"Camera?"

"Easiest way to copy anything. Drawing them by hand would have been very laborious and he didn't have the implements for it. Barcroft had plenty of pencils—which journalist doesn't?—but I didn't notice any ruler or T-square. They'd have been vital."

Halliday sighed. "This gets more baffling by the minute."

"Any more outbursts from Itzak Weiss?"

"No, thank heaven. He's still festering in his cabin."

"Word of the other thefts has spread, I'm afraid."

"We couldn't stop that." He slapped his thigh. "If only we'd made *some* progress. I feel so bloody impotent."

"Perhaps we have made progress," said Dillman, wanting to offer some encouragment, "though it must be treated with caution."

"Go on."

Dillman told him about his suspicions of Jeremiah Erskine and of Cyril Weekes's expertise with antique clocks. Mention of the name of J. P. Morgan was enough for Halliday. It set him off on a theory of conspiracy against the *Lusitania* by a rival shipping line. By the time he finished, he was ready to place Erskine under arrest and conduct a search of his cabin. Dillman calmed him down.

"Supposition is not proof, Mr. Halliday."

"Erskine sounds like our man."

"Why should he steal a violin or a clock or lady's purse? Weekes is much more likely to have done that, and I still find it difficult to believe that he's thief. No, sir, both men need watching carefully before we move in. If either or both are guilty, I'll be the first to jump on them."

"Do you think they could be accomplices?"

"It's crossed my mind. But I'd need a lot more convincing."

"You haven't been idle, anyway, Mr. Dillman. I can see that."

"What about those lists I asked you to get for me?"

"That's in hand. You'll get them tomorrow."

"Good. They may turn out to be crucial."

"Until then," said Halliday, suppressing a yawn, "I suppose that we'd both better try to get some sleep. We'll need all our strength to face tomorrow's batch of disasters."

"There may not be any."

"Pigs may fly!"

"How is Captain Watt taking it all?"

"Very well, considering. He gives nothing away. On the surface, he's behaving as if everything is fine but when he gets his hands on the culprit, there'll be hell to pay! The captain will make him walk the plank!" There was a tap on the door. "Not more problems, please! Who is it now?"

He opened to door to admit Roland Tomkins. Carrying a small case, the assistant surgeon moved to the center of the cabin and turned to face them. He gave a sheepish grin.

"You're not going to believe this," he warned.

"I'll believe anything!" wailed the purser. "What now?"

"Lionel and I have been taking it in turns to check that everything's in order in the freezer. Just to make sure that Mr. Barcroft is comfy, so to speak. We don't want him turning into a human iceberg."

"Don't tell me he's disappeared."

"No, Charles. But I found this lying beside him." He put the case on the desk. It was frosted with ice. "Brace yourselves," he said as he opened the case. They were both agog. "Took my breath away as well."

Inside the case was a lady's purse, a French Empire clock, and a number of other small items. Part of the afternoon's haul had been obligingly returned by the thief. Dillman's mind immediately began to grapple with the implications but Charles Halliday was inconsolable.

"He's laughing at us!" he howled. "The bastard is laughing at us!"

THIRTEEN

Charles Halliday was so jolted by the latest development that he felt the need of a restorative whiskey. Dillman declined the offer to join him, and Roland Tomkins was needed elsewhere so the purser had to drink alone. He poured a generous measure into a glass, taking a first desperate gulp. Dillman waited until the assistant surgeon had left before he spoke.

"It proves one thing, anyway," he said.

"Yes," moaned Halliday, staring into his whiskey. "He's running rings round us. It's maddening! The sod is toying with us!"

"No, he's just showing off a little, that's all. That was a mistake."

"Mistake?"

"He's given the game away, Mr. Halliday." He pointed to the case. "My theory was right. The murderer and the thief are one and the same man. Instead of keeping us guessing about that, he's admitted it."

"That gets us no nearer to catching him."

"Perhaps not, but it gives us a little insight into the way his mind works. That will be helpful. But let's come back to the body. I thought that it was locked away in a refrigerator."

"It was."

"Who had the key?"

"I did, Mr. Dillman. I took it from the kitchen staff. When we put Barcroft in there, I gave the key to Lionel Osborne in case he and Roland wanted to take another look at the body for some reason."

"Just as well they did. Is there only one key?"

"As far as I know."

"Then our man is something of a locksmith, obviously."

"He seems to be able to go anywhere he wants on this ship."

"Let's go back to the cabins," suggested Dillman. "The house-keeping staff must have keys to them, surely? How else could they get into the cabins to change the beds?"

"They only have keys to the cabins they service and each key is different. Only a master key will open every cabin and none of our master keys have been touched. I made sure of that." He sipped more whiskey. "How does he do it? How could he get into Fergus Rourke's cabin so easily? Or the Anstruthers'? Or Itzak Weiss's?"

"We might need to put another cabin on that list, sir."

"Another?"

"Henry Barcroft's," explained Dillman. "When there was no sign of forced entry, I assumed that the murderer had been a friend invited in to have a drink with him. But supposing he let himself into the cabin with a master key and took Barcroft unawares."

Halliday pulled a face. "He's certainly taken me unawares!"

"Look on the bright side."

"*What* bright side?"

"Stolen property has been recovered," said Dillman, looking at the objects in the case. "And not for the first time. You were able to give the chief engineer his diagrams back and you can now win plaudits from the lady who had her purse taken and from the Anstruthers. No harm seems to have come to their property." He picked up the clock and held it his ear. "Still working. When you give this back to the Anstruthers, you'll get a hero's welcome."

"But I didn't find the case. It was left in the fridge to taunt us."

"They don't know that, Mr. Halliday. I think you should take what credit you can. It will help to calm the other passengers' nerves if they think they've got Sherlock Holmes as their purser. And it'll put a stop to all the rumors flying around." He put the clock into the case. "This absolves Cyril Weekes of any guilt. A man who loves clocks the way he does would never subject it to severe cold in case it caused damage. We can cross him off the list of suspects."

"What about this Jeremiah Erskine?"

"I need to check up on him."

"Search his cabin. By force, if necessary."

"No," replied Dillman firmly. "By stealth. I'd like to take charge of that little operation, if I may. He could still be innocent, re-member. Charge in there to accuse him and Mr. Erskine could well turn nasty. You don't want to face litigation, do you? Erskine's a rich man. With some very powerful friends."

"J. P. Morgan among them!"

"I'm not sure that we should attach too much importance to that."

"We have to, Mr. Dillman!"

"Why?"

"Because J. P. Morgan has a controlling interest in our main rivals, the White Star Line. Morgan wants a complete monopoly. He'd gobble up Cunard if they didn't keep him at bay. The link with Morgan is the best evidence yet of Erskine's involvement."

"I wonder," said Dillman reflectively. "To start with, we don't know how close the two men are. They might just be business acquaintances. And J. P. Morgan is not just a shipping magnate. He has a vast empire to run. I don't think a man in his position would have time to worry about the day-to-day operation of his ocean liners."

"He's one of our chief enemies. That's enough for me."

"You'd know more about that than I do, Mr. Halliday."

"I feel it it in my gut."

"That may just be fatigue. You look very tired."

"I'm exhausted, Mr. Dillman. It's no fun trying to keep the lid on murder, theft, espionage, and who knows what else? I won't sleep a wink until this devil is caught."

"Then we'd better catch him soon or you'll drop in your tracks."

"Easier said than done."

"We get closer all the time."

"Do we?"

"Of course," Dillman reassured him. "Have you forgotten what you said when Mr. Barcroft was murdered? You told me that almost everyone on the ship was a suspect."

"Well over two thousand people."

"We've narrowed it right down now. We know he's male, strong and fit, and registered as a first-class passenger or he wouldn't be able to monitor the movements of people like Mr. Weiss and the Anstruthers. We also know," he added, tapping the suitcase, "that he has a weird sense of humor. I'd say that we had a pretty accurate profile of him. All we need now is to find his name."

"Jeremiah Erskine."

"Maybe, maybe not."

"When will you search his cabin?"

"At the opportune moment. Can you get me a master key?"

"Leave it to me."

"Make it soon, please." He watched Halliday drain his glass. "Now, why don't you cheer yourself up, sir?"

"I'm just about to—with another drop of scotch."

"There's a better way than that. I think you should restore this property to its rightful owners and bask in their gratitude. They needn't know where it was found."

"You're right," agreed Halliday, putting the bottle away. "This will solve nothing. And it will cheer me up to be able to give some good news for once. I just wish we'd found the Stradivarius in this case as well."

"No chance of that, sir."

"Why not?"

"He'd never hand back anything that valuable or risk leaving it in a refrigerator where it could suffer untold damage. No, Mr. Halliday, I'm fairly sure that our man has other plans for the Stradivarius."

Itzak Weiss was slumped in a chair with his head in his hands. Unable to console him, his wife busied herself in the cabin, tidying things that had no need to be tidied, opening and shutting drawers and cupboards that could just as easily have been left closed. Ruth Weiss was a woman who devoted herself to her husband and to his career. She had shared triumphs with him all over the world and been there to revive him during the odd moments of setback and disappointment. But she had never seen him so close to utter despair before. Nothing she could do or say could lift his spirits. While he brooded, she tried to keep busy in the vain hope that activity might take her mind off the tragedy they faced.

The violinist eventually looked up at her.

"Stop it, Ruth!" he complained.

"Stop what?"

"Pacing around, making noises."

"I have to do something, Itzak."

"It's getting on my nerves!"

"I'm sorry."

"Sit down!"

"Yes, Itzak."

"And just be quiet. Please!"

She touched his shoulder apologetically and brushed the top of his head with a kiss. Then she sat opposite him. Weiss heaved a sigh, sat back in his chair, and closed his eyes. His wife watched him with growing concern. She knew better than anyone what he was suffering. Having his beloved violin stolen was like losing a child. He was bereft.

A faint noise roused her and she turned round. Something had just been pushed under the door of the cabin. When she rose from her seat, she saw a small white envelope lying on the carpet.

She went over to snatch it up then opened the door to see who had delivered it. Nobody was in sight. Closing the door, she rushed out to her husband.

"Itzak! Itzak!" she said. "It's for you!"

He opened his eyes. "What? Why are you shouting, Ruth?"

"This letter was just pushed under the door. It may be good news. It may be something to do with your violin." She thrust it at him. "Here."

His gloom suddenly vanished and he tore open the envelope but the relief was only temporary. When he read the note, his face crumpled and tears began to stream down his face.

"What is it, Itzak?" asked his wife anxiously. "What does it say?"

Dillman needed thinking time. Instead of returning to the lounge, he went out on to the promenade deck where he found the stiff breeze stimulating. He walked slowly toward the stern, turning over in his mind everything that had happened since the theft from the chief engineer's cabin. Convinced that all the crimes were related, he sought to establish the connecting motive behind them. His contemplation was short-lived. As he walked past a pillar, he caught sight of a huddled figure on a bench in the shadows. She looked vaguely familiar.

"Miss Masefield?" he asked tentatively.

She came out of her reverie. "Oh, hello, Mr. Dillman."

"Isn't it rather cold to be sitting out here with no coat?"

"I have my stole."

"That won't keep out this wind." He began to take off his coat. "Why not put this around your shoulders?"

"No, no," she protested, getting up. "I wouldn't dream of it." She gave a sudden shiver. "It is rather chilly, now that you mention it. To tell you the truth, I hadn't noticed it before. I was miles away."

"Could I tempt you into a drink in the lounge?"

"Yes, please," she said, her teeth chattering slightly. "I think I need something to warm me up. Thank you for coming to my rescue."

"What were you doing out here on your own?"

"Escaping."

"From what?"

Genevieve gave a rueful smile. "Let's have that drink."

Dillman took her to the lounge and found two chairs in a corner. Drinks were ordered, brought, and sipped. Genevieve kept both hands closed around her glass.

"I needed that. Thank you."

"What's all this about escape?"

"A personal matter. Forget all about it. Well," she said, making an effort to compose herself, "if anyone had to find me, I'm so glad that it was you. If it had been someone like that odious journalist, I think I'd probably have turned tail and run. By the way, what's happened to Henry Barcroft? I haven't seen him all day."

"Probably working his way through the second-class passengers."

"The female ones, anyway."

"What do you mean?"

"It seems that I wasn't the only one he favored with the number of his cabin. He tried to lure Lady Carlyle's seventeen-year-old daughter there as well, apparently. And two other women complained about his attentions. Mr. Barcroft obviously worked on the principle that, if he asked us all, he would eventually find a volunteer. Well, he failed in first-class. I daresay he's issuing invitations left, right, and center to the young ladies elsewhere. Who knows? He might be in his cabin with one of them right now. It's on the shelter deck, isn't it?"

"Yes," said Dillman, thinking about two glasses beside an unopened bottle of Champagne. "You were very wise to reject his overtures."

"I never want to see the man again." She studied him quizzically. "But I'm surprised to see you on your own, Mr. Dillman. I thought you might have been spoken for by now."

"Spoken for?"

"Yes," she said, wondering if it was possible to embarrass him.

"You've been setting someone's heart alight. I had the most extraordinary conversation with her earlier. She wanted to make sure that I had no predatory intentions with regard to you so that she could have what she called a clear field."

Dillman sighed. "Miss Ellen Tolley, by any chance?"

"Attractive girl. I liked her."

"I like her myself, Miss Masefield. I had a drink with Ellen and her father after dinner. Nice people. Ellen is a little excitable, that's all."

"I blame you for that. You're the one who excited her."

"Not deliberately."

"No?" She gave him a shrewd look. "Ellen Tolley is not the only young lady aboard this ship who wants to solve the riddle."

"What riddle?"

"The one called George Porter Dillman."

"Am I such an enigma?" he said with a laugh.

"You trade on it."

"That goes for both of us. There's no more teasing riddle aboard this ship than Miss Genevieve Masefield. She goes out of her way to mystify and enthrall."

"Not with unqualified success," she muttered.

"So why were you sitting up there on deck like that?"

"For the same reason that you were strolling along it, Mr. Dillman. I wanted to be alone. I wanted to preserve my mystery. Just like you. Ellen Tolley tried to make me believe that she and I were soul mates but the truth is that we are worlds apart." She gave a half smile. "The only person aboard this ship with whom I have a real affinity is you."

"What about the Hubermann sisters?"

"Please!" she protested.

"They adore you."

"And I love them. In small doses."

"That leaves Lord Carradine."

Dillman thought he detected a slight wince. She took a second drink, then scrutinised him with interest. He felt a prickle of excitement.

"Why did you really do it?" she aked. "Why did you walk out on your family and the profession that went with it? You told me that you'd had enough of building yachts in Boston Harbor but I'm not sure that I believe that. You've got too much sense of purpose about you."

"Is that what you think?"

"My guess is that you didn't run *from* something, Mr. Dillman, you ran *to* it. You left Boston to go after something. Or somebody."

"Both," he conceded quietly. "The something I went after was the most precarious profession in existence. Acting. I've been stagestruck since the moment I paid my first visit to the theater. It was like a fire, smoldering inside me. Eventually it got too hot to ignore. That was the something I went off after. The theater."

"There was a somebody as well."

"George Porter, actor. I ran off in search of him. That was what my father could never pardon. I not only left him in the lurch to seek my fortune on the boards, I even dropped the family name of Dillman. My stage name was George Porter. Juvenile lead."

"You've certainly got the voice and appearance for it."

"But not the temperament, alas."

"Temperament?"

"I didn't realize that I'd spend most of my time out of work. That can be very galling, Miss Masefield. It's not simply unemployment. It's downright rejection. It means someone else is getting all the parts you think you ought to be playing." He hunched his shoulders. "I didn't have the temperament to cope with that. So I retired. After a couple of years as George Porter, the actor who never was, I've come back to being George Porter Dillman, the enigma."

"There's a lot of acting involved in being an enigma."

"I think we both know that."

Their eyes locked and they held their gaze, fascinated, tempted, enlarged with a new vision of each other. It was Genevieve who broke away. She finished her drink and got up, offering her hand.

"Thank you, again," she said as he covered her palm in a gentle handshake. "You saved me from freezing to death up there on deck. I've thawed out now but I still think I need a hot bath. Do excuse me."

Dillman was on his feet. "Good night, Miss Masefield."

"I can see what Ellen Tolley means about you."

"I can see why Lord Carradine is so attentive to you."

The wince was unmistakable this time. Genevieve hurried away. Dillman watched her go. Some sort of rift had clearly occurred with her aristocratic admirer but he had no time to speculate on her private life. Duty called. He had noticed Dorothea Erksine when they came into the lounge. She was sitting with Ada Weekes and two other ladies. Dillman strode across to them and exchanged greetings with the quartet.

"We missed you at dinner, Mrs. Erskine," he observed.

"Yes, we dined in private this evening," she said.

He looked around. "Is your husband not with you?"

"You'll find him in the smoking room, Mr. Dillman. At least, that's where he said he'd be. Jeremiah had somewhere to go immediately after dinner but he won't have stayed away from that card table for long."

"Cyril is the same," said Ada Weekes. "He's in there as well."

The ladies were enjoying a gossip over coffee and looked as if they might be there for some time. If Jeremiah Erskine was trapped at the card table, it would be an ideal opportunity to search their cabin. Dillman took his leave, adjourned to the smoking room to confirm that Erskine was there before going in search of Charles Halliday. The purser was already on his way to find Dillman. They met in a long corridor.

"I'm glad I found you!" said Halliday.

"Do you have that master key for me?"

"Yes, but I've got something else for you as well."

"What is it?"

"This," said the other, holding up an envelope. "It was put under Itzak Weiss's door. A ransom note. He can have his violin back at a price. An enormous price at that."

"Let me see it, Mr. Halliday."

"You may not be able to make head or tail of it."

"Why not?" said Dillman, taking the envelope.

"It's written in German."

When they got back to their suite, Violet Rymer announced that she wanted an early night, and fled to her own room. She wanted to escape her mother's incessant enquiries about her health and to have time alone to reflect once more on her relationship with Philip Garrow. Doubts still assailed her. The meeting in his cabin seemed to have created more problems than it solved and left both of them feeling unsatisfied. She loved him desperately and could not understand why their reunion had fallen so far short of what she hoped it would be. He had done the right thing, that was what she kept telling herself. In coming on the voyage, he had displayed love, loyalty, and bravery. Most young men in his position would have taken the money and deserted the young ladies to whom they had made such ardent promises. Not Philip Garrow. He was hers.

Still in her evening gown, she sat on the edge of the bed and gave an involuntary grin. Horrified when he first told her about her father's attempt to buy him off, she was slowly coming to appreciate the irony of the situation. Matthew Rymer was subsidizing their reunion. There was a poetic justice in that. The father who had treated her so harshly in the past was now unwittingly securing her future happiness. Yet there were still many obstacles to overcome. Philip would advise her. She promised herself that she would be more forthcoming when they met next day, more willing to let him dictate everything. He was much shrewder than she, more experienced, more mature.

Yet Violet was still uncertain about how fully she should yield herself. They were pledged to each other and would one day marry. In her opinion, that was the time to surrender her virtue, when their union had been blessed by God. His impatience was worrying. Though the idea of lying in is arms was exhilarating, it was also rather frightening to a young woman like Violet Rymer with a natural modesty reinforced by a sheltered upbringing. The studied absence of any physical contact between her parents had also helped to shape her perceptions.

Everything would become clear on the next day. Both of them would have been able to think over what had happened in his cabin. They would come to their second meeting with more realistic hopes and all doubts would vanish. Violet smiled wistfully. She missed Philip Garrow so much. While she languished in her cabin, she was comforted by the thought that he would be alone on his own bed, pining for her and planning for their future together.

"It's beautiful out here at night, isn't it?" said Philip Garrow.

"Beautiful but rather cold," she said.

"Look at those stars, Rosemary. Have you ever seen the like?"

"Not from the deck of an ocean liner."

"That's one new experience I've given you, anyway."

She gave an encouraging laugh and he slipped an arm around her shoulders. Rosemary Hilliard did not resist. Both of them had taken the precaution of putting on coats and hats before they came out on the boat deck. The sea was volatile but the *Lusitania* was undaunted by the angry waves, cutting its way across the ocean with a confidence that bordered on outright arrogance. Other couples had ventured on deck and the two lookouts in the crows' nest shared a quiet snigger when they turned their binoculars away from the sea ahead to snatch a glimpse at some of the budding romances taking place immediately below them.

"I'm sorry about last night," said Philip softly.

"Don't keep apologizing."

"I feel such an idiot."

"We were both to blame, Philip."

"I suppose so."

"Let's try to put it behind us."

"Yes," he said, tightening his grip. "I'm so glad you gave me a second chance. It will make up for everything."

"We'll see about that." She gave shudder. "The wind is getting up. I think I'm ready to go inside now."

"So am I."

He escorted her to the nearest door and they stepped through it.

"You can take your arm away now," she said pleasantly. "I'm fine now we're out of that wind. Well, thank you, Philip, it was a lovely idea of yours to go out on deck but standing out there has rather tired me."

"Let me walk you back to your cabin," he said with a grin.

"I can find it on my own."

"Oh." The grin vanished. "All right, Rosemary."

"Tomorrow, perhaps."

She kissed him on the cheek and walked away. Garrow grinned afresh. It was a firm promise. He would hold her to it.

Dillman moved swiftly. Charles Halliday had been stationed at the end of the corridor to keep watch in case the Erskines returned sooner than expected. Dillman did not wish to be caught in their cabin. There could be awkward repercussions. Letting himself in with the master key, he switched on the light and looked around. It was a large and luxurious cabin on the promenade deck with two portholes. Books, papers, and a box of cigars lay on the table. He checked each item, opened every drawer then searched the wardrobe. Dorothea Erskine had a large number of extremely expensive dresses but it was her husband's clothing that interested the visitor. Dillman went through the pockets of every jacket and pair of trousers. Then he found the tails.

He surmised that Erskine must have brought a second set because he would not seen in the first-class public rooms in a suit during the evening. The coat and trousers that he pulled out of the wardrobe must have been the ones he was wearing on the night when he blundered out of the smoking room after heavy losses at the card table. Dorothea Erskine had spoken of soiled clothing on his return. Dillman saw what she meant. One arm of the coat was smudged with what seemed to be grease and both cuffs had been stained with something. Dillman wondered if it was the blood of Henry Barcroft. Exposed shirt cuffs would also have been stained but he could find no dress shirt with blood on it. He decided that Erksine could have disposed of a shirt that might be beyond recall, whereas the coat could be cleaned more effectively.

When he replaced the items in the wardrobe, he saw something poked away in a corner. It was a large camera, complete with its own tripod. Taking both out to inspect them, he saw that the tripod was made of stout wood. Folded up and wielded with force, it would be more than capable of crushing a man's skull. Dillman put camera and tripod back where he found them and crossed over to the bathroom. Expecting to find nothing incriminating there, he was startled when he put on the light. A large metal tray stood on a shelf beside bottles of chemicals. More equipment rested on the floor. Jeremiah Erskine did not simply possess a camera. He had the means of developing his own photographs.

After a troubled night, Genevieve Masefield rose early to take a bath. It was time to reevaluate her situation. Lord Carradine had called her bluff and brought a premature end to the relationship. Though she had shown enough righteous indignation to cover her departure from his suite, she knew that she would never be invited into it again. Nor would she grace the captain's table in the company of the tobacco millionaire. It was a bitter disappointment but she had the resilience to overcome it. Instead of crying over spilled milk, she would simply look for another jug of it.

When she went off to have breakfast, her spirits were partially restored and there was no hint in her face or manner of the crippling blow dealt to her by Lord Carradine. She floated into the dining saloon with all of her usual aplomb. Only a scattering of passengers were there, but one of them spotted her instantly and signaled a greeting.

"Hello!" said Ellen Tolley. "Care to join us, Miss Masefield?"

Genevieve had hoped to be left alone but it was difficult to refuse the invitation. When she was introduced to Caleb Tolley, she sat down and studied the breakfast menu. Ellen began to recommend some items.

"What's the purpose of your visit, Miss Masefield?" Mr. Tolley asked. "Vacation? Visiting friends?"

"Both, Mr. Tolley. I'll be staying in New York for the first few couple of weeks, then I'll be going to Virginia to stay with the Hubermanns. Have you come across them yet?"

"The two sisters who are usually trailing you?"

"I see that you've been watching."

"Oh, I'm only part of a large and appreciative audience."

"What did I tell you, Miss Masefield?" said Ellen with a grin. "But what about Lord Carradine? He's done everything so far but fall to his knee and beg you to marry him. Will you be seeing him in America?"

"It's possible," said Genevieve, hiding her discomfort.

"Hey," Ellen said, winking at Genevieve, "do you reckon an English aristocrat would take his monocle out when he has a bath? Or goes to bed?"

"You're being very impertinent, Ellen!"

"Miss Masefield doesn't mind."

"Well, I do, young lady. Now act your age and show some manners." He turned to Genevieve. "Ellen should have gone to a finishing school in England. That might have knocked the rough edges off her."

"I rather like rough edges, Mr. Tolley," said Genevieve.

"That depends how close you have to get to them. Let's come back to this vacation of yours. How long is it due to last and where exactly do you intend to go?"

"Wherever I can."

Caleb Tolley moved his arm and accidentally knocked over the walking stick balanced against the table. Genevieve instinctively reached down for it at the same time as Caleb Tolley bent over from his chair. Their faces were only inches away from each other. Genevieve saw the curious look in his eye. She was not sure whether to be flattered or offended. Her hand closed on the stick and she gave it back to him.

"Thank you, Miss Masefield, he said, pulling himself back up into his chair. "I'm lost without that. Now, what were you saying?"

"What did I tell you?" said Dillman cheerily. "A trouble-free night."

"The calm before the storm."

"He's got what he wants. No need for anything else."

"There's still a lot of unfinished business for us, though."

"That's why we must have a hearty breakfast."

Charles Halliday had gone early to Dillman's cabin and they were discussing their tactics over the first meal of the day. A quiet night had done little to still the demons that haunted the purser.

"I still believe that we should challenge Erskine," he said.

"Not enough evidence."

"You found that photographic equipment in his cabin. You saw what might have been bloodstains on the jacket he wore the night of the murder. What more do you want?"

"A stolen violin, for a start."

"He may have stashed that away somewhere else."

"Along with the photographic copies of those diagrams? There was no sign of them either. That worries me. So does his wife."

"His wife?"

"Yes, Mr. Halliday. I think that Erskine is a very likely suspect. He certainly has strength and brutality enough to kill another man. And he has a strangely critical attitude toward the Cunard Line for a man who's used it so much. He was sounding off about disasters aboard your ships when I first met him."

"He's created the ones aboard the *Lusitania*."

"Has he? Could he keep such a series of crimes from his wife?"

"Mrs. Erskine must be an accomplice."

"Then she's a far better actress than I took her for," said Dillman, "and I do know a little about acting. Dorothea Erskine is not putting on a performance. She's perfectly innocent, I'm sure of it."

"That doesn't put her husband in the clear."

"No, but it introduces enough doubt to make us hold our horses. Why not leave Erskine to me?" he suggested. "I won't let him off the hook, I promise you. But I have other lines in the water as well. Coffee?"

"Black, please. Lots of it."

Dillman poured two cups. "That's how I feel this morning."

"I need sustenance before I face Mr. Weiss again."

"At least we know that his violin has not been destroyed. That must have given him some crumbs of comfort."

"Not when he has to stump up all that money to reclaim it. Besides," he said, fearing the worst, "how do we know that the thief will return it unharmed? We can't trust him to hand over the Stradivarius. It may just be a ruse to get the cash."

"I don't think that for one moment."

"Why not?"

"You translated the note for me. If your German is correct, what the thief is demanding is payment in U.S. dollars with notes of large denomination. But there are two very telling conditions."

"Yes," said Halliday, spooning sugar into his cup. "Weiss must get us to call off the search for the violin or it may no longer be there to be found. That really threw him into a panic."

"It was the second condition that interested me."

"The exchange will take place early on Friday morning."

"The day we arrive in New York. That minimizes the amount of time we'd have to organize a cabin-by-cabin search. And we can hardly frisk every male passenger from first-class as he disembarks."

"I told you, he's toying with us."

"No, Mr. Halliday, there's something else behind this. I still believe that the theft of the violin is a diversionary measure."

"A bloody expensive one, Mr. Dillman. Especially if we have to cough up the money. That's what Mr. Weiss is demanding. I can't see Captain Watt agreeing to pay for a violin we never owned in the first place. Though he may agree to loan the five thousand dollars."

"That's ridiculously cheap for a Stradivarius."

"Not if you've already paid out vastly more than that, as Mr.

Weiss must have done in Vienna. He must wish he had never traveled on this ship. And the story is bound to get out once we reach New York."

"Only if he's forced to pay the ransom. Retrieve the violin ourselves and Itzak Weiss will do anything we ask. You'd better finish that coffee and get off to see him." He drank some of his own. "No more problems with Henry Barcroft, I hope."

"I had a man on guard all night outside that refrigerator."

"Wise move."

"I've increased security throughout the whole ship."

"Discreetly, I trust."

"Very discreetly. What's your next move?"

"I need to question Erskine."

"To get a confession out of him?"

"To see if he can speak German."

The purser rose to leave. "I'll be off."

"Aren't you forgetting something, Mr. Halliday?"

"What? Oh, yes," he said, thrusting a hand into the pocket of his uniform. "Those lists you asked me to get." He passed them over. "The two table plans are complete but I've probably only got about three-quarters of the people who attended the music concert."

"That may be enough."

"Report back if you get a breakthrough."

"Aye, aye, sir," said Dillman with a mock salute.

When his guest departed, he looked at the first list, which contained the names of those who had dined with the Anstruthers on the eve of the thefts. Dillman knew none of the names. When he saw the list of those at the Anstruther table during luncheon on the day of the theft itself, however, he recognized several of them. One leaped up at him. Jeremiah Erskine.

"You're late," he complained. "I began to think that you weren't coming."

"I got held up in the hairdressing salon."

"What were you doing in there?"

"Pretending to have my hair done. It was the only way I could shake off my mother. Unfortunately, they were running late. That's why I was delayed. I only had my hair trimmed so that I could be out of there in as short a time of possible."

"You're here now, anyway," he said, squeezing her arm.

"Yes. You must've known that I'd come."

"I'd have waited all day."

They were sitting side by side on a wooden bench in the third-class lounge. It was not the ideal place to meet, but Violet Rymer had balked at the idea of going to his cabin again and selected neutral ground. Nobody would think of looking for them there. In the swirling crowd, they could be quietly anonymous.

"Did you think over what I said?" he asked.

"Yes, Philip, and I owe you an apology."

"For what?"

"Misjudging you."

"What do you mean?"

"Well, I was rather shocked when you told me about the money that Father gave you. Shocked that he should try to get rid of you like an unwanted beggar, and even more shocked that you'd used the money to pay for this voyage."

"I did it to be near you, Violet!"

"I see that now."

"So you don't think I'm simply being mercenary?"

"Far from it."

"Good."

"How much was it, exactly?"

"Enough to fund this trip and to pay for my accommodation in New York. All that I have to do is to keep my head down until the great day."

"What great day?"

Philip Garrow chuckled. "Your twenty-first birthday."

"I'd almost forgotten that."

"Well, I haven't," he said, fondling her arm. "I've thought about nothing else for months. That's the day when our lives will change forever. They won't be able to stop us then."

"No," she said.

"You might sound a little more pleased about it, Violet."

"I feel so inhibited in here," she said, glancing around.

"Would you rather go to my cabin?"

"I don't know."

"We could at least talk properly there. Without this din."

Violet wanted to acquiesce but something was stopping her. It worried her that she still had reservations about Philip Garrow. She felt so proud to be with him, so happy to feel him beside her. Yet she could not bring herself to move to the privacy of his cabin again.

"You're not afraid of me, are you?"

"Of course not, Philip."

"This is so *public*. Thank heaven I didn't travel third-class."

"It's like a cattle shed down here. All these people. The smell!"

"Your snobbery is showing, Miss Rymer!" he said with a mocking smile. "What happened to the young woman who once boasted that she'd live in abject poverty with me if only we could be together?"

"And I still would!" she said effusively.

"But it won't be necessary now, Violet. Don't you see?"

"Not exactly."

"Your twenty-first birthday. You come of age."

She beamed. "Yes! That means they can't stop me from marrying you."

"And they can't prevent you from coming into that money." Her face went blank. "The trust fund your father set up for you, Violet," he said. "On your twenty-first birthday, you come into a large amount of money and that will set me up in business and buy us our first house. How on earth could you have forgotten it?"

"I hadn't, Philip."

"So what's the problem? The trust fund has got the protection of the law around it. Your father signed and sealed that document. When you're twenty-one, you get the money whatever he says. And you can do anything you like with it."

"But I can't, Philip. I thought you'd guess that."

His smirk evaporated. "Guess what?"

"Father was so vengeful about you, it was terrifying. He altered the terms of the trust fund. A codicil was attached to it."

"Codicil? What are you talking about?"

"I only come into that money on condition that I never have anything to do with you." She saw his dismay and clutched at him. "But it doesn't make any difference, surely. If I have to choose between you and the trust fund, I'd choose you every time. We'll manage somehow, Philip. We'll be together. What more do we want?"

"Nothing," he muttered uneasily.

She clung to him. "Say something nice. Tell me you love me."

"You know I do, Violet."

"Then why have you gone so distant all of a sudden?"

"I'm thinking, that's all." He chewed his lip. "There must be a way of getting around this somehow. Tell me again about this codicil."

It was afternoon before Dillman finally cornered the Erskines. Elusive during the morning, they had not come into the saloon for luncheon. Both of them surfaced in the first-class lounge. Dorothea Erskine was part of a circle that included Matthew and Sylvia Rymer, Ada Weekes, Nairn Mackintosh and his wife, and Miguel, the Spanish artist. At a table in the corner, a card game was in progress. Edward Collins was dealing the cards to Cyril Weekes, Jeremiah Erskine, and three other men. Dillman wondered why they had shifted from the smoking room The move had clearly suited Erskine. He appeared to be winning for once.

Dillman strolled casually across to the group who were lounging in chairs. After an exchange of niceties, he saw a chance to use Miguel for his own purposes and plunged in with deliberate clumsiness.

"*Buon giorno, Miguel. Come stai? Sono Americano. Parla inglese?*"

The artist looked slightly baffled and the women were impressed.

Nairn Mackintosh laughed. "Faultless accent, Mr. Dillman, but you've got the wrong language, unfortunately. Miguel is Spanish and not Italian." There was general hilarity. "Why not just talk in English to him?"

Dillman apologized profusely to the Spaniard, then gave a sigh.

"Languages were never my strong point," he confessed. "I've got a smattering of French but I could never get to first base with German. It's such a complicated language. Anyone here speak it?"

"Jeremiah does," volunteered his wife obligingly. "He's fluent."

"He seems more interested in the card game at the moment," said Ada Weekes, keeping one eye on the table. "So does Cyril. If they don't finish soon, I'm going to break up that game. It's so antisocial."

Having learned what he wanted, Dillman only stayed a short while before finding an excuse to walk over to Caleb Tolley for a chat. Seated in an armchair, Tolley had his leg up on a footstool and was reading a book. Dillman talked to him for a few minutes, then his attention was taken back to the card table. Mild excitement was developing. A crucial game was in progress and the pot grew ever larger. Three players had opted out but Weekes, Erskine, and Collins were still raising the stakes in turn. Cyril Weekes removed his pince-nez and rubbed his temple with them while he stared at his hand. Jeremiah Erskine was glowing, as if certain that he could recoup all of his earlier losses in one glorious moment. Edward Collins was still the most relaxed man at the table.

Ada Weekes had taken enough. Tolerant of her husband's gambling until now, she marched across the room and stood behind Collins to wave across at her husband.

"How much longer will you be, Cyril?" she protested. "We promised to meet the Hubermanns in the Veranda Café for tea."

"All in good time, Ada. Give me five minutes."

"You've had far too many of those already," she said, going around to him and squeezing his shoulder. "Now, please. Make this the last game or I shall be cross. Very cross." She turned to the others. "Excuse me, gentlemen. I didn't mean to interrupt."

Ada Weekes flounced off to be greeted by words of praise from the other ladies, but Dillman's eye stayed on the game. More money went into the pot and the three players displayed their respective hands. Erskine was horrified that he had lost and Collins was evidently surprised by his defeat. It was Cyril Weekes whose podgy hands closed on a pot worth the best part of two hundred pounds. When he left the room with his wife, she was still berating him. Caleb Tolley gave a chuckle.

"Just as well she didn't stop him five minutes ago."

"Yes," said Dillman thoughtfully.

"Looks to me as if the game is over."

Collins was trying to deal but one of the men was already rising from the table and Erskine was shaking with fury. Picking up his cards, he hurled them down with contempt, said something to Collins, and stalked out of the lounge. His wife knew better than to follow him.

Dillman had other ideas. Excusing himself, he set off in pursuit of Erskine but lost him at the first staircase. Before he could follow the man up it, Dillman saw Genevieve descending it with such a friendly smile that he was stopped in his tracks.

"Henry Barcroft was right about one thing," she remarked.

"Was he?"

"Betting fever seems to be spreading. I've just had tea with two people who've each bet fifty pounds that we're going to win the Blue Riband on this trip. Apparently we're maintaining a steady twenty-five knots, which is faster than anything the German liners can manage."

Dillman looked at her in absolute wonder as an idea dawned.

"People are betting on it?" he queried.

"Dozens of them, from what I can gather. British patriotism."

"Thank you, Miss Masefield!" he said, reaching out to give her a kiss of gratitude on the cheek. "Thank you so much!"

Leaving her bemused, he went charging up the stairs past her.

FOURTEEN

The *Lusitania* was a tiny island of noise in the vast ocean. As the great ship powered its way toward an empty horizon, the clamor in its public rooms grew ever louder. Cleared of its chairs, the music room had been set aside for the dog show, open to all contestants and drawing the most astonishing range of animals from passengers in first, second, and—in the case of two spaniels and a mongrel terrier—third-class. A room that echoed to the harmonies of famous composers on the previous afternoon now reverberated with the yelps, snarls, growls, and barks of over forty dogs. Canine tempers were short, owners tried to shout their charges into submission, and partisan spectators cheered on their favorites.

Even this tumult could not compare with the pandemonium in the third-class lounge where a fancy dress parade was being held. Families with barely more than a few suitcases with which to start their new lives in America had begged, borrowed, or somehow improvised a wide array of costumes. Pirates competed with cowboys, fairy princesses with foul witches on makeshift broomsticks. There was even an infant Queen Victoria in a paper crown to fight for the throne of first prize. A tea dance for the second-class passengers combined with the roar of the ship's engines to swell the general commotion.

Some of the events helping to produce the cacophony had been suggested by Dillman as a means of keeping the passengers fully occupied but he did not pause to participate in any of them himself. His destination was the bridge, where he found the captain at his post with his officers. Hoping for some good news at last, Captain Watt took the visitor aside so that they could converse in private.

"Well, Mr. Dillman? Has any arrest been made?" he asked.

"Not yet, sir. But it is imminent."

"Purser Halliday keeps saying that to me but I see no sign of it."

"I believe that I have just made the breakthrough."

"Does that mean you've found Mr. Weiss's violin?"

"No, but I have every confidence that I will."

"You'd better, Mr. Dillman. The newspapers will crucify us if something like this gets out. And Itzak Weiss is threatening us with a lawsuit. A maiden voyage is supposed to be an act of celebration, not a publicity disaster. That Stradivarius must be found. I understand there's been a ransom note."

"It may be something else as well, Captain Watt."

"Something else?"

"A confession."

"What are you on about?"

"The language in which it was written," said Dillman. "I think that our man has unwittingly shown his hand. That's why I came to see you. Apparently everyone is starting to get excited about the prospect of our winning the Blue Riband on this voyage."

"Then the excitement is premature."

"Is there no chance that the ship will lower the record?"

"There's every chance, Mr. Dillman," said the captain proudly. "I'd stake my pension on it. What I can't guarantee is that it will happen on this trip. My orders are to take the *Lusitania* safely to New York, where we can expect a warm welcome, whatever time we arrive. I have not been urged not throw caution to the winds in pursuit of any record. That will come in time. The *Lusitania* is a greyhound of the sea, Mr. Dillman. It won't be long before she wins the race for the Blue Riband, and I expect to be on this bridge when she does it."

"We seem to be maintaining a high speed now."

"Yes," said the other, "and we'll continue to do so while we can. But the North Atlantic is the most dangerous ocean of them all. The weather can change for the worst so quickly. A heavy swell would slow us right down. And reports are already coming in about ice ahead. We *could* still break that record, Mr. Dillman, but I'd advise you not to bet your life savings on it."

Dillman grinned. "I don't *have* any life savings, Captain. But what I really came to ask you is this. How big a triumph would it be if the ship did capture the Blue Riband on its maiden voyage?"

"An enormous triumph. Our rivals would never forgive us."

"You'd seize business from them at one fell swoop."

"Of course, everyone wants to travel on the fastest liner."

"She's rather more than a liner, Captain Watt."

"Not at the moment."

"What about the future?"

"Your guess is as good as mine, Mr. Dillman," said the captain with a weary sigh. "But there's no point in trying to bamboozle a man like you. I know you've got a nautical background. You understand the principles of marine architecture." He took Dillman to the window and they looked down toward the bow of the ship. "What do you see down there?"

"A narrow prow, designed for speed."

"And?"

"Reminiscent of a destroyer."

"What else do you see, Mr. Dillman?"

"A foredeck that could easily be reinforced to take guns."

"Go on."

"A compass platform could be added on top of this bridge. A second could be placed in a number of locations. Decks, fore and aft, could be cleared. Passenger accommodation could be restricted to allow more room for cargo. Do you want me to go on, sir?" said Dillman. "This ship was designed for peace but is also ready for war."

"It won't be of our choosing, sir. But we're bound to take note of the way that the Germans are building up their navy. They're flexing their muscles. We need to be ready in case they start to swing punches."

"In the meantime?"

"We win the battle of the Atlantic with the *Lusitania*."

"Perhaps even on this voyage?"

"Nothing would gladden my heart more. I've spent a lifetime competing with German skippers who think they own this ocean. High time someone wiped that arrogant grin off their faces." He looked around. "And we've finally got the ship that can do it."

"Thank you, sir." Dillman moved off. "You've been a great help."

"You're going?"

"I have to, Captain Watt."

"But you haven't told me about this so-called confession."

"I have to find the man who wrote it first."

Dillman ducked out of the bridge and descended the stairs. While the captain deserved to be kept informed of every development, there were some things the American felt obliged to keep from him. He still believed that his own camouflage was the best means of catching the man they were after. He made light of the personal danger involved. The visit to the bridge had provided vital confirmation. He was tingling.

"Hold on, Mr. Dillman!"

A loud voice cut through the crowd on deck and he turned to see Carlotta Hubermann waddling toward him. She had a mischievous glint in her eye, which was never there when her sister, Abigail, was with her. Dillman waited until she came panting up to him.

"You sure are a difficult man to find!" she said.

"I didn't realize you were looking for me."

"Genevieve said you'd come in this direction. Like a bullet from a gun, that's how she put it. What's the rush? This is the life of leisure, Mr. Dillman. Enjoy it while you can."

"I intend to, Miss Hubermann."

"Good! That means you'll join Abigail and me for dinner this evening. We'll meet you for drinks in the lounge beforehand." She raised a hand to stop the protest that rose to his lips. "I won't take no for an answer, Mr. Dillman. You're needed for compassionate duty."

"Compassionate duty?"

"I'm seating you next to Genevieve Masefield. Something's upset her. She can't hide it from me. I reckon it's to do with that Lord Carradine. Abigail may have been right all along. Perhaps he is sinister. Anyway," she said, squeezing his arm, "Genevieve needs brightening up and I think you're just the man to do it. She really likes you."

"I'm glad to hear that, Miss Hubermann."

"See you later, then. Oh, by the way, don't go near the music room. They're holding a dog show down there and the noise is earsplitting. A dog show! What lunatic came up with an idea like that?"

Matthew Rymer had reverted to his more usual mood of suppressed anger. Pacing the lounge in their suite, he fired rhetorical questions at his wife, who sat meekly in a chair and toyed with her purse.

"Where the devil has she got to? How long does it take to have your hair done, for heaven's sake? Violet should have been back by now, surely? What's got into the girl? We practically had to drag her aboard last Saturday, yet now she goes prancing off whenever she can. Is there something I should know about, Sylvia?" He stopped to tower over her. "Well, is there?"

"No, Matthew."

"So what is happening?"

"I'm as much in the dark as you."

"Violet has been gone for hours."

"Perhaps she met a friend at the salon."

"What friend? She hardly speaks to anybody."

"That's not true," said Sylvia Rymer. "She often talks to Mrs. Weekes. They get on well together. Then there's that Mr. Dillman. Violet likes him. She's been agitating for us to invite him here to dinner one evening."

"Well, she's wasting her time."

"Why?"

"Something about the fellow," he said, on the move again. "Can't say what it is but it worries me. I'm certainly not going to encourage any friendship between my daughter and him."

"Mr. Dillman is so courteous."

"Sylvia, he's an *American*!" He sneered. "Besides, I've invited Nairn Mackintosh and his wife to join us for dinner here tonight. Violet can forget all about Mr. Dillman. I want her on her best behavior. Mackintosh is coming round to my suggestion."

"That's good to hear, Matthew."

"It's one of the rewards of this voyage."

"Not the only one, I hope,"

"Oh, no," he said, stifling a smile. His tone hardened. "I think that we should watch Violet more carefully. Too much freedom could be dangerous. Who knows what she might get up to?"

"I can't keep an eye on her all the time."

"We can share the load. All three of us."

"Three of us?"

"You, Mildred and I. No point in bringing a maid unless we make full use of her," he said airily. "Next time Violet wants to go to the salon or wander off on her own, we'll send Mildred with her."

"If you say so, Matthew."

"I do say so. I insist."

The cabin door suddenly opened and he swung round. Violet Rymer came into the room and saw the grim expression on her father's face. She tried to control the turmoil inside her head and force a smile.

"Where on earth have you been?" demanded her father.

*   *   *

234

Dillman caught the chief engineer as he was about to leave his cabin. Fergus Rourke grinned at his visitor's immaculate appearance.

"No need to wear white tie and tails to call on me," he joked. "I don't stand on ceremony here, Mr. Dillman."

"Could you spare me a minute, please?"

"As long as you're not going to tell me any more lies."

"I've come to ask your advice, Mr. Rourke."

"Well, that's different."

They went into the cabin and Rourke switched on the light again.

"I wondered if I could possibly glance at those diagrams of yours again," said Dillman, pointing to the folder on the desk. "The ones that were stolen."

"You mean, the ones that you found by sheer chance under a pile of sheets in a linen cupboard? I hope you didn't prick your fingers on the drawing pins." He opened the folder and stood back. "Help yourself. Then you can tell me what all this is in aid of."

Dillman looked first at the cross section of the boiler room but reserved his real concentration for the wiring diagram. Miles of cable had been used, snaking its way around the entire vessel to feed electricity to its control panels, appliances, and countless thousands of bulbs. He checked to see where the generators were, then matched their position against another diagram. The chief engineer peered over his shoulder.

"You're on to something, Mr. Dillman."

"Possibly."

"What is it?"

"Let's just say that I may have seen the light."

"Share it with me."

"When I have more proof, Mr. Rourke."

"Proof of what?"

"Call it maritime envy."

"Could you put that into English for me?"

"Wrong language, sir."

"Eh?"

"It would be more appropriate in German."

Leaving him openmouthed in bafflement, Dillman went out.

Itzak Weiss shuttled between anger and sadness with no intervening stage. When the purser tried to console him, he was met either with a stream of vituperation or with a series of tearful pleas. Ruth Weiss was perched on the arm of her husband's chair, alternately calming him when he shouted and patting him when he sobbed. Charles Halliday did his best to bring a modicum of cheer to the cabin.

"Your violin is safe, Mr. Weiss. At last, we know that."

"Do we?"

"Yes, sir. Why else send the note to you?"

"It could just be a cruel joke."

"The thief wants to exchange it for money."

"Well, I'm not paying it out of my own pocket," insisted Weiss. "Why should I? This is the responsibility of the Cunard Line. My property was stolen aboard one of their ships. That makes them culpable."

"Not necessarily, sir."

"It must," said Ruth Weiss. "Passengers are insured against loss or damage to luggage. We saw the rates in your brochure."

"This is a slightly different matter, Mrs. Weiss. Luggage stored away is indeed covered by the insurance premium. But we did not envisage a loss on the scale of a Stradivarius."

"You will pay the ransom money!" howled the violinist, pointing an accusory finger. "And if the instrument is not returned to me in perfect condition, I will demand full compensation. I still have the receipt for that violin. Do you know how much it cost me?"

"I'd rather not," said Halliday, "and I do beg of you not to fear the worst. We've already picked up a number of vital clues and may well be able to reclaim the instrument before Friday."

"You saw the ransom note. You must suspend the hunt."

"We have done, Mr. Weiss. In one sense. That's why you do not see anyone in uniform charging around the ship to search cabins. That would be the quickest way to ensure that your violin is tossed through the nearest porthole or smashed to pieces."

"*O mein Gott!*" said Weiss, clutching at his chest.

"Do not say such things, Mr. Halliday," chastised Ruth Weiss. "My husband has suffered enough as it is. We have not had the strength to leave this cabin since the tragedy. Look at him—he is in pain!"

The purser apologized and did his best to soothe both of them. His words eventually began to have an effect. When he ignited a faint hope in Itzak Weiss, the violinist reached out to grab him by the hand.

"Find it, Mr. Halliday!" he implored. "Find my Stradivarius, please. If you can bring it safely back to me, I will not sue your company or release a word of this to the press. I will be so grateful that I will give a free concert to your passengers in the music room!"

"That's a most generous offer, sir!"

Charles Halliday smiled, but his stomach was churning restlessly. Too many unanswered questions still remained. He feared that the man they were after would always be a few steps ahead of them. The only real hope lay with George Porter Dillman, and the purser was beginning to wonder if his confidence in the American was misplaced. When he left the cabin, his smile froze and his apprehension soared.

After drinks in the lounge bar that evening with Genevieve Masefield and the Hubermann sisters, Dillman made his way to the dining saloon. Helped by his daughter, Caleb Tolley was lowering himself gingerly onto a chair at a table near the door. When she saw the newcomers, Ellen Tolley intercepted Dillman with a mock frown.

"Seems as if I lost out, after all," she complained. "And there was Miss Masefield, telling me that I had a clear run at you."

"Another time, perhaps," he appeased her.

"Another man, I think."

"I'm just being sociable, Ellen."

"I know," she said with a grin. "And who can blame you? Just remember that I'm still around, will you? Before this voyage is over, I'm determined that someone is going to take me out on deck for a look at the stars. Don't let me down, George."

"It's a promise."

The promise was easily given but not so easily kept. Dillman had no wish to be caught in a private tug-of-war between Ellen Tolley and Genevieve Masefield. What might be extremely pleasurable under other circumstances was a major distraction at the present time. All his energies needed to be focused on the task in hand. Dinner with Genevieve and the Hubermanns would be enjoyable but he would use it to scan the dining saloon and to keep watch. As soon as he sat down, he saw something that alerted him. The Anstruthers, the retired couple whose property had now been restored, were coming through the doors with Jeremiah Erskine. Were they walking beside the thief who had broken into their cabin?

Dillman was seated between Genevieve Masefield and Carlotta Hubermann. He suspected that the latter had been in charge of the seating plan. Abigail Hubermann still treated him with mild disdain but her younger sister was much more amenable.

"You have to hand it to the royal family," said Carlotta. "They do add a bit of tone. Like any true American, I'm a diehard republican, but there's something so grand about having a king and queen."

"Only if you have the jack as well," observed Dillman, gently teasing her. "From the same suit, of course. Do you play poker?"

"No, you naughty man!" she reproached him with a laugh. "That wasn't what I was talking about, as you know only too well. I think that King Edward is just wonderful. I'm not sure that I'd like him as a house guest, mark you, especially with Abigail around, but I think he looks magnificent in an open carriage. Such style, such dignity. We've got nothing to touch it."

"I disagree, Miss Hubermann. I daresay that President Roosevelt cuts a fine figure when he stands on the steps at the White House." He turned to Genevieve. "Will you be going Washington at any stage?"

"I'd like to, Mr. Dillman," she said. "If I can fit it in."

"We'll make sure you do, honey," Carlotta assured her, waving the menu at her. "Have you seen what they're giving us this evening?"

"A meal fit for a king," said Dillman graciously, "and for the two queens I have the good fortune to be sitting between."

Carlotta Hubermann grinned but Genevieve's response was more muted. Glasses were filled and the meal was served. A couple of hours seemed to float past. Dillman kept up polite conversation while his mind wrestled constantly with more urgent questions concerning a ransom note and a wiring diagram. His gaze constantly roved the room. Genevieve wanted to know why he had given her the spontaneous kiss earlier on.

"Was it so objectionable?" he asked worriedly.

"No, not at all. Just rather unexpected. I suppose that's all part of being a man of mystery," she said with a mocking smile. "You do the unexpected. But what did I do to deserve that kiss?"

"A big favor."

"In that case, I must do you another sometime."

It was dinner table banter rather than anything more serious, but Dillman was still ignited by the remark. As the meal came to an end, the guests began to disperse. Dillman made an excuse to slip across to the nearby table where Jeremiah Erskine was seated, hoping to engage him in casual chat about his knowledge of German. Before the conversation could get under way, however, he heard a scream of surprise behind him and turned to see Genevieve Masefield staring in distress at her silk evening gown. While gesturing in the course of conversation, she inadvertently knocked over her wineglass and spilled its contents down the front of her gown. She dabbed at it with a napkin then hurried toward the door. Dillman noted her consternation. Carlotta Hubermann came swiftly across to prompt him.

"The lady needs help," she said with a nudge.

"Yes, of course."

"Well? Go after her, man."

Dillman nodded and picked his way through the crowd.

Genevieve had a head start on him but he knew that her cabin was on the deck below. While she would descend by means of the grand staircase, he headed for the narrow companionway that would afford him a shortcut. It was at the end of a long corridor and he hurried toward it. In his haste, he did not realize that he was being followed.

Reaching the top of the steps, he was about to descend them at speed when someone gave him assistance. Two strong hands grabbed him by the shoulders and pushed him with vicious force. Dillman went headfirst down the companionway, turning somersaults and buffeting himself hard on the walls. His head struck the floor at the bottom of the stairs and he lost consciousness.

Genevieve Masefield was very annoyed with herself. Having removed the silk evening gown, she laid it on a towel in the bathroom and sponged the wine stain with cold water, hoping that it would save the dress. A loud bang on her cabin door made her look up. When it was followed by a second, even louder, bang, she put a dressing gown on over her underwear and answered the door.

"Mr. Dillman!" she cried. "What's happened to you?"

"Fell down the stairs."

"Your head is bleeding!"

"Banged it as I came tumbling down. Any chance I could come in?"

Genevieve helped him inside at once. Her visitor was clearly dazed and barely able to stand. His tie had come undone, a button was missing off his tailcoat, and he looked thoroughly disheveled. Sitting him on an upright chair, she closed the cabin door and rushed back into the bathroom. Dillman's wounds took priority over the stain on her dress.

"How did it happen?" she asked, bathing the gash on his temple.

"I tripped."

"But why were you coming down the stairs in the first place?"

"It was Carlotta Hubermann's idea," he explained. "When you rushed out, she dispatched me after you to lend assistance. I tried to cut you off by coming down a companionway used by the staff but I made a faster descent than I intended." His head was clearing. "Now I know how Jack must have felt."

"Jack?"

"In the nursery rhyme. Remember Jack and Jill? Isn't there something to the effect that Jack fell down and broke his crown?"

"And Jill came tumbling after! I should forget that, if I were you. Unless you wanted to have your head mended with vinegar and brown paper." Having bathed the wound, she stemmed the bleeding with a handkerchief, using a scarf to bind it into position. "If you go to the surgery, they'll bandage that properly."

"I'd prefer you as my nurse any day."

"How are you feeling now?"

"Much better, thanks."

"You were really groggy when you first came in."

"A glass of water and I'll be as good as new."

She fetched the water and watched him drink it. He was rallying.

"Now, suppose you tell me the truth, Mr. Dillman."

"About what?"

"That little tumble you took. You look like one of the fittest and most surefooted men on this boat. And you've spent many years going up and down narrow companionways on your father's yachts. It's second nature to you, isn't it? You didn't fall, did you?"

"I'm not sure. It all happened so quickly."

"Please, Mr. Dillman. Don't insult my intelligence."

"All right," he admitted, "maybe somebody did help me on my way."

"Why?"

"Who knows? Jealousy, perhaps. Someone saw me rushing off to your cabin and tried to stop me. That's all I know."

Genevieve set his glass aside, then took him by the shoulders.

"Why don't we stop fencing?" she said. "I told you that we had an affinity. Both of us have something to hide. I know what my secret is, but what's yours? Haven't I earned the right to share it by now?"

Dillman searched her face to see if he could trust her. From the moment he had first seen her on Euston Station, she had exercised a fascination for him, but that did not mean he could safely reveal his true purpose on board the ship. Genevieve saw his hesitation.

"What have you got to lose?" she encouraged. "I'm as close as the grave. Whatever you tell me, it will go no further. Besides, I may be able to help you, Mr. Dillman. We can play Jack and Jill for real, if you like. Now that I've mended your broken crown, we can go back up that hill to fetch a pail of water. And this time, neither of us will come tumbling down."

"I'll hold you to that," he said with a grin. "Let me give you the shortened version. What I said about leaving the family firm and going on the stage was all true. The thing I didn't tell you was what happened afterwards. I may have failed in the theater but I put my acting abilities to great use elsewhere. Have you ever heard of the Pinkerton Detective Agency?" She nodded eagerly. "I became one of their operatives, working under cover to expose all sorts of crimes. You *really* have to act in those situations, Miss Masefield, or it can get dangerous."

"So I see."

"Then you'll also have worked out that I'm now employed by the Cunard Line. How that came about is another story. Suffice it to say that I earned my spurs on an earlier voyage. So I had my passage booked on the *Lusitania*. I was hoping for a quiet trip," he said, "but it hasn't worked out that way."

"I heard there have been some minor thefts aboard."

"We've had rather more serious crimes than that, I fear. And one of them was used to flush me out. I realize that now."

"Flush you out?"

"The man we're after knew there'd be a private detective aboard. I see now why he staged one of the thefts. It brought me out of cover. I'd bet my last cent that he saw me going into the victim's cabin." He put a hand tenderly to his temple. "This is the result."

"He attacked you?"

"He's an opportunist. Been lurking in readiness."

"Who is he?"

"That's the problem. I'm not entirely sure. Which means he holds a crucial advantage because he knows exactly who I am." He got to his feet. "On the other hand, he doesn't realize that I survived the fall without any broken bones. Plenty of bruised ones, maybe," he said ruefully, stretching himself, "and one heck of a stiff neck, but I'm still in one piece. The advantage may swing back my way. He thinks he's taken me out of the game and that the field is clear."

"For what?"

"That's one thing I can't tell you. But, if you want to help me, say that I met with an accident. When you go back up to the lounge, put it about that I had a nasty fall and have been carried off with concussion."

"If you wish."

"I do wish. It might lull him into a sense of security."

"Who? Who is this man?"

"Your turn to provide a few answers, Miss Masefield. I've taken you into my confidence," he reminded her, "why don't you do the same? I don't think you're simply going on vacation, are you?" She shook her head. "You're on the run, I think. What from?"

"A terrible mess I left behind me," she admitted, moving to sit on the sofa. "Not entirely of my own making, I may say, but I have to bear much of the responsibility. The name of Lord Wilmshurst will mean nothing whatsoever to you, will it?"

"Does he wear a monocle as well?"

"No," she said, "he spends most of his time in a bath chair, nursing his gout. And he doesn't look in the least like an English aristocrat. I was engaged to his son, Nigel. It was quite an achievement, believe me, because I don't exactly come from a titled family. Let me be honest with you. To some extent, I went hunting for him. I was very fond of Nigel, but I won't pretend that I was madly in love with him. What really attracted me was his family and his position. I suppose I was infatuated with the idea of sharing them. To understand why, you'd have to come from my background." She gave a hopeless shrug. "It all went hideously wrong. I began to have guilt feelings about the whole thing then my fiancé did something which I found unforgivable. It involved another man. We had a fierce row. I snatched off my engagement ring and threw it in the river. At that point, of course, I forfeited control of the situation."

"Control?"

"Yes," she sighed. "Technically, I'd broken off the engagement but it was Nigel's account which was believed. He portrayed me as a callous gold digger, who was only after his title and money. He claimed that he'd found me out and discarded me. There was an element of truth in that, I admit, but it was by no means the whole story and I really had been having second thoughts. Even without the row, I don't think that I could have gone ahead with the marriage. But Nigel was in control. His version became the official one. I had proof of that on this very ship. I was branded as a social outcast, Mr. Dillman. It seemed to me that the only sensible thing was to leave England and start afresh elsewhere."

"It was a dramatic move to break off the engagement."

"As an actor, you would have appreciated it."

"Why?"

"Because I wasn't reckless enough to throw a valuable diamond ring into the river Thames. What I took off my finger was a paste ring I inherited from my mother. For sentimental reasons, I was sorry to lose it, but it had no commercial value."

"What happened to the engagement ring?"

"This," she said, indicating the cabin. "I sold it to pay for my passage and to stock my wardrobe. I felt that I'd earned that ring. It was the least Nigel could give me in return for the loss of my good name. So I booked a passage on the *Lusitania*," she continued. "At the back of my mind was a silly idea that, during the voyage, I might even find another gentleman to dance attendance on me."

"With or without a monocle."

"I want to forget Lord Carradine."

"Do you?"

"He was *my* fall down the stairs."

"Then we have more in common than I thought."

"At least my life isn't in danger," she said with concern. "Yours is. You could have broken your neck when you fell. Don't you have any idea at all who could have pushed you?"

"I think so," he said, "though I can't be certain yet. When I first regained consciousness, I had this ridiculous idea that it might have been her. Acting out of jealousy when she saw me rushing to your aid. I almost believe that she's capable of it."

"Who?"

"Ellen Tolley. She seems to have developed a strong interest in me."

"It's much more than that, Mr. Dillman."

"Is it?"

"She's been breathtakingly frank on the subject. Miss Tolley even cornered me in the ladies' room for cross-examination. She thought I might be a potential rival for your affections."

"Was she that blunt about it?"

"Oh, yes."

"That's very disturbing," he said, pursing his lips. "I think I shall have to start dodging her in future. Both of them."

"Both?"

"Ellen and her father."

"But Caleb Tolley is not her father."

Dillman gaped. "What do you mean?"

"I shared a table with them. It took me a while to work it out, but I got there in the end. Ellen may have fooled you, but I'm a woman. What you would probably call a designing woman. The advantage is that I can recognize one of my own kind."

"I don't follow."

"The Tolleys are not father and daughter."

"Are you sure?"

"Yes," she said confidently. "Because if they are, you've got a nasty case of incest aboard."

Dillman needed only a second to assimilate the information.

He reached out impulsively for her. This time the kiss was on the mouth.

As the message came in through his earphones, the operator scribbled it down on his pad with pencil. When the Morse code stopped clicking in his ear, he turned to his colleague.

"Message from the *Haverford*," he said with a cynical laugh. "She's sailing east and wanted to wish us Godspeed. I bet she does! Since when does a steamer from another line want to see a Cunard ship get the Blue Riband back?"

"Why not send a witty reply?" suggested his companion.

"I've sent enough messages for one day," said the other, vacating his chair so that the other wireless operator could relieve him. "My favorite was an old lady who wanted an urgent message sent back to her daughter in Liverpool. It was to remind her to feed the canary. I ask you!"

Dillman burst in while they were still laughing. He had smartened himself up and removed the makeshift bandaging from his head but his face still made them both stare. The ugly red gash on his temple was glistening and there was a dark bruise flowering on his chin. His hair was unkempt.

"I wasn't looking where I was going," he said by way of explanation. "Look, this is important. When I came in here before, you showed me some messages sent by a Mr. Barcroft." He pointed to the man who had just come off duty. "Remember? You told me you kept every wireless sent from this room. Is that true?"

"Yes, sir."

"I need to go through them all."

"But there are hundreds!"

"No other way," said Dillman, "unless you happen to recall a Mr. Caleb Tolley. You couldn't miss him. Uses a stick."

"Passengers don't come directly here, sir. Their messages are brought in. Most of them, anyway. We do get the odd passenger who tries to jump the queue by sneaking in here in person. That Mr. Barcroft was a case in point, but I don't remember any Mr. Tolley. Victor?"

"Nor I," said the other man.

"Then let me see those messages."

It was a long search. Aided by the two men, every message that had been dispatched was checked, then set aside. Since they worked backward chronologically, they took time to find the one short message sent by Caleb Tolley. One of the operators read it aloud.

"Here it is, sir. 'Wonderful trip. Everything is fine.' Man of few words, isn't he?" He handed the piece of paper to Dillman. "Take it."

"Did you see where this was sent?" asked Dillman, studying it. "Not to Liverpool or New York. But to the *Deutschland*."

"That's right, sir," said the man. "She passed us in the dark last Sunday. Case of ships in the night, eh? She's part of the Norddeutscher Lloyd Line. Mr. Tolley must have a friend aboard."

Dillman saw the time at which the message had been sent. His mind went back to the nocturnal meeting with Ellen Tolley on Sunday night. She told him that her father had gone back to his cabin with a headache. Their encounter took on a new meaning. It was not the coinicidence he had assumed. The friendly young American girl with whom he had collided was not lost at all. She was deliberately preventing him from continuing his pursuit of Barcroft. Dillman believed he knew why.

He thanked the operators and charged off. Caution advised him to seek help from the purser, but he was in no mood for a sensible option. His blood was too hot for that. Dillman wanted revenge. A deliberate attempt had been made to disable him. Someone wanted him out of the way while they made a decisive move. That thought was enough to send him racing off to the chief steward. Startled by his appearance, the man willingly gave the detective the information he wanted, and Dillman went off to the cabins allotted to Ellen and Caleb Tolley. He knocked hard on the first door but got no reply. The other cabin also seemed to be empty when he tapped repeatedly on its door.

Dillman was glad that he had kept the master key provided by the purser. It let him into the first cabin, which he immediately identified as belonging to Caleb Tolley. Expecting to find damning evidence, he was dismayed to see nothing even remotely incriminating. When he went into the adjoining cabin, however, it was different story. Nominally belonging to Tolley's daughter, the room bore few indications of a woman's touch. What Dillman first noticed was the sketch pad, pencils, and ruler on the desk. He recalled seeing Ellen at work on deck and admiring her draftsmanship. Further examples of her skill with a pencil soon came to light. When he opened a drawer, he found exact copies of the diagrams that had been stolen from the chief engineer's cabin. There was a bonus and it gave Dillman a surge of pleasure. On the wiring diagram was an obliging little cross.

The search was not yet complete. In the wardrobe, concealed behind Ellen's dresses, was a large black valise. He flicked the catch and opened it up. Dillman could not resist a little shout of delight.

Charles Halliday was looking more haggard than ever. Too anxious to enjoy his dinner, he had returned to his cabin immediately afterward to brood on the vicissitudes of life as a purser aboard an ocean liner. Pressure was being applied from all sides and it was threatening to squeeze him to a pulp. Captain Watt was pushing him hard for results, so was Fergus Rourke, so was Itzak Weiss, and so were the dozens of other passengers with more minor concerns. The accumulated pressure was stifling. A tap on his door promised no release valve.

"Come in!" he called, sitting up. "Mr. Dillman!"

His visitor stepped into the cabin with fire in his eye, blood on his temple, and a bruise on his chin. Draped over his arm was a large towel embroidered with the Cunard emblem.

"What in God's name happened to you, man?"

"They tricked us, Mr. Halliday."

"They?"

"The couple who've been behind us all along. The raid on Itzak Weiss's cabin was partly a ruse to bring me out into the open. Once they knew who I was, they could choose their moment to pick me off, as you see. Luckily, I survived the fall."

"What fall?"

"One of them pushed me down a companionway."

"One of whom?"

"The Tolleys. Father and daughter. Man and mistress. Whatever their relationship, I'm sure of one thing. They're in this together. They killed Barcroft between them."

"How?"

"Think back to those two glasses with the bottle of Champagne," said Dillman. "They weren't for Barcroft and a male friend. He had an assignation with Ellen Tolley. Set up by her, I've no doubt. According to what I've heard, he propositioned a number of young ladies and must have thought he finally hit the jackpot with Ellen."

"Who are these Tolleys?"

"First-class passengers. And first-class performers," admitted Dillman with reluctant admiration. "They took me in. Ellen is clever enough and cunning enough to take in any man. She obviously hypnotized Barcroft. He invited her to his cabin, but she took someone along with her. It wouldn't have been difficult to distract Barcroft. In the state he was in, he probably wouldn't have heard a cavalry charge coming through the door behind him."

"Yet they didn't get what they came for, Mr. Dillman."

"Oh, yes, they did, sir."

"But they didn't find that brown envelope."

"They didn't need to, Mr. Halliday. They took it into the room with them. Think back. The body was positioned in the one place from which that envelope would be spotted. We were meant to find it there so that we would assume it was Barcroft who stole the diagrams from the chief engineer's cabin."

"And he didn't?"

"No. They copied what they stole, then planted it on him."

"How do you know?"

"I've just seen concrete proof in Ellen Tolly's cabin."

Halliday sprang to life. "Let's arrest them at once!"

"Stay where you are, sir!" warned Dillman. "Going after them is the worst thing you can do. It would not only cause a scene in public, it would end in violence and some of the other passengers might get hurt. Caleb Tolley is a strong man. He uses a walking stick because he claims to have a bad leg but I don't believe there's anything the matter with him. I have a horrible feeling that he used that stick to batter Henry Barcroft to death. Do you want him flailing it around in the lounge?"

"Of course not."

"Then play this quietly, sir. Let him come to us. I know exactly where the rendezvous will be. I'll tell you where to station your men. If we plan this with care, we may be able to tidy up this whole mess in one night and none of the other passengers would be any the wiser." He gave a broad grin. "How does that sound?"

"Too good to be true!"

"Won't anything put the color back in your cheeks?"

"Yes, Mr. Dillman."

"What?"

"A stolen violin."

"I was forgetting that," said Dillman, removing the towel from his arm. He held up the Stradivarius. "This was hidden away in a valise in Ellen Tolley's cabin. Why don't you do yourself a supreme favor, sir?" He handed the instrument over. "Take it back to Itzak Weiss now and win yourself a friend for life."

Violet Rymer was more distressed than ever. The afternoon's meeting with Philip Garrow had started so well but ended so badly. Money had once again been the stumbling block. It was his turn to be shocked this time. When she told him that her marriage to him would jeopardize the payment of the trust fund to her, his manner had altered completely, and before they could talk the matter through properly, the third-class lounge had been invaded by a fancy-dress contest. Driven out, they parted in the most unnerving way, Violet seeking assurance that looked like it was never coming from him. Pulsing with frustration, Philip Garrow, the young man she loved and with whom her whole future was entwined, had pushed her away and run off. Violet had been spurned. It was demeaning.

Another gap had suddenly opened up between them. Yet it was not irremediable. In her heart, she knew and believed that. Philip loved her. All that she had to do was to demonstrate the full strength of her love for him and everything would be all right. That was the thought that helped to sustain her through dinner and through the long conversation that followed. When the guests departed, she retired to her own room and left her parents in the parlor. They would not remain there long. Her father had drunk quite heavily and her mother, a woman of delicate constitution, did not like late nights, preferring instead the solace of a sleeping pill prescribed by the family physician.

Violet waited, listened, and bolstered her resolve with thoughts of what lay ahead. Philip would be so pleased that she was ready at last to sacrifice herself wholly to him. It would bind them forever. Lying fully clothed in the dark, she watched the light under her door go out. Her parents had left the lounge and gone to bed. Another half hour would be a sufficient safety zone. Each minute was separate torment. When she felt certain that the coast was clear, she let herself back into the lounge and went out through the door to the passageway. In giving her a key of her own to the suite, her parents had never imagined it might be used during a bold escapade at night.

A mixture of elation and foreboding took her onward. She was stepping into the unknown. It was not at all as she had hoped or envisioned but there was no helping that. Only by throwing herself into Philip's arms could she prove what he meant to her and receive the answering assurances from him. It seemed an age before she reached his cabin and she was trembling like a leaf as she tapped on it. There were sounds from within. She tapped harder. Afraid that someone might see her, she banged on the door with more purpose. A lock clicked and the door inched open. Two dark, guilty eyes peered out at her.

"Violet!" said Garrow in a hoarse whisper.

"Let me in, Philip."

"I can't. I mean, not now."

"Don't you want me to come in? You did yesterday."

"Well, yes. But—"

"Let me in!" she begged. "Please!"

"Who is it?" asked the voice of Rosemary Hilliard.

Violet Rymer staggered back. Philip Garrow opened the door to reach out to her, then realized that he was stark naked. He immediately retreated back into the room. But she no longer needed him now. Ashen-faced and feeling sick, she supported herself against a wall while she took in the full horror of what she had discovered. The door clicked shut and Philip Garrow went out of her life forever. Raised voices were heard inside the cabin. Minutes after Violet had trudged slowly away, a fuming Rosemary Hilliard stormed out of his room and left her host to enjoy another cold night alone in his bed.

On the long walk back to her suite, Violet went through the tortures of recrimination. Cruel as they had seemed, her parents had been right about Philip Garrow all along. He was not worthy of her. At least she had made that discovery for herself before it was too late. She would not have to carry any more false hopes in her breast. Finding him with another woman had been a shattering experience for her and left her walking in a trance. Yet her night of disillusion was not over. As she turned into the passageway that led to her suite, she saw her father at a distance let himself out of the door and creep along to the cabin occupied by Mildred. When he let himself in with a key, Violet's misery was complete.

She fell to her knees and wrapped herself in her arms as if protecting herself from any more blows. Self-pity gradually passed off, however, as she considered the implications for her mother. Subdued by a sleeping pill, Sylvia Rymer was dreaming happily in her bed, quite unaware that her husband was no longer beside her. Violet's dismay turned to anger and she hauled herself up. The two most important men in her life had betrayed her but they had left her feeling vengeful and strangely empowered now. She knew exactly what to do.

Letting herself into the suite, she went into her parents' bedroom, pushed home the bolt behind her, then looked down sadly at the sleeping figure. Violet took off her dress, climbed into bed, and enfolded her mother in her arms. They needed each other now.

Caleb Tolley went down the steps, then strode swiftly along the corridor. There was no sign of his limp now and his walking stick was tucked under his arm. Having waited until most of the other passengers went to bed, he was confident that he would now be unobserved and unobstructed. His destination was a room on the orlop deck, and it took him only a matter of seconds to pick the lock. Once inside, he pushed home the catch on the door and used a torch. Its beam played across the wall until it located a large fuse box. Tolley grinned. A small explosive device would cause untold havoc. It would knock out the lights in a substantial part of the vessel and achieve his objective in the simplest way.

He was about to place the miniature bomb in the fuse box when the light was suddenly switched on. Tolley swung round to see Dillman standing with his back to the door.

"You can see better with the light on, Mr. Tolley. So can I."

"What are you doing here?" growled the other.

"Waiting for you," said Dillman calmly. "Only this time, I won't turn my back to you. That was a nasty shove you gave me down those stairs."

"I can do worse than that."

"I know. I was the one who found Henry Barcroft."

"Barcroft was a fool," sneered the other. "He stumbled on to something which was no business of his and had to be eliminated."

"Well, before you try to eliminate me, Mr. Tolley, I'd better warn you now that there are two armed men stationed at either end of the corridor outside. You didn't switch on the light in case it was seen under the door. An unnecessary precaution," said Dillman calmly. "I knew exactly where you'd come because you were obliging enough to mark the spot on the wiring diagram that Ellen so cleverly copied. It was in your daughter's cabin. Not that I believe for a moment that she really *is* your daughter, of course."

Watching him carefully, Tolley put down the explosive device and reached for his walking stick. The torch was still in his other hand. He gave a slow smile as he studied his captor.

"You're an astute man."

"I tend to get results."

"What do you want, Mr. Dillman?" he asked.

"You, sir."

"Don't you realize what else you might have, man?"

"Caleb Tolley is prize enough."

"But there's money in this. Big money, I promise you. Let me go and I guarantee that you'll have your share."

"How? There's no escape for you from here."

"Yes, there is. When I blow out the lights, there'll be pandemonium everywhere. I'll be able to slip away in the dark."

"Where to? You've got nowhere to hide."

"There are other ways of protecting oneself."

"Just give me the walking stick," said Dillman, approaching with caution. "Then we can talk this over. You're far too intelligent to try to fight your way out of this, aren't you?"

Caleb Tolley tensed into a defensive posture, then he seemed to accept the hopelessness of his situation. He tossed his stick to the floor. Dillman moved to kick it aside, knowing what brutal damage the stout handle could inflict on the human skull. Tolley acted quickly. Without warning, he hurled the heavy torch at Dillman and caught him a glancing blow on the temple that sent him reeling. Tolley retrieved his stick in a flash and lifted it menacingly. Dillman backed away.

The voice of Charles Halliday came through the door.

"Are you all right in there?" shouted the purser.

"Stay out!" called Dillman."

"We've sealed off the corridor!"

"I'll be there in a minute!"

"You're a brave man," taunted Caleb Tolley, circling his man. "There's only one problem, Mr. Dillman. In order to leave here, you'll need a couple of stretcher bearers. Henry Barcroft was not the first victim of this stick—and he certainly will not be the last."

He lashed out with the stick but Dillman parried the blow on his left arm. Ignoring the pain, he flung himself hard at his adversary. Tolley was knocked to the ground with such force that he dropped the walking stick. Grappling with him, Dillman rolled over a few times as he fought to secure an advantage. Tolley was strong and resourceful, punching, gouging, and even biting his opponent but he had met his match this time. Forcing him onto his back again, Dillman sat astride him and pummeled away with both fists until resistance finally stopped.

Dillman was exhausted, dripping with perspiration and gasping for breath. His fists were bloodied, his left arm still smarting from the blow. Tolley was in a far worse state. His face was streaming with blood and his clothes were torn. He gulped in air noisily. Yet he was still not vanquished. When Dillman crossed to flick open the catch on the door, the wounded man was unperturbed by the sight of the revolver in the purser's hand.

"Get up!" ordered Halliday.

"You heard him," said Dillman, hauling Tolley up by the scruff of his neck. "He wants to lock you up where you won't do any more harm."

Tolley gave a weary grin. "Didn't you tell him?"

"Tell him what?"

"About my profession,"

"We've discovered what that is."

"My other profession."

"What are you talking about?"

"Insurance, Mr. Dillman," said Tolley, still fighting for breath. "You don't think I'd take such risks without adequate insurance, do you? I arranged for a hostage to be taken."

"Hostage?" echoed Dillman, fear stabbing at him.

"Yes. I believe that you know the lady in question."

Genevieve Masfield was in a state of agitation for the rest of the evening. After her visitor had departed with a kiss, she put on another dress and went everywhere in search of him, but Dillman seemed to have vanished. While tending his wound, she had come to realize just how much she liked him and she could not believe she had been so honest with him about her situation. At the same time, she knew that Dillman would not betray a confidence. She could trust him as implicitly as he trusted her. Though she feared for his safety, she was eventually forced to give up the search and went back to her cabin, hoping that he would at least get a message to her in due course. Opening the porthole to let in some fresh air, Genevieve sat on the bed and waited.

It seemed an age before the knock came. She went bounding across the cabin with alacrity. Flinging open the door, she spread her arms as if to welcome Dillman back but she saw that her visitor was in fact Ellen Tolley, carrying a valise and a carpet bag. Genevieve's pleasure vanished instantly.

"Say, could I ask you a favor?" said Ellen, pushing past her with the luggage. "It's a terrible imposition, I know, but could I bring these in here for a while?"

"No," replied Genevieve, asserting herself. "You certainly can't. You have no right to barge in here. Take them back to your own cabin."

"That could be difficult."

"Well, you can't leave them here."

The slap across the face was so violent and so unexpected that it sent Genevieve flying. When she sat up on the floor, she saw that the door had now been closed and that Ellen Tolley was now standing over her with a gun in her hand.

"Don't think I won't use this," warned Ellen. "It wouldn't be the first time I've fired in anger. Now sit over there, on the bed," she added, motioning her with the barrel of the weapon. "And take that stupid expression off your face."

Genevieve crawled to the bed then perched on the edge of it. Her cheek was on fire. Ellen Tolley was no longer the chatty young American woman who followed her into the ladies' room. She was an armed intruder, standing between Genevieve and the door. When the latter opened her mouth to speak, the gun waved her into silence.

"All you need to know is this," said Ellen, moving to sit on the chair. "I'm the one with the loaded weapon. You're the one with the serious problem. So do as you're told. I was hoping that we wouldn't have to resort to this but something has obviously gone wrong."

"Wrong?"

"Caleb didn't come back in time so he must have encountered some obstacles. Our insurance policy had to be activated. You, Genevieve."

"Me?"

"You're our way out." She laughed harshly. "And it's no use squinting at me like that. You're going to have to get used to having me around. Caleb and I plan to share your cabin until we reach New York. You're our hostage, you see. Our landing card. They'll have to release Caleb or they'll have a first-class passenger with a bullet between her eyes and you would be extremely bad publicity for the Cunard Line."

Genevieve quailed. She looked across at the luggage.

"What have you brought?" she asked.

"A few overnight things. Oh, and I packed another hostage into that valise. As secondary insurance. They wouldn't dare try anything heroic while we have that in our possession."

"That?"

"Yes. It's worth far more than that diamond necklace of yours, I can tell you. It's the most valuable item aboard this ship. When Caleb gets here, we'll show it to you." She gave a mocking grin. "I don't suppose you've ever shared a cabin with a man and a woman, have you? Don't worry. Your virtue is not in danger. My husband will not touch you."

"So he's your husband? I knew he was not your father."

"That was very perceptive of you."

Genevieve was slowly recovering her composure. Her cheek still burned but she was not going to give Ellen the satisfaction of watching her put a comforting hand to it. She took a deep beath.

"Why me?" she asked. "Why pick on me?"

"Because you're his weak point. Men always have one somewhere and I'm an expert in finding it out. The only person on board this ship whom George Dillman would never endanger is you. He's far too chivalrous. That's why we chose Genevieve Mase-field. To exploit his weak spot. You're his Achilles' heel."

"And who is yours?"

"I don't have one."

The gun remained pointing at her and Genevieve had to make an effort not to stare at it. There was no doubt in her mind that her unwanted guest would use it if necessary. She probed for more detail.

"Why do you need a hostage?" she said. "Is this something to do with Mr. Dillman being pushed down those steps earlier on? He crawled along here so that I could bathe his head wound."

"Now, isn't that touching?" said Ellen with sarcasm. "And so symbolic. He came to you on his hands and knees. We were rather hoping that he wouldn't have the strength to get up again. Ever!"

"So much for the interest you showed in him!"

"Oh, that was genuine at first. I liked the guy. Until we discovered that he was the resident detective. That put us on opposite sides."

"And what sides are those?"

"Winners and losers. We're the winners. No question of that."

"Who are the losers?"

"You, George Porter Dillman and the dear departed Henry Barcroft."

Genevieve was shocked. "Mr. Barcroft is dead?"

"He made the mistake of inviting me to his cabin."

The tap on the door removed the cold smile from Ellen's face. Keeping the gun on Genevieve, she put a warning finger to her lips. Carlotta Hubermann's anxious voice pierced the door with ease.

"Genevieve?" she called. "Are you there? Do let me in. There's been the most terrible accident. Mr. Tolley has been killed and Mr. Dillman seriously injured. He's calling for you, Genevieve. You must come before it's too late. Mr. Dillman sent for you."

Ellen Tolley only half-believed the story. Suspecting a trap, she nevertheless found Carlotta Hubermann's tone very convincing. She stood up and moved tentatively towards the door, not knowing whether to open it or leave it locked. Genevieve knew exactly what to do. Feeling for a pillow with one hand, she took a firm grasp on it then hurled herself across the cabin and swung the pillow violently at the gun. As the weapon was deflected, Ellen's finger closed on the trigger and a bullet was discharged harmlessly into the ceiling.

It was the cue for Dillman to make his entrance. Throwing himself at the door with full force, he broke the catch and burst in to make a swift appraisal of the situation. Before Ellen could point the gun at him, he caught her by the wrist and twisted the weapon out of her hand. She was pushed forcefully back into the cabin, but she was not finished yet. Ellen pounced on the valise and pulled out the violin that was inside, holding it up in triumph.

"Stay where you are!" she cried. "This is a Stradivarius. We stole it from Itzak Weiss. It's worth a fortune. Think of the ugly repercussions if any harm should come to it." She held the violin close to the wall. "Now, let me have my gun back or I'll smash it to pieces."

"Go ahead," encouraged Dillman. "It can be replaced."

"A Stradivarius?"

"Take a close look at the instrument, Ellen. It belongs to a member of the orchestra. I borrowed it from him when I found the Stradivarius in your valise. The real Stradivarius is safely back in Mr. Weiss's hands."

Ellen stared at the violin in disbelief. As Dillman moved toward her, she threw it at him but he ducked out of the way. He got a firm grip on her. She fought hard but was soon overpowered. Charles Halliday entered with two armed men to march the captive unceremoniously out. Genevieve was so relieved that she burst into tears and fell into Dillman's arms. He pulled her close and let his own emotions show.

Carlotta Hubermann interrupted the romantic moment. Eager for praise, she put her head around the door and beamed hopefully.

"How was I?" she asked. "Convincing?"

* * *

It took the remainder of the voyage for the full truth to emerge. Caleb and Ellen Tolley were awkward under questioning but a series of wireless messages gradually elicited information about them and their activities. Meanwhile, the *Lusitania* sailed calmly on with none of its passengers or crew any the wiser about the recurring crises that it had undergone. True to his promise, the grateful Itzak Weiss gave a recital on the eve of their arrival in New York. Dillman attended it with Genevieve Masefield on his arm. Reunited with his beloved violin, Weiss played with enormous passion and earned a standing ovation from his audience. When many of the spectators adjourned to the lounge immediately afterward, Dillman and Genevieve were among them. Cyril Weekes made a point of seeking out the former for a quiet word alone.

"I'll say good-bye now, old chap," said Weekes, "in case I miss you in the morning. I'm off to the smoking room now."

"Another game of poker?"

"I'm afraid so. It's become an addiction."

"You'd play much better in here, Mr. Weekes," said Dillman with a knowing smile. "Your wife might bring you luck. In the smoking room, you'll find Mr. Collins more of a handful. They tell me that he plays like a professional gambler."

Weekes chortled. "That's why I had to clean him out at least once, Mr. Dillman," he admitted. "You have sharp eyes, sir. So does my wife. When I give a signal at a critical point in a game, Ada comes to my rescue. It's amazing how much information she conveys by squeezing my shoulder and issuing an order. I know exactly what my chief opponent is holding in his hand." He looked defensive. "It's not really cheating, you know. And I had to get back at Mr. Collins somehow."

"It might teach him a lesson."

"Most of the time, it really is luck," said Weekes. "Meeting Ada was my first stroke of good fortune. Her father wouldn't countenance a friendship between his daughter and a very junior member of his staff so we had to meet in secret. In a potting shed, actually. That's where I proposed to her." He gave another chortle.

"In the circumstances, I felt that it was the gentlemanly thing to do. I've been lucky ever since. In love, in my business life, at the card table. Good-bye, Mr. Dillman." They exchanged a warm handshake. "You may have found me out but I wasn't entirely taken in by you either. Your story about bumping into a lifeboat. That isn't how you got those bruises on your face, is it?"

"Perhaps not, Mr. Weekes."

"No, I think that you and old Erskine indulged in a spot of fisticuffs. The fellow is mad about boxing. He even tried to lure me into a sparring contest. Yes, that's how you came by those injuries, isn't it?"

Dillman did not disillusion him. He waved his friend off to another session at the card table before returning to Genevieve, who was talking to the Hubermanns. Carlotta was still preening herself over her part in the deception which had momentarily distracted Ellen Tolley. Sworn to secrecy, her sister had been told of the emergency and now viewed Dillman through much more sympathetic eyes. After chatting with them for a few minutes, the two sisters excused themselves and moved tactfully away as if giving the flowering relationship a discreet seal of approval. Genevieve watched them go.

"That was a stroke of genius," she observed.

"What was?"

"Getting Carlotta Hubermann to knock on my cabin door."

"She was the only person I could think of," said Dillman. "Ellen Tolley would hardly have opened up if I'd come calling."

"She was caught off guard by Carlotta. That gave me my chance."

"Thank goodness!"

"I was so angry at the thought you'd been injured. I lashed out."

"And all because of Miss Hubermann's talents as an actress." He squeezed her hand affectionately. "It's ironic, isn't it?"

"What is?"

"Caleb Tolley was so determined to prevent the *Lusitania* from claiming the Blue Riband on her maiden voyage that he was prepared to commit murder and slow the vessel down by destroying part of its electrical system. And yet, ironically, there's no chance that we will break the record now. Tolley needn't have bothered."

"I thought that was a false name, George."

"It was. Their real name was Blauner. Carl and Ellen Blauner."

"So he had no insurance company in New Jersey?"

"Yes, he did. That was their cover, Genevieve. But most of their money came from the German government. I don't know much about European politics but what I do know is that the Germans are spoiling for a fight."

"There have been articles to that effect in all our papers."

"The British won't run away," he said seriously. "In launching a ship like this one, they're waving a huge Union Jack at the Germans. The Blauners were paid to tear that flag down and steal vital information about the *Lusitania* at the same time."

"What about Henry Barcroft?"

"An innocent bystander."

"Did they have to murder him?"

"It was curiosity that really killed him, Genevieve," he explained. "He wanted to know everything about the ship even if it meant poking around without official permission. The night that I followed him, he saw Caleb behaving suspiciously in a part of the vessel where no passengers were allowed. Caleb got out fast, not knowing if he'd been recognized or not. Ellen was his lookout and she made sure that I didn't see anything untoward by blocking my path. Barcroft was a potential danger, but he was also the ideal person on whom they could plant the stolen diagrams." He gave a shrug. "The rest, you know."

"Not quite," she told him. "There was a time when you believed that Mr. Barcoft had taken those plans from the chief engineer. Why?"

"Because he was so nosy. I was wrong about him and even more wrong about Jeremiah Erskine. It took me ages to unravel the true relationship between the two of them. No wonder Barcroft was so keen to butter him up."

"Mr. Erskine? The ugly man with the beard?"

"He owned something very beautiful," said Dillman. "As far as an aspiring author like Barcroft was concerned, anyway. Among his many other American assets, Erskine owns a publishing company. Quite a large one, I understand. It has close links with George Newnes Limited, the British publishing house."

"So?"

"Barcroft wanted to elevate himself out of journalism and into the realms of literature. He'd already got a British publisher interested in his idea. That's what he was doing on this maiden voyage," he said quietly. "Researching a novel. Collecting situations and characters."

"Characters?"

"Look around you, Genevieve. This ship is full of them. Who could resist the Hubermanns, for instance, or the Rymers, or our aristocratic travelers?" He gave a chuckle. "It's even possible that a certain Genevieve Masefield and George Porter Dillman may have featured in the novel, albeit under different names."

"I'm not sure that I like the sound of that," she said with a shiver. "Have you any idea what the book was going to be called?"

"Yes—Erskine told me."

"Well?"

"*Murder on the Lusitania.*"

POSTSCRIPT

The *Lusitania* reached Sandy Hook Bar at 9:05 A.M. on Friday, September 13, 1907. Though she had failed to beat the record time for an Atlantic crossing, she was given a tremendous welcome in New York, comparable to the scenes in Liverpool at her departure.

In Germany, there was great jubilation that the *Lusitania* had not captured the Blue Riband on its maiden voyage, which had been carefully monitored by their press and by their maritime companies. Albert Ballin, chairman of the Hamburg Amerika Line, used the occasion to make some disparaging remarks about the help that the British government had given to their rivals, the Cunard Line.

On her second voyage from Liverpool, the *Lusitania* did take the Blue Riband from German hands. She left the Mersey at 7:00 P.M. on Saturday, October 5, 1907. Leaving Queenstown at 10:25 A.M. on the following day, she maintained good speed and reached Sandy Hook on Friday, October 11, in a record time of four days, nineteen hours, and fifty-two minutes.

On Friday, May 7, 1915, the *Lusitania* was making her 202nd Atlantic crossing when she was sunk by a German torpedo with the loss of 1,195 civilian lives, including those of over a hundred American passengers. The tragedy represented a turning point in the First World War as it mobilized opinion against Germany and led indirectly to the involvement of the United States in the war.